W9-AQK-785

Black Trails and Bloody Murder

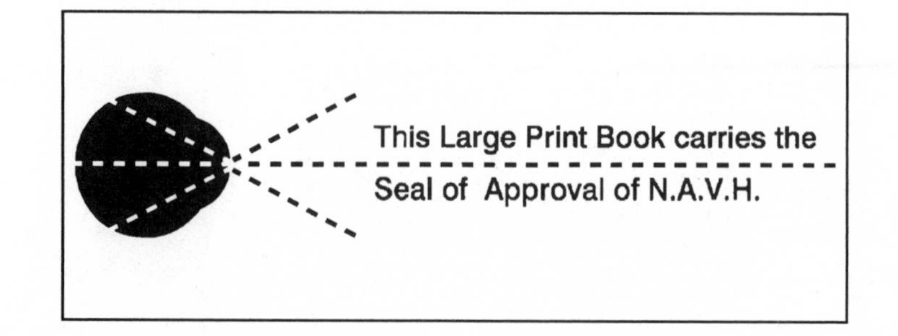
This Large Print Book carries the
Seal of Approval of N.A.V.H.

ROGUE LAWMAN:
A GIDEON HAWK WESTERN

BLACK TRAILS AND BLOODY MURDER

A WESTERN DUO

PETER BRANDVOLD

THORNDIKE PRESS
A part of Gale, a Cengage Company

Francisco • New York • Waterville, Maine
• Mason, Ohio • Chicago

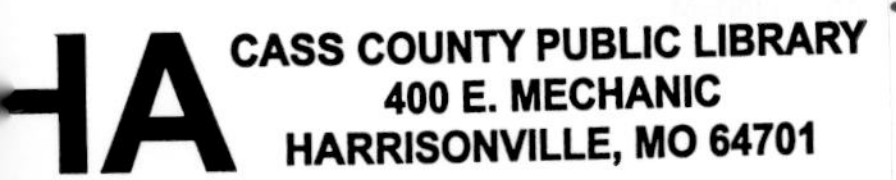

This novel is a work of fiction. Names, characters, places and incidents are either the product of the author's imagination, or, if real, used fictitiously.

The publisher bears no responsibility for the quality of information provided through author or third-party Web sites and does not have any control over, nor assume any responsibility for, information contained in these sites. Providing these sites should not be construed as an endorsement or approval by the publisher of these organizations or of the positions they may take on various issues.

Thorndike Press® Large Print Western.
The text of this Large Print edition is unabridged.
Other aspects of the book may vary from the original edition.
Set in 16 pt. Plantin.

**LIBRARY OF CONGRESS CIP DATA ON FILE.
CATALOGUING IN PUBLICATION FOR THIS BOOK
IS AVAILABLE FROM THE LIBRARY OF CONGRESS**

ISBN-13: 978-1-4328-4712-8 (hardcover alk. paper)

Published in 2019 by arrangement with Peter Brandvold

Printed in the United States of America
1 2 3 4 5 6 7 23 22 21 20 19

CONTENTS

Undertaker's Friend

Chapter 1

Gideon Hawk found a sheltered place to camp for the night along a pristine mountain lake. From a high ridge, the lake had resembled a heart-shaped nugget of ornamental turquoise shimmering against the gauzy green velvet of a fir and spruce forest.

Hawk stripped tack from his grullo mustang, rubbed the horse down thoroughly and carefully with a swatch of burlap, then picket-pinned the stalwart, loyal, but nameless animal in the trees at the edge of the camp.

The bivouac sat on a ledge maybe thirty feet above the lake. The ground was spongy and layered with pine needles and other forest duff. The cool air owned the heady tang of pine resin. Tall evergreens protected the campsite on the side sloping down from the ridge. On the north side was the lake over which a cool, refreshing breeze whispered.

No trouble was likely to come from the

lake. If trouble came from the ridge, the grullo would give a warning.

Hawk gathered wood and built a small fire. He made sure his Henry repeater was loaded and leaning nearby. He brewed a pot of coffee on an iron tripod mounted over the stone fire ring he'd built to contain the flames, and sat back against the woolen underside of his saddle to smoke a cigarette and to enjoy the piping hot brew as well as his view of the lake.

As the sun angled down in the west, tree shadows stretched long and dark across the water. The breeze died. The water turned to glass.

Hawk lifted one knee, leaned back on an elbow, and looked around. A rare serenity settled over the rogue lawman, though the perpetually grave set of his face did not betray this fact. He was alone here. He might have been the last man. All was quiet. A bald eagle dropped low over the lake until the curved talons hit the water with a splash.

The raptor rose skyward on its heavy wings, a writhing, silvery fish trapped in its feet. It gave a shrill cry of satisfaction as it caromed off toward a darkening northern ridge where it would dine on its fish.

The only sounds were the breeze playing in the crowns of the pines up near the top of the southern ridge, and, nearer, the pleasant snapping and crackling of Hawk's small fire. The smoke smelled good. Occasionally, when a vagrant breeze turned the smoke toward him, it burned his eyes and peppered his coffee with gray ashes. But even that was pleasant here on this lonely promontory over an isolated mountain lake, at the end of another hard-fought blood trail.

Hawk sipped his coffee. Staring out over the lake, he sat up straighter and narrowed his jade-green eyes, which shone in sharp contrast to his dark skin tone and the severe facial features he'd inherited from his Ute war chief father. The eyes were the same color as his Norwegian immigrant mother's.

Hawk's heartbeat quickened slightly.

He wasn't alone, after all.

On the far side of the lake, someone had walked out of the trees and was striding purposefully toward the shore, which dropped gradually to the darkening water. The figure, tall and slender, appeared from this distance to own the curves of a woman. The fading light flashed salmon on the white blouse and touched the long, auburn hair gathered into a tail, which was pulled forward to hang over her right shoulder.

Hawk grabbed his field glasses and adjusted the focus.

A woman, all right. Fairly young, judging by how fluidly, lightly she moved. How straight and plumb the line of her body was, the breasts firm and pointed behind the blouse. She wore a long, dark skirt and dark boots.

Where in the hell had she come from?

She walked down the slope to the edge of the water, where she paused, staring into the lake.

That side of the lake was maybe seventy-five yards from Hawk. In the sphere of his magnified vision, he saw the grave, pensive expression on the young woman's oval-shaped, even-featured face. She'd likely be pretty if he saw her close up. She stood there for a time, not looking around, not seeming to enjoy the scenery of the place, but only staring at the water.

A strange apprehension touched Hawk.

"What're you thinkin' about . . . ?"

It was as though his throatily uttered muttering had prompted her to action. She stepped forward into the water. She kept walking straight ahead, as though she thought she was walking on dry land. The water quickly moved up past her ankles to her knees, the soaked skirt clinging to her legs.

The water rose from her knees to her

thighs . . . and higher . . . to her waist.

Still, she kept walking until the water was up to her breasts. Then her head slipped under and she was gone.

Hawk lowered the glasses, scowling, narrowing his eyes. He raised the glasses again. All he could see of the woman were the ripples ringing out from the place on the water where she'd disappeared.

Hawk fiddled with the focus wheel, as though that would somehow bring her head back to the surface.

"What in tarnation . . . ?" he grumbled, lowering the glasses once more.

His heart thudded.

He set the glasses down, rose quickly, and, casting anxious glances at the far side of the lake, kicked out of his boots and peeled off his socks. Working hastily, muttering to himself, he shrugged out of his cracked leather, wool-lined vest and chambray shirt and skinned out of his black whipcord trousers and longhandles. Naked, he ran to the edge of his camp, leaped onto a flat rock overlooking the water, and dove forward off the balls of his feet, lifting his arms straight up above his head.

He drew a deep breath as his large, muscular body arced through the chill air, and then the lake wrapped itself around him, feeling warm until he reached the nadir of his plunge. Then the icy mountain chill bit him deeply. He arced back to the surface, lifting his head, quickly getting his bearings, and started swimming quickly but fluidly toward the lake's far side, keeping his head above the surface.

When he thought he was near the place where the woman had disappeared, he drew his knees toward his chest and flung his arms and head forward and down. He swam toward the bottom, reaching ahead and pulling the water back behind him.

The water was as clear as polished glass, so he saw her right away — a slightly blurred figure floating below him and to his right. She appeared to be kneeling in the water roughly two feet above the lake's sandy bed, as though she were giving praise. Her hair and blouse and skirt billowed around her. Her arms floated upward. As Hawk swam to her, he saw that her eyes were closed and that she wore a serene expression. Air bubbles rose from her nose and slightly parted lips.

Hawk grabbed her around her waist and pulled her to the surface. He thrust his head out of the lake and drew a deep breath, shaking water from his face. He slid his left arm up beneath her shoulders, lifting the woman's head out of the water, as well, and then began swimming toward the nearest shore, the one she'd come from.

Letting her head rest against his shoulder, he dragged her through the water as he swam awkwardly, using one arm. His feet scraped the lake's shelving bottom. He stopped swimming and trudged up the steep shelf, grunting with the effort of pulling the woman along, the level of the lake dropping down his chest to his knees and finally to his ankles.

He picked the woman up in his arms. She was much heavier now than she'd been in the water, the lake streaming off her sodden body and her hair, which hung now like a single, soaked, brown rag. As Hawk carried her onto the shore, he looked down to see that she still wore the same serene expression as before.

Hawk laid her on the grass several feet up from the gravel and sand. He stared down at her, puzzled. He placed a hand on her belly. She didn't appear to be breathing. He'd never tried to save anyone from drowning before. He drew a deep breath, thought it through.

He had to get the water out of her lungs.

He reached down and began to press on her belly, then, reconsidering, turned her over so that she lay belly down against the grass, and placed his hands on her back. He leaned forward, putting a good bit of his own weight on her body.

Nothing.

He pressed again, released the pressure, then leaned against her, pushing hard on the middle of her back. He did this several times, putting more and more weight on her, imagining her lungs expanding and contracting, until she convulsed and made a gurgling sound.

Her face was turned to the side. Her eyelids fluttered. Her mouth opened. Water gushed out of it onto the grass.

Hawk pressed down hard on her back again.

Again, she convulsed.

When no more water issued from between her lips, which appeared thin and blue, Hawk turned her over onto her back. The serene expression was gone. Now deep lines scored her pale forehead, and her lips were stretched back from her teeth. Her eyelids fluttered. She writhed on the ground, shaking her head.

"No," she moaned. "No, no."

She shivered, lips quivering, teeth clacking.

Hawk looked around. The sun was almost

down. The lake had turned nearly black. Only a little green light remained in the sky.

He glanced back over his shoulder to stare across the lake. He could see the flickering orange flames of his cookfire on the stony ledge on the lake's far side, gray smoke unfurling skyward. Imagining the caress of those warm flames against his cold, soaked body made him shudder with anticipation.

He had to get himself and the girl — she was somewhere between a girl and a woman, he thought — to the fire.

Hawk rose, pulled his charge up by one arm, crouched, and settled her onto his right shoulder. As she continued to choke and cough, convulsing on his shoulder, occasionally mumbling, "No, no," he began walking along the shoreline, following the curve toward the far side and the gray smudge of his stony bivouac.

Hawk looked around cautiously, making sure that he and the girl were alone out here. He was naked and unarmed. Being a hunted man, such a state was deeply uncomfortable.

It was nearly dark by the time he gained the base of the ledge on which he'd camped. He had to look around for a time to find a way up into the outcropping. Finding a long, narrow, steeply meandering cavity, he shifted the girl onto his other shoulder and began climbing. By the time he'd reached his camp, he'd scraped his bare feet raw and bloody. His fire had burned down to feebly glowing coals.

He lay the girl down beside the fire, on his own spread soogan, by his saddle and saddlebags. She was shivering and groaning, writhing and muttering. Hawk set some crumbled pinecones on the fire, and blew on the coals. When small flames began licking against the tinder, he slowly added slivers of dry firewood. The flames grew, crackling, snapping, and smoking.

Hawk, shivering, turned to the trembling woman.

"Gotta get you out o' them duds," he grumbled.

She stared up at him now, but he wasn't sure she saw him. She seemed only half conscious, maybe in shock.

He unbuttoned her blouse, then slid it off her shoulders. She did not resist but only stared up at him, shivering. He lifted her camisole and chemise over her head, and tossed them onto the rocks to dry by the fire. The pale globes of her breasts sank against her chest, perfectly round and full, the pink nipples jutting. He removed her boots, wool stockings, and then her skirt.

He was going to leave her drawers on, but when she began fumbling with them, trying to peel them down her thighs, he helped her.

He tossed the drawers onto the rocks.

He looked down at her lying before him, naked. She had a beautiful body — full-busted, flat-bellied, round-hipped, and long-legged. Her lips were beginning to get some fullness and color back. Her eyes were lilac blue.

Hawk knelt between her spread legs. He stared down at her. Her eyes held his.

The warmth of the fire pushed against him, and he stopped shivering. He became aware of the desire warming his nether regions, and he glanced down to see that he was fully erect. She lifted her arms and opened her hands, reaching for him, staring at him, parting her lips.

Her breasts were rising and falling heavily, her belly contracting and expanding sharply as her breathing quickened.

She closed her hand over his jutting shaft. At first, her hand was cold. He flinched. Quickly her hand warmed, warming him. His heart thudded.

She kept her gaze on his. Her eyes were slightly crossed. She canted her head slightly to one side and made a grunting sound of desperate desire, hardening her jaws.

Hawk lowered himself over her. She spread her legs farther apart, grunting and raising her knees. Hawk lowered his head to hers, mashed his mouth against hers, and slid into her warm, wet opening.

Chapter 2

Hawk hadn't made love with such raw power and passion in a long, long time. The woman seemed to devour him. She writhed beneath him, bucking against him, moaning. Anyone watching would have thought, wrongly, that she was fighting him.

At the apex of their coupling, she gave a long, guttural groan and clung to him as though he was all that was holding her back from a fall into a dark abyss. Finally, long after they'd stopped shuddering together, she released him. Her body relaxed against the ground.

Hawk rose and, warm now from exertion, gathered his clothes and dressed. She sat up and, raising her knees to her breasts, watched him. Her wet hair, littered with dirt and pine needles, clung to her shoulders. She looked like some wild woman of the forest.

Hawk said nothing as he built up the fire.

Still, she watched him, saying nothing. She arranged her clothes on rocks nearer the fire, to quicken the drying, and then sat on the ground again, a blanket wrapped around her shoulders. She watched Hawk in hushed silence as he set about putting another pot of coffee to boil on the tripod.

When the coffee was done brewing, he poured two cups and handed one to her.

Behind him, the grullo whinnied.

Hawk spun, his .44 Russian instantly in his right hand, the hammer clicked back. The flickering firelight shone in two eyes staring at him from the forest. Two horse eyes. The horse's ears twitched, curious.

"It's all right," the woman said, her voice husky and hoarse behind Hawk. "He's mine."

Hawk turned back to her. She looked at the silver-chased revolver in his hand. Hawk depressed the hammer, dropped the popper back into its holster positioned for the cross-draw on his left hip, and snapped the keeper thong in place over the hammer.

Hawk sat on a rock, picked up his coffee, and studied her through the wafting steam. He didn't know what to make of her. Something told him she would entertain no questions. That was all right. She likely wouldn't ask any, either. That, too, was fine with him.

He didn't much like talking about himself. In fact, he didn't like to talk much at all about *anything.*

He didn't know why she'd tried to drown herself, and it wasn't his business to know. People had their reasons. They didn't always feel the need to share those reasons with others.

It hadn't been Hawk's place to save her. He'd done so automatically, without thinking about it. Maybe he hadn't been sure she'd wanted to die. Now, having saved her and made love to her — if you could call what had happened here around the fire anything close to love — he knew that's exactly what she'd attempted to do. She'd wanted to die.

Maybe she'd try it again. It was no business of his. If he chose a similar course of action, which wasn't out of the question, he wouldn't consider it anyone else's business. In fact, he felt a little guilty now for intervening. He didn't usually trifle in other people's business as long as they didn't trifle in his.

Hawk drank half of his coffee, then reached into a saddlebag pouch for a small burlap sack of jerky. He placed a couple of pieces in his left hand, drew the top closed, and handed the sack across the fire to the woman.

She shook her head, sipping her coffee.

Hawk set the sack down, then leaned back against his saddle. He drank his coffee and ate the jerky. He built up the fire again and then set to work cleaning and oiling his guns. He could feel her eyes on him, watching. By the time he was finished with that chore, she rose, removed the blanket from around her shoulders, gathered her clothes, which appeared nearly dry, and started dressing.

She didn't look one bit shy about dressing in front of him. Why should she, after what they'd done? Still, some women would.

When she was finished, she threw her hair, which was also nearly dry but still dirty, out from the collar of her blouse, and said, "I'll be going."

Hawk frowned as he slipped his Colt into its holster. "Dark out there."

She jerked her chin toward the southeast. "Moon on the rise. Small one, but I know the trail."

She walked over to her horse, which was saddled, and toed a stirrup. She swung up into the saddle.

"Here," Hawk said, taking the blanket to her, holding it up to her. "It's a cold night.

You'll need this." She didn't have a jacket, and he knew her clothes were still damp.

She took the blanket, wrapped it around her shoulders, and dipped her chin. It was an acknowledging nod. She looked at Hawk. It was as though she wanted to say something but couldn't find the words. He gazed back at her, waiting.

She sucked her cheeks in, then reined her horse around, touched heels to its flanks, and rode away. The hoof thuds dwindled gradually.

Hawk was sitting by his fire, sipping another cup of coffee, when he heard the thuds of her horse's hooves again on the far side of the lake. She'd ridden around to the side he'd first seen her on, and was retracing her route to wherever she'd come from.

The night was so quiet, the air so still and dense, that he heard her horse kick a stone. The stone rolled briefly, clattering. The hooves continued to thud for a time, the sounds dwindling again gradually, until there was only the silence of the night weighing down around the solitary man by the fire.

Hawk finished his coffee. The fire burned down to glowing embers.

He rolled up in his soogan, tipped his hat over his eyes, and slept.

■ ■ ■ ■

Arliss Coates rode her gelding, Frank, out of the forest and onto a shaggy, two-track wagon trail touched with blue light shed by the kiting quarter-moon. She stopped the horse and looked both ways along the trail.

Which direction was town?

Getting her bearings by the moon's position, Arliss reined Frank to the left and began heading northwest along the trail. As she heeled the horse into a trot, however, she began to feel an invisible hand pushing her away from the town of Cedar Bend.

She did not want to return there. Or, more specifically, she did not want to return to the house she shared with her husband, Roy. But there was nowhere else for her to go.

Or was there?

She gave a shudder as she imagined the lake's dark chill. Of walking into it again, at this time of night, of taking a deep breath of water to push the life out of her, and reclining on the sandy bottom forever.

Again, she shuddered. The mountain night air was cold, and her clothes were still damp. They smelled of the lake she remembered walking into as though it had been a dream she'd dreamt several weeks ago.

Had she really done that? Tried to *drown herself*?

When she'd ridden out of Cedar Bend that afternoon, she'd had no intention of doing anything like what she'd ended up doing. She'd merely felt the walls of that house — of *Roy's* house — closing in on her, with its baskets of Roy's laundry to wash and dry and iron and Roy's meals to cook, and his wood to split because he'd been grazed by a bullet a couple of months ago when he'd been trying to stop a fight between two drunks in Miss Pearl's Red Light Parlor, and he claimed it still bothered him.

But, of course, any work bothered Roy. Arliss had found that out not two days after they'd been married and Arliss had moved into the house he'd built when he'd become town marshal of Cedar Bend. He'd built the house for himself and his then-wife, Charmian, who'd died during a stagecoach robbery two years ago. Ten years Arliss's senior, Marshal Roy Coates had seemed so strong and capable. A strong, noble man. Maybe a little stern, but, like her father had told her, good men were stern. Weak men were soft.

Well, Roy had turned out to be both stern of temperament and soft of character . . . at least when it came to doing anything except coming home from work and sitting in his rocking chair and drinking whiskey or ale and lamenting the death of his beloved Charmian.

Of course, Arliss didn't know for sure that lamenting his dead wife was what he was doing, but she'd once caught him studying a tintype of Charmian with a look of longing in his eyes. Arliss suspected that Charmian had been Roy's first love, and losing her had been the heartbreak of his life. He'd married Arliss because she was young and pretty, and she was the daughter of a wealthy man.

But he hadn't loved her. In fact, Arliss got the very real sense that her presence in Coates's house was almost an affront to Roy's memory of Charmian. Arliss only reminded Roy of who *wasn't* there. Arliss was an imposter. After the first few months of marriage and his initial delight in her young, supple body, Roy had turned away from Arliss. He'd started to resent her. She'd seen it in his eyes, which hardly ever looked upon her anymore, and when they did, it certainly wasn't with anything akin to fondness.

When he was drunk, which he was nearly every night, he often regarded her with a toxic mixture of lust and shame. Never with love.

So those walls had been closing in on Arliss Coates, formerly Arliss Stanley, who'd grown up on her family's Circle S Ranch in the mountains and was accustomed to some space around her. She'd never been a stranger to work, but somehow working for Coates was far different from working around the ranch with her mother and her brother, Johnny. That work had been fun. There'd been camaraderie in it, and there'd always been a hired man around to flirt with and to make Arliss feel young and alive and desirable.

Now, there was nothing but Coates's laundry and his cooking and his firewood to split and his garden to tend — a garden that Charmian had likely tended so much better — and the incessant ticking of the wooden wall clock that had been an heirloom of Charmian's family.

So the walls had been closing in . . . and Arliss had saddled Frank for a ride in the mountains, and the next thing she knew, she'd been walking into the chill waters of Pine Lake. Her family had once picnicked on Sunday afternoons around the lake when Arliss was a little girl. Her father had taken

Arliss and Johnny hunting near the lake, as well.

She supposed walking into those cold waters had been her way of going back in time, of returning home when she had no other home to return to. She was no longer welcome at the ranch.

Again, she gave an involuntary shudder, thinking how much colder and darker those waters were now, so many hours after the sun had set . . . imagining herself lolling in the lake's frigid depths.

She recalled the man who'd pulled her up out of those depths. She remembered the heavy, rugged weight of his body atop hers, the sweet pain of his hardness inside her, sliding in and out of her, making her feel young and alive and desirable again, just as she had in what now seemed so many years before . . .

Arliss reined Frank to a halt on a low dike, and stared down the rise's far side and into the night-cloaked valley in which Cedar Bend lay. Again, she felt that invisible hand pressing against her chest, holding her back from the town. Revulsion for Coates's house, Coates's life, was a heavy brick in her belly.

She must have ridden for close to an hour after leaving the dark, green-eyed stranger on the ledge above the lake. She'd been so deep in thought as Frank had negotiated his own remembered way out of the mountains that it seemed like only a few minutes had elapsed since the stranger had reached up to give her the blanket that was still wrapped around her shoulders.

It smelled of him.

Earthy and musky with man sweat and old leather, and a faint touch of juniper, maybe cedar . . .

She found herself turning her head to stare up into the dark mountains blotting out the stars behind her. Her breasts tingled as she remembered his hands kneading them, his mustached lips suckling them. Warm blood of remembered desire pooled in her lower regions.

She shook her head, turning forward to gaze out over her horse's raised ears. The warmth of chagrin crept into her cheeks.

My god — what a harlot she'd been. Toiling like a she-bitch in heat with some aimless drifter, possibly an outlaw, judging by all the guns he carried and how well he carried them. Yes, an outlaw. He was probably holing up in the mountains, on the run from the law. Arliss doubted she'd ever see him again, which was as it should be.

Still, the thought gave her a vague but bitter disappointment as she booted Frank down off the rise and headed along the trail toward the flickering lamplit windows of Cedar Bend and the only home she had.

CHAPTER 3

Arliss found herself so deep in thought again that instead of circling around the outskirts of the town, she rode right through the heart of Cedar Bend via the town's broad main artery. Right past the town marshal's office, where Roy likely was — unless he was "patrolling" one of the parlor houses, as Arliss was well aware he tended to do.

She knew he frequented such places because she herself had seen him coming and going from Miss Pearl's or another house called the Alley Cat on the town's rough-hewn southern end, when she'd been strolling around the town's backstreets on nights she'd found herself feeling especially homesick and claustrophobic and unable to sleep or focus on needlework.

At first, she'd been hurt and angry that her husband was being unfaithful to her. Not so recently, however, she'd become glad

Roy visited those places. It meant he'd come calling on his wife for such pleasures less frequently, though Arliss suspected that it wasn't so much pleasure he sought from her. What he really wanted was to punish her for being there in his house, taking the place of Charmian. His lovemaking had been pleasant for maybe the first few times. Forever after, it had been most unpleasant, indeed — more angry and violent than passionate.

Fortunately, he didn't force himself on her more than once every two or three weeks these days.

Arliss gritted her teeth as she watched the marshal's office slide past on her right. It was a low, L-shaped, mud-brick building with bars over the windows, and a wooden front veranda. A sprawling cottonwood abutted its right end, offering shade on sunny summer days. A lamp lit the two front windows, but Roy usually left a light on, even when he wasn't in the office.

He was likely out on "patrol," which was just fine with Arliss. She released a held breath of relief as Frank trotted on past the place, but then she gritted her teeth again when hinges gave a dry squawk from the direction of Roy's office.

"Arliss?" Roy's voice.

ɔund herself keeping up the pretense that
ıey were a happily married couple — that
he loved him, that he loved her. She wasn't
ure why. Maybe because the truth seemed
o harsh and raw and terrifyingly lonely that
he didn't really want to believe it deep
own, though she did.

"Where've you been, Arliss?"

"I told you. I went for a ride in the
ıountains. I got turned around. When I
inally realized I was heading in the wrong
lirection, the sun was nearly down." She
huckled, though it sounded phony and
vooden even to her own ears.

"You grew up in those mountains. You
ouldn't get lost up there."

"I guess I got distracted."

Roy reached up and felt the arm of her
ılouse. It was a quick, brusque movement
vith absolutely no tenderness at all. He
ould have been cleaning his fingers on the
abric.

"You're blouse is damp." He grabbed her
kirt, rubbing it between his fingers. "The
kirt, too."

"Frank spooked and pitched me into a
reek." Arliss chuckled again, her heart
hudding apprehensively. "I'm fine."

"Frank, huh?" Roy sneered. "I never did
rust that horse. Has a look in his eye. Too

Oh shit, oh shit, Arliss thought.

She kept her head forward and continued riding, the blanket billowing out in the night air around her, like wings.

"Arliss, is that you — where you been? I been lookin' all over for you!"

She glanced over her shoulder as she continued putting distance between them. "Just went for a ride, Roy. Heading home!"

"Arliss!" Roy shouted. She cringed at the exasperation in his voice.

On her left, men's laughter sounded. Arliss glanced over to see three or four townsmen standing outside the Arkansas River Saloon, a couple with their hips hiked on a porch rail. They held drinks and cigarettes or cigars in their hands. They laughed with subtle mockery as they switched their gazes from Roy to Arliss, then back again.

"Arliss, goddamnit, get back here!" Roy bellowed. She could really hear his anger and frustration now. It caused his voice to gain that brittle shrillness she knew so well.

"I'm chilled, Roy," Arliss called behind her again. "I'll be at home!"

She rammed her boot heels into Frank's flanks, and the horse broke into a gallop.

Louder laughter erupted behind her.

A minute later she rode up to the stable flanking Roy's house on a barren lot at the northeast edge of Cedar Bend. Having been raised on a ranch, she knew that tending her horse took precedence over her own needs. When Frank had been rubbed down, fed, watered, and led into the small corral that abutted Roy's stable, Arliss drew the stranger's blanket more tightly around her shoulders and strode from the stable past the single-hole privy and a small, dead tree to the house's rear door.

She grabbed an armload of wood from the pile by the door and let herself inside the house. She shivered in delight at the thought of a hot bath. She carried the wood up through the short hall and was surprised to see the glow of a lantern on the other side of the flowered curtain that partitioned the hallway off from the kitchen and small parlor.

Tentatively, Arliss slid the curtain aside. Her stomach dropped when she saw Roy sitting at the end of the kitchen table over which the hurricane lamp hung, sputtering slightly, smoking.

"Roy," she said in surprise.

He sat casually in the chair, one arm hooked over the back. One boot was hiked on a knee. Roy was an austere-looking man, thirty-two, with wavy, dark-red hair and a thin mustache. His gray eyes were set too

far to either side of the bridge of his we
like nose, which was a little flat and kn
due to its having been broken and no
correctly.

His forehead was broad, high, and li
freckled behind an unnatural pallor s
where between cream and tan. He w
red bandanna wound tightly and kn
around his thick neck, at the open coll
his powder-blue work shirt.

A five-pointed star was pinned tc
shirt's breast pocket. A Remington rev
was holstered on Roy's right thigh.

He rested one thick hand on the tabl
fingers slightly curled inward.

His eyes were hard as he studied
Through them she could see the rc
anger inside him.

"I didn't expect you home so soon,"
said, faking a smile and trying to s
casual.

"Come here."

"What?"

"Come over here. Stand in front of
Let me get a look at you."

Arliss hesitated, then swallowed. Sl
she walked around the table to stand b
her husband. Again, she smiled.

"Sorry if I worried you. I didn't mea
be gone so long." For some reason, she

much stable grain. What he needs is a good, hard quirtin'. Don't you worry . . ." He rose from his chair and started toward the curtained doorway.

"What're you doing?" Arliss asked.

Roy stopped. "I'm gonna quirt that horse long and hard. He needs some of that contrary taken out of his hide."

"Don't you dare!"

Roy looked incredulous. *"What?"*

"Frank is my horse, remember? My father gave him to me for a wedding present. He's *my* horse — not yours. And no one will ever lay a hand on him!"

"He needs a good, hard quirting, I tell you, Arliss. He's gotta learn to respect . . ."

"Or maybe I . . . *I* gotta learn." Arliss's heart was beating fiercely. Rage burned her ears. It was all coming out now — all the pent-up anger and frustration. It was like opening a window in a shut-up room, letting the stink out. "Isn't that right, Roy? Maybe it's I, your wife, who has to learn some respect? Isn't that what you really mean?"

Roy turned full around to her, glaring down at her, his own rage burning like a flame in his distant eyes. "Why did you back-talk me out there on First Street, for all to hear?"

"Is that what this is about?"

"Those men — good friends of mine . . . they were laughin' at me. Laughin' about the way you talked *back* to me!"

"I see," Arliss said, crossing her arms on her breasts, smiling without humor. "Now I see what this is about."

Roy curled his upper lip and turned back to the curtained doorway. "That horse needs a good quirtin', all right. And I'm just the man to give it to —"

"Stop, Roy!" Roy always kept an old Remington revolver hanging from a peg in a square-hewn ceiling support post by the range. Arliss grabbed the gun now and, holding it in both hands, aimed it at her husband. She hardened her jaws and narrowed her eyes. "If you go anywhere near my horse, I will blow your head off, Roy!"

Again, Roy turned full around to her. Fury bleached his face, drawing down his mouth corners. His right cheek twitched. He walked toward her, his nostrils expanding and contracting, his broad chest rising and falling sharply.

"You put that gun down."

Arliss ratcheted back the hammer. "You stay away from Frank."

"I'll do whatever I think is right. Now, put that gun down. I won't tell you again!"

"Stop!"

Roy kept coming, taking one slow step at a time. His mustached lips stretched a challenging grimace. "Go ahead," he said. "Pull the trigger. I dare ya."

Arliss wanted to. Oh, god — how she wanted to! She'd never known how badly she wanted to shoot him, probably *had* wanted to since the second month after they were married, when she saw him leaving Miss Pearl's with a sheepish grin on his face and she realized that their marriage was a sham.

As Roy kept moving toward her, she tried to squeeze the trigger. But her finger seemed frozen in place, merely resting against the trigger. She bit her lip, but she couldn't fire the gun.

Roy jerked his arm up and sideways, against her hand holding the gun. The gun discharged with an angry *crack.* The bullet tore into the ceiling, causing dust to sift onto the table. The gun flew over the table to bounce off the front wall and clatter onto the floor.

"Bastard!" Arliss screamed.

Roy backhanded her hard. She twisted around and flew forward against the table. She tried to push off the table but Roy pressed himself up against her backside, pinning her there. He sniffed her neck and then the blanket hanging off her left shoulder.

"What's that smell?" Roy sniffed the blanket again, like a dog. "What is that?" There was a stretched pause. He lifted the blanket to his face, scowling down at it, giving it a good, long sniff. "That ain't no smell I recognize. That's a *man's* smell."

"Roy, let me go!" Arliss screamed, trying to push him away from her.

He held her fast against the table, pinning her arms to her sides. "Who's that smell, Arliss? Who does that smell belong to?"

"Roy, no!"

"Who?"

"Roy!"

"That's why you're wet — ain't ya? You tried to wash his smell off. But you didn't do it." Roy sniffed the blanket again, then tossed it away. "You tried, but you couldn't wash his smell off, Arliss. Who was it? You tell me, you hear? I'm gonna ride up into them mountains, and I'm gonna kill the son of a bitch!"

"Roy, you're crazy! Let me go!"

"You think so, do you? You think I'm just gonna forget that you rode up into them mountains and rutted like a back-alley cur with some man? Ha!" Roy started to slide her skirt up her legs. "You lie beneath me like I'm somethin' you're just toleratin', waitin' for it to be over. But you go up into them mountains and you rut like somethin' *wild*! Ain't that right, Arliss?"

"Stop!" she screamed.

"No, I ain't gonna stop!"

He continued to slide her skirt up her legs. She could feel his heart beating fiercely against her back. She could also feel his desire. His body was hot, fairly trembling with lust. Imagining her with another man had aroused him!

"Oh, god — stop, Roy!"

He slammed her face down against the table. Keeping her pinned to the table with his body and with one forearm pressed against the back of her neck, he reached up and pulled down her pantaloons and drawers. He was breathing hard, grunting and sighing. Arliss tried to lift her head but there was no give in Roy's arm nor in his body rammed against her.

He ripped the pantaloons off her with a loud, grating grunt, and flung them away. He did the same to her drawers.

"Roy . . . Roy, goddamn you," she sobbed, feeling him moving around behind her, bending his knees, unbuttoning his pants. "Roy, stop," she said, her voice trembling, tears trickling down her cheeks. "Stop this, right now, Roy! I'll tell my father!"

"You do that," Roy said, and then she could feel his engorged manhood pressing against her as he spread her legs apart with his right knee. "You do that, and you also tell him about the man you fucked in the mountains!"

Arliss gave a grating cry against the tearing burn as he rammed himself into her, his arm pressing even harder against the back of her neck.

Mercifully, he finished quickly.

He pulled away from her with a grunt and stumbled backwards, his breath rasping in and out of his lungs. Arliss was too weak to stand. There was a horrendous burning in her belly. She dropped down the end of the table and collapsed onto the floor.

She lay on her side. She snaked one arm across her belly and drew her bare legs up. Roy stood over her. He was still breathing hard, shoulders rising and falling heavily. He glared down at her, stretching his lips back from his teeth.

"Now that we've come to an understandin'," he said, his voice phlegmy, "I reckon I'll get back to work."

He grabbed his Stetson off a hook by the door, and left.

Arliss drew her knees to her belly, gritting her teeth against the pain of the vicious attack, against her rage and hopelessness.

She closed her eyes and cried.

CHAPTER 4

The next day, late morning, Hawk halted his grullo on a rise and found himself staring across a broad valley toward a town sprawled across a chunk of dun-colored prairie about one-mile square.

He hadn't known there was a town out here. But, then, he'd never been to this neck of the frontier before. That was why he was here now. Since he lived to kill those who deserved killing, he tended to cut broad swaths and burn bridges. He figured few people would recognize him here. With this neck of the territory being fairly well off the beaten path, he likely wouldn't be hunted here by those who were hunting him, either — namely, deputy U.S. marshals and bounty hunters, the occasional Pinkerton.

While Hawk hadn't known there was a town out here, he'd figured there must be one around somewhere. When he'd left his bivouac earlier that morning, he'd come across a trail that had appeared well traveled, scored as it was by both horse and wagon prints. It had appeared a well-maintained stagecoach run.

Most well-used trails, especially stagecoach trails, eventually led to towns.

He was gazing across a valley at such a town now.

An instinctive apprehension touched him. He usually avoided towns. For such a man as Hawk, towns often meant trouble. But since he'd never visited this one before, the chances of trouble catching up to him here were slim.

Also, he didn't intend to let any grass grow under his feet in the town beyond. He was low on trail supplies. He'd stop in town long enough to fill a couple of croaker sacks with possibles, including a few bottles of whiskey, and then he'd ride south and west. His intention was to wend his way back to a cabin he maintained in the remote San Juans. He'd hole up there for a month or two while his back trail cooled and then, before the autumn cold and snows came to the high country, he'd ride south to spend the winter in Arizona or northern Mexico.

Surely, he'd find some men who needed killing in Arizona or Mexico. Most likely, both places. Everywhere on the frontier were men who needed killing. Even some women. Hell, Hawk couldn't think of a place on god's green earth that wouldn't be better off with its human herd culled. That's how he saw himself — a culler of the human herd.

He looked down at the badge he wore pinned to his shirt, partly covered by the left flap of his wool-lined leather vest. It was a deputy U.S. marshal's badge that he usually wore upside down, for that's also how he saw himself — as an upside-down lawman. There was no need to advertise himself here, however. He unpinned the badge and shoved it into a pocket of his vest, where it snuggled with the small horse his late son, Jubal, had carved from a chunk of oak.

The horse and an ambrotype photograph of Jubal and his dearly departed mother, Hawk's beloved wife, Linda, was all that Hawk had to remind him of his family so brutally taken some years ago now by "Three Fingers" Ned Meade.

Hawk brushed his hand across the Russian revolver positioned for the cross-draw on his left hip, then lifted his reins and clucked to his horse, which started down the rise. Fifteen minutes later, he walked the horse along the main street of the town, which a badly weathered sign jutting up from a clump of rocks and buck brush at the town's outskirts had identified as Cedar Bend.

A fairly typically rough-hewn ranching supply town, Hawk thought. A dozen or so wood frame or adobe brick false-fronted building establishments, some a combination of both, some shaded by a cottonwood or two. Nothing made the settlement stand out from any of the other such places he'd visited on his travels across the frontier.

Hawk angled the grullo toward one of the three hitchracks fronting the Arkansas River Saloon. He had few weaknesses, but a drink in a quiet saloon now and then was one of them. He'd have that drink, possibly two or three drinks, then stock up on trail supplies in the mercantile he'd spied another block to the south, then head back to the mountains long before sunset.

Now and then he'd imbibe in the pleasures of a whore, if he could find one to his liking. One that wasn't liable to leave him with a burning case of the Cupid's itch. That was another weakness of Hawk's. The occasional need for a woman. He wished it wasn't, but he was a man with a man's desires, and there it was.

Fortunately, his carnal sojourn of the evening before with the pretty young woman he'd saved from the lake had satisfied that need for the time being. Hawk wondered about her in a vague sort of way. He didn't like to get sidetracked by abstractions, and ever since she'd ridden out of his camp, that's what she was. An abstraction.

Hawk tied the grullo to the hitchrack, mounted the veranda, and pushed through the batwings. The place was pleasantly quiet. It smelled of sawdust and beer. There were only five other customers drinking at various tables in the long, narrow room, and two business types in bowler hats standing facing each other at the bar, sudsy mugs of brown ale in their fists.

They all looked at Hawk, raising their brows with interest. The wanted circulars his face adorned notwithstanding, such wistful gazes were to be expected. Hawk knew he cut a singular figure. Not only was he tall, dark, and green-eyed, he also wore two big, well-kept pistols. Obviously, he was no traveling minstrel.

When Hawk was satisfied none of the men around him were bounty hunters or federal lawmen or Pinkertons, he walked straight ahead to the bar at the back of the room. A snarling bear's head was mounted above it and so were several sets of deer and elk antlers. A dapper little man, bald-headed and wearing armbands on the sleeves of his ruffled shirt, stood behind the bar, gazing at the newcomer through wide, light-blue eyes.

The eyes had a childlike quality. They were filled with awe now at the impressive-looking stranger standing before them. The mustache of a proud lion mantled the small barman's upper lip. It must have been the little man's way of compensating for his diminutive, otherwise nondescript stature.

"Help you, stranger?" the little man asked in a little man's feminine voice, giving one sweep of his mustache an absent tug.

"I'd like a bottle of whiskey. Not one you brew in a stock trough out back, but somethin' you got with a label on it. I'm gonna take it over there and drink down part of it, and if I like it, I'll take two more."

"Oh," said the little man, as though he found the order somewhat peculiar and maybe a little fascinating. "Well, all right, then." He turned to look up at the shelves of his back bar, lifting a delicate hand and brushing his tapering fingers across the labels. "Well, then . . . let's see. How 'bout this one here? It comes up from Texas. A little spendy, but if it's good tangleleg you're lookin' for, then this is probably the best one I sell."

"You recommend it?" Hawk said.

"Uh, well . . . yes," said the little man, flushing a little as he ran his pale-blue gaze across his customer's broad shoulders. "But, uh . . . with reservations . . . and a nod to individual taste, of course. If you don't like that one, I'll buy you a taste of somethin' else. How would that be?"

He suddenly seemed a little worried the newcomer might get colicky and start shooting up the place.

"All right," Hawk said, typically taciturn. "How much?"

"Let's just see if you like what you drink out of the bottle, and then we'll settle up," said the little man, holding up his delicate hands in supplication.

"All right," Hawk said, picking up the bottle in one hand and grabbing a shot glass off a near pyramid with the other. "Obliged."

He started to turn away. The little man said somewhat sheepishly but affably, "Where . . . where you from, stranger?"

Hawk glanced back at him, brows ridged.

The little man slid his eyes to the two others standing to Hawk's right. They both looked down. The little barman moved his pale, thin lips inside his mustache, as if to speak, but no sounds came out.

Then he just held up one of his pale hands

again in supplication, waving off the ill-advised query and smiling.

Hawk took his bottle and glass over to a table at the side of the room, about halfway between the front wall and the bar, kicked out a chair, and sank into it. He kept his back to the wall.

He glanced at the other customers. They were watching him furtively. When his eyes met theirs, they turned away quickly and resumed the conversations they'd been involved in when Hawk had walked in and they'd found themselves distracted by the curious newcomer.

Hawk popped the cork on the bottle and filled his shot glass. He sipped the whiskey, rolled it around in his mouth, let it wash to the back of his tongue, and swallowed. He looked at the barman. The little man was watching him expectantly. Hawk pooched out his lips and dipped his chin with approval.

The barman smiled and gave an end of his outlandish mustache a tug.

Hawk finished off the first shot of the whiskey. Already, the forty-rod was warming him, sanding off the sharp edges. The saloon was cool and dark. He liked the molasses-like tang of drink that permeated the air. He liked the hushed murmur of the conversations. He liked the crude but homey way the place was outfitted. He even found himself liking the little barman with his preposterous mustache, who was now running a rag over the top of the bar and conversing with the two businessmen drinking before him.

Hawk kicked out a chair to his left, and crossed his boots on top of it. He refilled his glass and sank back into his chair, enjoying himself. He sipped the whiskey slowly. It wasn't the best he'd tasted, but he'd tasted worse. It would do for these parts.

He'd drunk down half of his second shot when the drum of galloping hooves rose in the street fronting the place. The men around him stopped talking and, frowning, turned to stare through the dusty front windows. Hawk squinted against the outside glare. Three horseback riders galloped past the place, a couple of pedestrians hurrying to keep from being trampled. When the riders had disappeared to the north, their dust hung heavy in the air behind them.

The other men in the saloon muttered darkly, one grimacing and shaking his head. One said, "That's what happens when you spare the rod."

"Ain't that a fact?" said the man he shared a table with.

Hawk finished off the second shot and refilled his glass. He liked it here. He'd stay another twenty minutes or so, then head over to the mercantile. Besides, his horse needed a rest before it climbed back into the mountains.

Hawk raised his shot glass to his lips but pulled it down when two men walked quickly past one of the two front windows. They wore dusters similar to those of the three who'd galloped past the saloon. They were moving too quickly for Hawk to get a good look at them, but he thought both wore neckerchiefs up over their faces. A second later they pushed through the batwings, guns raised. They had their faces covered, all right.

"Everybody just sit still and there's a *chance* you won't get hurt!" said the one wearing a red neckerchief with white polka dots drawn up over his mouth and nose. A curl of thick blond hair hung down over his right eye.

"Oh, shit!" said one of the customers sitting directly across the room from Hawk.

"Oh, shit, is right!" said the second man who'd entered the saloon with his gun drawn. He laughed, grinning behind his green bandanna. He was shorter than the first man but broader through the waist and shoulders.

A door flanking the bar opened, and a third man entered the room wearing a bandanna over his face. This man was more fashionably dressed than the other two. He seemed to fancy himself a gunfighter, for he wore a low-slung holster thonged on his thigh. The holster was trimmed with three hammered silver *conchos.*

Conchos also decorated the leather belt around his waist, below his cartridge belt. He wore Mexican *charro* slacks with the traditional flared cuffs, and a light-blue shirt embroidered with fancy red stitching tracing the outlines of two curvy, naked girls. His crisp tan Stetson had a snakeskin band.

"This here's a holdup, Mister Pevney," the third man said, proudly, waving his silver-chased Colt pistol around. He pulled a burlap sack out from behind his cartridge belt, and tossed it onto the bar. "Kindly fill that sack for me, please, and don't be holdin' out on me. I know you did a whoppin' business last night, it bein' payday out to the Crosshatch, and every Crosshatch rider spendin' the whole long night in town!"

The dapper little barman glowered red-faced at the holdup man who fancied himself a border tough. "Johnny Stanley, who are you tryin' to fool with that neckerchief up over your face? Don't you think I know it's you?"

He thrust a hand over the top of the bar, pointing out the other two hardtails also waving their pistols around. "And that's Avril Donnan and Dave Yonkers. You boys put away them guns and get the hell out of here before I send for Coates!"

"Can't fool an old fool, I reckon, boys!" Chuckling, the would-be border tough jerked his bandanna down off his face. He aimed his pistol toward the bar, narrowing one eye and clicking back the hammer.

The little barman gave a yelp and pulled his head down as Johnny Stanley blasted a forty-four round into the back bar mirror. The mirror shattered, the glass raining onto the floor.

The little barman lifted his head and turned to his mirror in horror. "Good god! *You got any idea what that mirror cost me?*"

Stanley aimed his pistol at the little barman. "The next one's gonna be drilled right between your beady little eyes, Mister Pevney . . . less'n you get to fillin' that bag right quick." He turned to slide his gaze across the other customers, including Hawk. "The rest of you start diggin' your valuables out of your pockets and layin' 'em out on your table. My pals Avril and Dave will walk by to collect momentarily, and if all goes well, and none of you hoopleheads piss-burns me too bad, we'll be on our way. If I even *think* any of you upstandin' citizens of Cedar Bend is holdin' out on me, I'm drill you a third eye. Understand?"

The little barman grabbed the burlap sack off the bar and, looking constipated, took it over to where he apparently kept his cash-box under the bar. The others in the room began emptying their pockets onto the table. Avril and Dave began making the rounds, holding their own bags open so the customers could drop coins and bills and wallets and timepieces into them.

The toughnut who Pevney had called Dave — the stockier of the first two men who'd entered the saloon — walked over to Hawk's table. He'd removed his neckerchief from over his face, as had Avril. Dave scowled at Hawk, who was staring at Dave over the rim of his half-raised shot glass.

Hawk's boots were still crossed on the chair.

"Hey, you — what makes you think you're so special? Empty them pockets. Lay it all out on the table, now, you hear?" Dave aimed his cocked Schofield at Hawk's face.

Chapter 5

Hawk stared at Dave over the rim of his shot glass, which he was turning very slowly in his fingers.

Dave looked aghast, frustrated. He turned to Johnny Stanley, who was just then accepting the burlap sack back from the little barman. "Hey, Johnny — this son of a bitch 'pears to be wantin' for that third eye you was talkin' about."

Johnny cradled the bag in his left arm and looked at Hawk. "Oh, yeah?"

Sneering, he walked over to stand beside Dave, scowling down at Hawk.

"What?" Johnny said. "You think you're too good to get robbed, Mister?"

Hawk sipped his drink and then set it on the table. "No. And you three ain't too good to get dead."

"What's that supposed to mean?" Dave asked. "Can't you see we both got our guns aimed at you, you cork-headed fool? Who are you, anyways, and what makes you think you can talk to us like that? We're here to rob you, and that's just exactly what we're gonna do. You ain't no better than these other hoopleheads."

He glanced at the barkeep and the other customers.

"You'd best think it through," Hawk said, staring up at Johnny through those cold, green eyes.

Johnny's scowl deepened. His dimpled cheeks flushed, and his eyes blazed with anger. "No, you'd best think it through, you simple fool!" He wagged his Colt at Hawk. "You get your valuables up here on the table or I'm gonna blow your head off!"

Hawk stared back at Johnny for a full five seconds. Then he turned to Dave, also scowling at him but looking a little skeptical, fearful. His cocked Schofield was shaking slightly in his hand.

Hawk cast his glance over Johnny's left shoulder, toward the bar, and lifted his right cheek with a shrewd grin. Johnny and Dave both did exactly what Hawk knew they'd do. Believing someone was making a play behind them, they cast quick, cautious glances toward the bar.

Hawk gave his table a violent shove with both hands, ramming it into both Johnny and Dave. The two would-be saloon-robbing desperadoes were pushed backward, off-balance.

As they yelled and swung their pistols back toward Hawk, the rogue lawman drew his Russian with his right hand and his Colt with his left hand.

The Russian roared a wink before the Colt, knocking Johnny backward. Screaming, Johnny triggered his own Colt into the ceiling while Dave drilled a round into the very edge of Hawk's table.

Rising from his chair, Hawk calmly clicked the hammers of both his pistols back. He aimed at Johnny, still stumbling backward, raking his spurs along the floor. Hawk's Russian punched a round into Johnny's right shoulder, evoking another shrill, girlish scream.

Meanwhile, Dave was reestablishing his balance after tripping over a chair. Just as he got his Schofield leveled on Hawk again, Hawk's Colt roared, drilling a round into the dead center of Dave's chest. Dave triggered his Schofield into the wall behind the rogue lawman, then threw his arms up as though he was surrendering. Then he dropped straight back onto the table behind him, jerking and flopping his arms and legs as he died.

The third toughnut, Avril Donnan, stood on the other side of the room from Hawk. He was dancing around, yelling, trying to get a clear shot at the man who'd just trimmed the wicks of his pards. Before Avril could get a single shot off, Hawk triggered both his Russian and his Colt at the same time, carving two holes, one directly beside the other, in the upper center of Avril's chest.

He yelped and dropped his pistol, twisting and raising both forearms to his chest. He threw his head back as he stumbled around as though drunk, the two businessmen standing at the bar sidling away from him. (By now, the other customers were all lying belly down on the floor, their heads in their arms.) Meanwhile, Johnny awkwardly gained his feet and, crouched forward, ran in a shambling fashion, dragging his boot toes, out the front batwings, screaming, "Help me — I've been killed!"

He ran off the veranda and into the street, still screaming, "Help me — I've been killed!"

Hawk strode casually across the room in which the gun smoke wafted thickly, and pushed through the batwings. Johnny was out in the middle of the street, staggering and bleeding. Horseback riders and wagon drivers and pedestrians all stopped to stare incredulously at the screaming young man in the gaudy garb of the southwestern border *bandito.*

"Help me!" Johnny screamed again, swinging around to point accusingly toward Hawk. "My name is Johnny Stanley an' that bastard over there done me in! Someone get my father! That bastard killed me!"

"Apparently I haven't yet," Hawk grumbled, stopping on the saloon's front stoop. He raised both pistols, cocked them, aimed, and narrowed his green-eyed gaze down both barrels at once.

The Russian and the Colt bucked and roared simultaneously.

Johnny was punched back off his feet and lay dead, limbs spread out, in the street. The driver of a freight wagon couldn't get his team stopped in time. The heavy rig ran over Johnny and left the young, dead, would-be saloon robber rolling in the dust like an oversized ragdoll.

The freight driver bellowed at his mules, checking them down. Once the wagon had stopped, the driver hitched around in his seat to look at the dead man lying under a cloud of wafting dust behind him.

"I'll be damned," the driver said, running a beefy forearm across his mouth. To no one in particular, he asked, "Ain't that Johnny Stanley?"

The bearded freighter shuttled his shocked gaze from Stanley to Hawk, still standing on the veranda of the Arkansas River Saloon.

"I reckon it *was,*" the rogue lawman muttered, holstering both his smoking pistols. "Now at least he's *quiet.*" He turned toward the batwings but stopped when he saw a man wearing a five-pointed star walking along the main street, angling toward what remained of Johnny Stanley. The lawman's wary eyes were on Hawk. He had a pistol in his hand, aimed in Hawk's direction.

Hawk winced, then sighed. The lawman was an unwelcome complication. Lifting his hat and running his hand through his hair, Hawk walked back into the saloon while the other customers, looking harried and owly as they collected their valuables, brushed past him on their way out. They sidestepped the rogue lawman as though taking the long way around a stalking panther.

The little barman, Pevney, stood staring wide-eyed toward Hawk. "Is . . . is he . . . dead?"

"Unless he can digest lead bettern' most," Hawk said, and returned to his table.

He sat down, finished what whiskey was

left in his shot glass, then poured himself another drink. He knew he was due a visit from the local law, so he might as well wait here and get it out of the way. He didn't have to wait long. Boots thudded on the veranda. The lawman looked over the batwings. His eyes found Hawk, and then he stepped inside, aiming his Remington out from his right hip, keeping that elbow close to his belly.

He was an odd-looking gent with an understated, well-trimmed mustache and a nose that hadn't received the doctoring it had required.

He stopped inside the batwings and looked at the two dead men still spilling blood onto the sawdust-covered puncheons.

Pevney cleared his throat and said haltingly, "Johnny and his two buddies there, Dave an' Avril Donnan . . . they was . . . tryin' to rob me, Marshal Coates. Johnny blew out my mirror there. They was . . ."

He let his voice trail off when Coates stopped and cast a scowl at him. "Did I ask you a single question, Joe?"

Pevney just stared at the local lawman, pale-blue eyes round as saucers.

"Did I?" Coates asked again, louder, tighter.

Joe Pevney shook his head.

"Then kindly shut the fuck up," Coates said.

Pevney swallowed.

Coates walked over to Hawk's table.

"Who're you?"

Hawk lifted his shot glass, sipped his whiskey, and then set the glass back down on the table. "Hollis. George Hollis."

"Cold steel artist, eh?"

"Nah. Just a man who don't like to empty his pockets unless it's my own idea."

"Think you're smart, do you?" Coates curled his upper lip. "Well, Hollis, you're in a fine pickle."

Hawk said nothing. He turned to gaze out one of the two windows facing the street on that side of the room. A small crowd had gathered around Johnny Stanley. Several in the crowd were gesticulating wildly.

"Did you hear me, Hollis?"

Hawk turned to Coates. "I heard you. I ain't in no kind of pickle — fine or otherwise. The barman there told you what happened."

Coates glanced over his shoulder at Pevney, who looked sheepish. "I didn't hear a goddamn word that fool said." He turned back to Hawk and gestured with his revolver. "Stand up. Slow."

Hawk sighed. He picked up his shot glass

and threw back the rest of his whiskey. Then he slid his chair back too quickly for Coates's taste.

"I said slow, damnit! And get those hands up!"

Slowly, Hawk raised his hands to his shoulders. Slowly, he rose from his chair.

"Now, just as slowly," Coates said, taking a wary step back, "set them pistols on the table."

Hawk set first the Russian, then the Colt on the table.

"Get them hands up!" Coates barked.

Hawk raised his hands to his shoulders.

Coates shoved each of Hawk's pistols down behind his own cartridge belt.

"Now, then," Coates said, waving his cocked revolver and taking another cautious step backward, "let's go on over to the jail. I'm gonna lock you up and go through my wanted circulars. Just got a fresh batch in off the stage last week."

He gave a shrewd grin. "I got me a suspicion I'll find your half-breed face on one of 'em."

Keeping his hands raised, Hawk walked slowly across the room toward the door, stepping over Dave's bleeding carcass. As he did, Coates bent down behind him, scooped the burlap pouch off the floor, and tossed it over to the wide-eyed Joe Pevney. "Put that away, you damn fool!"

Pevney caught the pouch against his chest, and staggered backward, his eyes on Hawk and Coates.

Hawk pushed through the batwings. He glanced over his shoulder at Coates. The lawman was staying about six feet back behind him, just out of Hawk's reach.

"North," Coates said when Hawk had dropped down the steps and into the street. "Any fast moves, Mister, and I'll drill you right here and leave you to the wild dogs that come into town every night to scavenge."

"All right," Hawk said, heading north along the main street. "Don't be so nervous."

"Nervous, hell!" Coates hurried forward and gave Hawk a hard, angry shove and then stepped back again, out of his prisoner's reach. "You're the one that oughta be nervous. When Mortimer Stanley gets wind of what you done to his boy — his only boy — he's gonna throw a necktie party in your honor!"

Coates chuffed with delight.

As Hawk walked north, he glanced to his left. A box wagon had been drawn up in front of Burt Schweigert's Harness Shop.

Several townsmen and even a few women in feathered picture hats stood around, watching as a thin younger man with a limp and a much older, gray-haired gent loaded young Johnny Stanley into the back of the wagon. On a side panel of the wagon had been painted in ornate red lettering CHARLES AND BUSTER McCAULEY UNDERTAKING.

"Well, you made a friend in the McCauleys anyway," Coates said.

When Hawk reached the town marshal's office, he moved up onto the porch. Coates's boots thudded on the steps beside him.

"It's open," Coates said.

Hawk paused in front of the closed door. He turned his head to peer at the crowd still gathered in front of the harness shop. The tall man and the older, gray-haired man were now driving away with Johnny Stanley's body flopping lifelessly in the back, beneath a ratty gray blanket. They were heading for the saloon to pick up the other two cadavers.

"I told you, it's open," Coates said, louder.

"I was just wonderin'," Hawk said.

"Wonderin' what?"

He glanced over his shoulder at Coates, narrowing one eye in speculation. "I never been sure what's appropriate in this situation. Should I send flowers?"

Hawk grinned as he tripped the door's steel latch. Behind him, Coates's face reddened with anger. He lunged forward, raising his pistol, intending to slam the barrel down against the back of Hawk's head. "You smart-ass son of a — !"

Hawk wheeled quickly right, throwing up his right arm. Coates's gun slammed into it, and fell to the floor of the porch. Coates gave a surprised grunt. Hawk brought up a right haymaker and laid it across the lawman's left cheek with a resounding smack that sent Coates hurtling backward off the porch steps and into the street, where he fell in the dirt on his butt.

Hawk moved down the porch steps as Coates grabbed Hawk's own Colt from behind his cartridge belt and, snarling, raised the revolver and thumbed the hammer back. The gun roared. Hawk kicked it out of the man's hand but not before the bullet had torn into Hawk's upper left arm.

Coates screamed and clutched his injured right wrist in his left hand.

Hawk grabbed the man by his shirt collar, hoisted him up out of the dirt, and pummeled the man's jaws. Coates grunted and dropped to a knee. He fumbled for Hawk's second gun. The rogue lawman pulled his

Russian out from behind Coates's cartridge belt, and tossed it away.

He grabbed Coates again by his shirt, lifted him up, and, fury radiating from the raging fire in his wounded left arm, sent four right jabs into Coates's mouth.

The man's lips exploded like ripe tomatoes.

Coates fell in the dirt, spitting blood flecked with teeth. With the bellowing roar of an incensed grizzly, he hoisted himself up and came at Hawk with both fists flying. Hawk's left arm was useless, but rage was a living thing inside him. Coates managed to land a single right cross on Hawk's left cheek, but Hawk ducked another one and came up slamming his right fist again and again into Coates's ribs.

He could feel bones snap beneath the pummeling.

Hawk kept battering the lawman as Coates stumbled backward, screaming, futilely trying to shield himself from the vicious blows of an enraged, unabashed fighter who outweighed him by twenty pounds. Unlike Coates, who had a doughy midsection, very little of Hawk was anything but taut sinew and bulging muscle.

When Coates crouched to shield his ribs, Hawk hammered the man's ears until they looked like red cauliflowers.

Coates fell on the sun-bleached boardwalk fronting the Wells Fargo office and post office, on the far side of the street from the jail. He lay on the boardwalk, legs curled into the street, breathing hard and wagging his head. He spat more blood. Both eyes were swelling like purple eggs.

"Enough," he said so softly and gratingly that Hawk could barely make it out. "Enough. Fer . . . chrissakes . . . *enough* . . . !"

Hinges squawked.

Hawk looked up. An old man with a long, gray beard and wearing a leather-brimmed cap with the Wells Fargo insignia sewn into the brim stared warily out through a ten-inch gap in the office door.

The Wells Fargo agent looked from Hawk to the bloodied local lawman writhing like a landed fish on the boardwalk before him. He looked at Hawk again. His gaze slid to Hawk's bloody left arm.

Hawk followed the man's gaze. Blood oozed from a hole about halfway between Hawk's shoulder and elbow. Shit. He'd have to get it sewn up before he left town. There was no telling when he'd find another town . . . not that he felt inclined to set foot in another one again. Not after his experience in this one, which didn't figure on improving any time soon.

Hawk removed his neckerchief and began wrapping it around his arm. He looked at the old man. "Sawbones hereabouts?"

CHAPTER 6

Arliss sat in Roy's kitchen, sipping the tea she'd just brewed.

She'd thought that with time she'd come to see the kitchen, the house, as both hers and Roy's. But now, after yesterday's savage attack, she knew she'd never see the house as anyone's but Roy's. Roy's and Charmian's.

Arliss would continue to live here, a stranger, in Roy's and Charmian's house. When she could find somewhere else to go and a way to support herself, she'd pack her bags and leave. Roy and Charmian . . . the dearly departed Charmian, crawling with worms and maggots in her cold, dark grave . . . could have the place to themselves.

Until then, Arliss would live here. But she no longer considered herself Roy's wife. If Roy ever considered her his wife again, she'd take the butcher knife down off the wall over the range and geld him with it.

That would clarify the situation right well.

She gave a satisfied snort. Then, feeling the burn in her left cheek, which had been scraped raw when he'd taken her atop the table, she brushed her fingers across the scrape, which she'd lightly dabbed with arnica.

"Bastard."

Arliss lifted the tea to her lips once more. She frowned, staring down at the steaming brew. It was missing something . . .

Arliss got up from the table, walked into the parlor area of the house, and retrieved Roy's bottle of rye from the cabinet by his rocking chair. She returned to the table, sat down, pried the cork out of the bottle with a grunt, and splashed a goodly portion into the tea. She sipped it.

"Mmm," she said, licking her lips. "Better."

She was about to take another sip when she heard a stumbling sound outside. A man was out there, breathing hard, grunting. The stumbling grew louder. She looked at the post where Roy usually kept his spare revolver, the old Remington. It was no longer there, however. He'd probably hid it or taken it with him to the jailhouse after she'd nearly shot him with it yesterday, before he'd raped her.

Arliss froze in her chair, not sure what to do — how to defend herself.

Boots thumped on the stoop and then the knob rattled and the door was shoved open. Roy lurched halfway in; then, one hand remaining on the doorknob, he dropped to his knees. At least, Arliss thought it was Roy. His face looked like a swollen, bloody mask, the lips torn and ragged.

"Arliss!" Roy bellowed throatily, blood dribbling down his chin.

Arliss's heart thudded. She started to rise from her chair, then, feeling a strange, devilish satisfaction, sank back down in the hide seat.

"Arrr-lissss!" Roy bellowed again, louder. He hadn't seen her sitting at the table, only eight feet away from him.

With malevolent casualness, she said, "What happened, Roy? You look like you got run over by an ore wagon." She almost laughed.

Roy jerked his head toward her. His eyes glistened between the swollen lids. He dropped his hand off the doorknob, and said, "Help me upstairs!"

Arliss sipped her whiskey-laced tea and arched a brow at him coolly. "What happened?"

Roy ground his teeth. He spoke as though

he had rocks in his mouth. "Will you just get your ass up out of that chair and help me upstairs? Then fetch the doc!"

"Get yourself upstairs."

"Arliss!"

"Get yourself upstairs, Roy."

He looked at her. Then he dropped to all fours with a groan. "Goddamn . . . goddamn you . . ."

Arliss slid her chair back and rose. "No. Goddamn you, Roy." She walked around the table and glared down at him. "What happened? The Chain Link boys?" When the boisterous Chain Link hands got drunk on payday, Roy often had trouble controlling them, despite his toughness. He'd had several deputies over the years, but the job didn't pay well enough to compensate for Roy's pugnaciousness, so none had lasted long and Roy had given up on trying to fill the position.

He shook his weary head. He was looking at the floor. "You help me upstairs, I'll tell you." He glanced up at her through his swollen eyelids. "I'll tell you about your brother."

Arliss frowned. So her brother had something to do with this. Somehow, she wasn't surprised. When there was trouble in town or in the county, Johnny usually had some part in it. He'd been running off his leash for the past several years.

Arliss no longer had any sisterly feelings for Johnny, but out of mild curiosity, and because she wanted to get Roy out of her hair, she grabbed his arm and helped him to his feet. She struggled to get him upstairs and into the room she now considered to be his alone. His and Charmian's.

After yesterday, Arliss had moved into the spare bedroom — the room originally intended for Roy and Charmian's child, which, because Charmian had been barren, had never materialized.

Arliss got Roy on the bed. He lay huffing and puffing and grunting in agony.

"Whiskey," Roy groaned, glancing at the whiskey bottle on the small, round table near the upholstered armchair in the corner.

The table sat beneath the bright, oval-shaped spot in the otherwise sun-faded wallpaper that marked where the tintype wedding photograph of Roy and Charmian had been hanging until Arliss had moved in and taken it down.

Arliss poured whiskey into the glass. She held the glass out to Roy. When he reached for it, she jerked it back.

"Johnny," she said.

Roy scowled up at her, shifting his smoldering gaze between her and the whiskey that shone a pretty amber in a ray of sunlight angling through a near window.

"Dead," he said, snidely. He almost smiled.

She felt her lower jaw loosen. She didn't know why she was surprised. She'd always figured her brother would end up killed in one of the dustups he was always getting involved in. Still, the information took her off-guard. Johnny gone. She didn't feel any emotion about the loss, for she and Johnny had been alienated for years. Still, the world suddenly seemed a little stranger than it had a moment ago.

Roy reached for the glass. Again, Arliss pulled it away.

"Did you kill him?" she asked.

"Hell, no." Roy chuckled without mirth. "He was tryin' to rob the Arkansas. Some stranger shot him and those two worthless trail pards of his."

"What happened to you?"

"The stranger resisted arrest." Roy stretched his lips back with a grimace, then grabbed the glass out of Arliss's hand before she could pull it away again. He scowled down into the glass and said through a snarl, "He got his, though. I put a bullet in him."

Roy tossed back half the whiskey in the glass. Pulling the glass down, he smacked his lips and gave a phlegmy sigh. "Just wait till your pa hears about this." He shook his head fatefully. "Hell's gonna pop. That firebrand could do no wrong in old Mort Stanley's eyes. The more shit he pulled . . . the more men he killed . . . your pa just puffed his chest out a little bigger."

Arliss was deep in thought, staring down at the bed. She jerked when Roy barked, *"Fetch the doc, goddamnit. My ribs need settin'!"*

Arliss shot him a withering glare. "You go to hell!"

She swung around, stomped out of the room, and drew the door closed behind her.

"Arliss, you fetch the doc!" Roy yelled on the other side of the door. His tone grew desperate, wheedling. "I told you I was sorry about what happened yesterday. I was in a real bad mood. I won't ever do it again. You fetch the doc, now — all right, honey?"

She strode into the smaller room at the end of the hall and sat on the edge of her bed. She folded her hands in her lap and stared out the curtained window at a cottonwood branch. She could hear Roy's labored breathing edged with frequent groans on the other side of the wall.

She sat there for maybe a minute, pondering. Coming to a decision about what she would do, she got up, grabbed her felt riding hat and her gloves and light wool jacket, and left the room. As she dropped down the stairs, her heels clicking on the uncarpeted steps, Roy yelled from behind his closed door, "Goddamnit, Arliss, you fetch the doc for me, you contrary bitch!"

Arliss went out and drew the front door closed behind her.

She strode out of the yard and traced the shortest route to the heart of town, where Doctor Donleavy housed his practice. She hadn't intended to fetch a doctor for Roy. He deserved to suffer. But then she realized that his suffering would only make her suffer more. Best get him patched up and out of the house as soon as possible.

"You lookin' fer the doc, Miss Arliss?" asked George Howe, who was arranging hoes and other hand implements in a barrel outside Howe's Mercantile. Arliss had started up the outside stairs that gave access to the doctor's office in the mercantile's second story.

Howe gave a weak, knowing smile. He knew she was fetching the doctor for Roy.

Arliss stopped three steps up from the bottom of the stairs. "Is he in?"

Howe shook his head and shuttled his somewhat sheepish gaze kitty-corner across the street. "He's over at the hotel. Whitehall fetched him a half hour ago."

"Oh," Arliss said, puzzled. "All right."

She glanced at Howe once more, then headed across the street to the Colorado Hotel.

"Sorry about Johnny, Miss Arliss," Howe called behind her, smiling weakly.

"No, you're not, Mister Howe," Arliss said over her shoulder. She doubted that anyone in the county would miss Johnny Stanley. She doubted she'd miss him. At least, she wouldn't miss the firebrand he'd been for the past five years. The only one who'd miss him was their father.

She went into the hotel and learned from Chester Whitehall, the hotelier, that the doctor was tending a patient on the second floor, in room nine. Arliss climbed the stairs to the second floor, and knocked on the door of room nine. She hadn't realized the door wasn't latched. Her first knock nudged it open far enough that she could see a gun being jerked in a blur of fast motion from a holster. The gun was cocked and aimed at her.

Arliss gasped, then froze.

She looked up from the gun to the face of

the man wielding it. Her heart fluttered, and her mouth went dry. The doctor, who stood beside the man sitting on the bed aiming the pistol at her, turned toward her, wide-eyed. He'd been wrapping the knuckles of the sitting man's right hand with a white flannel bandage. The sitting man's upper left arm was also wrapped. A spot of red shone on it.

The sitting man's torso was bare.

Arliss remembered looking up at that same bare chest as it hovered over her. She remembered the masculine smell of it, the sensation of the man's slab-like muscles against her kneading hands as he'd toiled between her legs.

"Arliss . . . ?" the doctor said.

The sitting man depressed his revolver's hammer. He lowered the gun to the bed and stared at her, expressionless. His green eyes burned in deep sockets. They threatened to mesmerize her.

Arliss tore her gaze away from his. She cleared her throat, swallowed, and looked at the doctor. "I just wanted to let you know that Roy could use some tending, too, Doc."

Doctor Donleavy was tall and gaunt with a beak-like nose and pewter-gray hair combed to one side, a rooster tail licking up at the top of his head. He blinked his somber eyes, and said, "I don't doubt that he does. Is he home?"

Arliss nodded.

The doctor said, "I'll head over to your place just as soon as I'm done here. Only be another minute or two."

Arliss nodded. She glanced once more at the man on the bed. He stared at her with the same blank expression as before. Again, her heart fluttered. She looked at the bandage on his arm, then at the hand the doctor was wrapping. She could see that the knuckles were scraped and bloody.

As he continued to wrap the sitting man's hand, Donleavy looked at her again. "Was there something else, Arliss?"

Arliss shook her head and turned away.

She walked down the hotel stairs and stepped out onto the front veranda. She pressed her hands to the rail and leaned forward, breathless. Of course, she hadn't forgotten about the stranger, but she hadn't expected to see him here in town. She certainly hadn't expected their paths to cross in this way.

No, nothing like this.

Johnny was dead and Roy was home in bed, badly beaten by the man she'd . . .

Arliss turned to look up at the hotel's second story. She gazed at the window of what she thought was room nine. She found herself strangely drawn to it. To *him* — to the man who'd killed her brother and beat her husband half to death.

Who was he? What was he doing here? How was it that he had come out of nowhere to so quickly and improbably affect her life in such a large way?

Arliss turned to stare out into the street. Several townsmen and townswomen were walking past the hotel. They saw her standing on the hotel veranda, and they stared, obviously having heard that her notorious brother had been killed. They were wondering how she was taking the news. Most importantly, however, they were likely wondering how her father would take the news.

Johnny dead.

Arliss still couldn't quite wrap her mind around that fact herself. But a fact it was. She wasn't sure why, but she felt the need to be the one to tell her father. She certainly didn't owe it to him to be the one. He deserved to be told by someone outside the family. By one of his several agents in town. Maybe that's what he'd prefer, in fact. Maybe, if she told him, he'd realize that a large part of her motivation was to rub his nose in it.

So what if he did?

Arliss dropped down the veranda steps and headed over to the furniture store that doubled as Charles and Buster McCauleys' undertaking business. The shed in which the undertaking took place was behind the main store. Arliss walked through the store cluttered with mostly rough-hewn, handmade furniture toward the shed in the back. Mrs. McCauley was sitting in a chair behind the cluttered rear counter — a strangely masculine-looking woman wearing a green visor as she flipped through a ledger book, a pen in her ink-stained fingers.

She looked at Arliss but said nothing, her eyes grim, her thin mouth turned down at the corners.

Arliss walked out the main store's back door and found Charles and Buster in the undertaking shed. The elder McCauley was rolling a cigarette as Buster, taller and leaner than his father, and walking with a limp he'd been born with, fitted a lid onto one of the two caskets that were propped on sawhorses. Both men jerked with starts as Arliss walked into the shed and stopped between the open double doors. Charles jerked with a more violent start than Buster, dropping his cigarette and makings sack on the shed's earthen floor.

"Lordy, you gave us a fright, Miss Stan . . . I mean, Mrs. Coates!"

"I came to see my brother." Arliss nodded at the casket that Buster was standing next to. He'd taken a stumbling step back when Arliss had appeared so unexpectedly. "Is that him there?"

Chapter 7

Remembering his manners, Charles McCauley doffed his hat and held it over his heart. "We're so sorry for your loss, Miss Arliss — Buster an' me is, an' the missus, too of course."

"Is that him there?" Arliss asked again, staring at the coffin.

Buster looked at his father.

Charles said, "Yes, it is. We just got him laid out and ready to be planted. Where would you . . . ?"

"I want to see him." Arliss walked toward the diamond-shaped coffin.

Charles stepped forward, as well. "Oh, you wouldn't want to see him, Miss Arliss," the elder McCauley said tenderly. "He's shot up awful bad, and a freight . . . well, a freight wagon rolled over him."

Arliss looked at Buster. "Open it."

Buster looked from Arliss to his father. Arliss kept her commanding gaze on him.

Charles sighed. "Well, all right, then." He and Buster pried up the coffin lid, and removed it. They held it between them, stepping back as though to give Arliss some room with her brother.

Arliss stepped up beside the coffin and closed her hands over the edge. She looked down at her brother glaring up at her. Arliss heard herself give an involuntarily groan of revulsion at the hideous sight.

"See, now," Charles said, stepping forward again with the coffin lid. "I told you that ain't somethin' you need to —"

Arliss held up her hand. "Give me a minute!"

Charles stopped. He and Buster shared a look.

Arliss drew a deep breath and looked down once more at her brother. Johnny lay with his hands crossed on his belly. He was a bloody mess. His face was relaxed but his eyes were open as though maintaining the same expression as when Johnny had realized he'd been killed. It was as though he were still staring at the man who'd killed him.

The man in room nine of the Colorado Hotel.

Arliss was a little surprised to feel no sadness about her brother's demise. She was shocked to see him lying here, but only because he'd cut such a broad swath for such a long time, been such a big story around here for so many years, that he'd grown to myth-like proportions.

She also felt a little sheepish and it took her a minute, searching her feelings, to realize that her guilt stemmed from the fact that she'd lain with the man who'd killed him, and enjoyed it. As if that somehow made her complicit in Johnny's death.

Which, of course, it did not.

No, there was no reason for her to feel guilty. She did, however, feel repelled now by the man she'd lain with. By the man in room nine. He'd caused the crumpled, bloody, glaring mess before her . . . the mess that had once been a living, breathing man.

True, that man had turned sour years ago and become a blight on the county. Still, he'd been alive. And the man in room nine had killed him.

Obviously, what Arliss had suspected about that man was true.

He was a killer. Likely, a hired killer. A shootist. One who'd been holing up in the mountains, likely trying to stave off the punishment due from recent transgressions not unlike the one glaring up at Arliss now.

A killer. She'd lain with a killer. The killer

of her brother.

And she'd enjoyed it.

In fact, she hadn't been able to get that night out of her mind. She'd found herself thinking about it even more intensely after Roy had raped her. Odd, how two such similar acts could have such dissimilar effects.

One had caused her to feel in a way she hadn't known was possible.

The other had been torture. Because of it, she'd vowed she'd never let Roy touch her again. She'd kill herself first.

Arliss stared down at her dead brother.

No, she didn't feel any sadness. Even her guilt was quickly diminishing, now that she knew there was no cause for it. The feeling moving in to replace it was one of . . . what?

Satisfaction.

Johnny's death was proof — as though any was needed — that their father was a monster. And Arliss couldn't wait to show the man the irrefutable evidence.

Mortimer Stanley had turned Johnny into what he'd become, and he'd turned his only daughter over to the town marshal of Cedar Bend as a bribe, keeping the lawman in his pocket. Another reason he'd forced her into marriage with a man she hadn't loved was to simply be rid of her. He hadn't wanted her on the ranch anymore, reminding him how her brother had turned out. He especially hadn't wanted her around after Arliss had seen what she'd seen, what she knew about the death of her mother.

Arliss looked at Charles and Buster McCauley staring at her curiously, holding the coffin lid vertically between them.

"I'm going to need your wagon," she said. "I'm going to take my brother home to our father."

The McCauleys shared another dubious look.

An hour later, Arliss sat in the driver's seat of the undertakers' wagon, staring up at two dead men hanging over the trail. Each man wore a noose around his neck. Both ropes had been tied off near the bottom of the pine tree from which the two men hung, twisting slowly in opposite directions in the mountain breeze.

Each was dressed in drover's attire typical of the area — wool shirts, neckerchief, vests, and brush-scarred chaps over faded denims, the denim nearly worn through on the insides of the thighs. The marks of men who spent most of their days in the saddle, riding for the brand.

One man wore a beard. His hair was long,

thick, and tangled.

The other wore a two- or three-day growth of beard stubble. He was blond, with a broad face and misshapen nose. The death grimace twisting his lips showed several missing teeth. His name was Early. He'd grown up in these mountains. Arliss had seen him out on the range when she was still living at home, and, more recently, she'd seen him in town. Last time she'd seen him, he'd been driving her father's supply wagon. He'd worked for her father as a ranch hand.

She didn't recognize the bushy-headed drover, but he'd likely worked for Mortimer Stanley, as well. They'd been hanged here together, on the Circle S range. Their faces were badly cut and swollen. They'd each been given a savage beating not unlike the one Roy had taken. Their shirts were torn and soiled.

Arliss grimaced, then shook the reins over the back of the gelding in the traces. She continued on up the trail that would take her to her father's ranch headquarters. Pines stood tall on both sides of the trail, at times nearly blocking out the sky. The trail followed the course of an old ravine. The route became impassable during the rainy season and during the spring snowmelt, making travel to town impossible for at least two months out of every year.

Arliss knew that fact very well — and the closed-in feeling it had given her every year she'd lived out here, having been born on the ranch. The closed-in feeling hadn't been such a bad thing, however. It had been a fact of life, and she'd come to even enjoy the feeling of living on an island of sorts.

Besides, she'd been happy most of those years. This was back before four years ago, before her mother had died and everything had gone to hell, including her father and her brother.

And herself, as well.

Now everything was changed. The ravine trail looked dark and menacing to her today, as it curved slowly up the mountain to the pass on the other side of which lay the ranch in a broad, grassy bowl along the North Fork of Diamond Creek. Home to her once. Now she felt as though she were on the trail to hell.

She was maybe two hundred yards from the top of the pass when a pistol cracked in the forest somewhere around her. The report echoed hollowly. It was followed by one more blast and the ensuing echoes.

Arliss's heart lurched. The gelding whickered testily.

"Hold up!" a man shouted. Because of the echoes, it was hard to tell, but Arliss thought the voice had come from her right.

She stared up the slope on that side of the trail. Her eyes picked out movement in the forms of two horseback riders coming down the slope, their horses picking their way, tails arched. The men rode out onto the trail ahead of Arliss, turned toward her, and reined up.

One of the horses whinnied and shook its head.

The gelding pulling the undertakers' wagon whinnied in kind.

The men stared grimly out from beneath the brims of their weather-stained Stetsons. It didn't take long, however, before both sets of eyes acquired the glassy cast of male lust. They looked at each other, smirking, and rode forward.

"Well, now," one of them said, approaching the wagon.

He opened his mouth to continue, but Arliss cut him off with, "I'm Arliss Coates. Your employer's daughter, if you ride for Stanley. And since that's the Stanley Circle S brand on both your horses, you do. Unless you're horse thieves, that is." She didn't recognize either man. That wasn't unusual. She hadn't been out here since she'd been married off to Roy, and her father's payroll was forever changing.

Both men sobered up quickly. They gave each other a quick conferring glance, and the first one said, "Oh, well, we're sorry if we spooked you, Miss Arliss. Mister Stanley's given the order we should check everyone we see out here. Rustlin' has been a problem of late."

"Oh?" Arliss said. "Who'd be foolish enough to rustle Stanley beef? Doesn't everyone know my father's reputation for not tolerating long-looping by now?"

"You'd think so," said the second rider, hiking a shoulder. "But . . ."

Arliss hooked a thumb over her shoulder. "What about those two decorating that pine tree back there? I recognized one as Lyle Early."

"That's Early, all right," said the first rider. He was a small, lean rider in a pinto vest and funnel-brimmed hat. He also had two smart-looking pistols on his hips. "Your pa thinks him and Newton was stealin' beef right out from under his nose."

"What do you think?" Arliss asked him, blocking the sun from her eyes with her gloved right hand.

The small, lean rider glanced at the other man — a tall man with a long, angular face covered with a cinnamon beard streaked with gray. He wore two pistols in shoulder rigs. He shrugged and grinned without humor at Arliss. "Like your pa tells us every morning before he sends us out on the range, we ain't paid to think, Miss Arliss. We're paid to work."

He grinned again. Then he glanced into the wagon box. "Who's that?"

"My brother."

Both men stared at her, their eyes widening, pupils expanding. They didn't seem to know how to respond to the information. They'd obviously known Johnny. They probably knew what a close relationship Johnny had had with their father.

They probably knew how the old man would take the news of Johnny's demise, as well.

The infamous Johnny Stanley . . .

"Well, if you two will excuse me," Arliss said, lifting her reins in her hand.

"We'll ride point for you, Miss Arliss," said the smaller man, turning his horse around and starting up the trail. "A purty girl shouldn't be travelin' alone out here!" He threw up an arm, beckoning.

The news had energized both men. Arliss knew from her own experience how any news, even bad news, could excite those who dwelled this far off the beaten path. The news of the demise of Johnny Stanley, welcome news to some, unwelcome news to others — namely, Mortimer Stanley — was nevertheless big news indeed.

They both galloped on up toward the pass, their yells echoing off the surrounding slopes.

Arliss shook the reins over the gelding's back. The wagon lurched up the trail, over the pass, down the other side, and into the yard of the Stanley Circle S.

CHAPTER 8

Arliss watched the drovers angle their horses over to the bunkhouse, which sat next to the breaking corral and one of the headquarters' two barns. As the riders pulled their horses up in front of the bunkhouse, the door opened and several men ducked out onto the stoop to join the three men who were already sitting there, smoking.

They were a ragged-looking lot. Long-haired, scraggly-bearded, mean-eyed, and dirty. They also wore guns — even the one who sat on the stoop, kicked back in his hide-bottom chair wearing only his balbriggans, hat, and boots.

No one seemed to be working. It was the middle of the week, but all of the hands appeared to be sticking close to the bunkhouse. The bleary cast to their gazes told Arliss they'd been drinking. Not working. Drinking.

Was it a holiday?

Puzzled, she looked around the ranch yard — at the tack shed, at the blacksmith shack, whose doors were closed, as if no one had been working there so far today; at the two corrals in addition to the breaking corral, and at the springhouse and the windmill and the stock tank ringing the base of it.

Aside from the men now standing or lounging around outside the bunkhouse, staring at Arliss dubiously, the place could have been deserted. The buildings looked rundown and unoccupied. Weeds had grown up around all three corrals. A corral gate hung askew. Several shake shingles were missing from the roof of the blacksmith shack. Both barns needed the chinking replaced between their stout logs, and they needed the weeds cut down along their stone foundations.

The dozen or so horses milling in the corrals needed currying.

Arliss cast her gaze up the rise to the south. Her heart fell at the shape the main house was in. Her father had built the place soon after he'd established the ranch, after he'd spent his first two years out here alone in a small, one-room log shanty he'd built himself.

Mortimer Stanley had taken pride in the building of the house, which resembled a manor house from the Antebellum South he'd taken his leave of several years before the war had broken out. Not long after he'd moved their mother out here, they'd welcome their first baby — their one and only boy, Johnny. Three years later, Arliss had come along.

They were a small family for such a large house, but Arliss had enjoyed the vast, airy rooms with their rich furnishings shipped to these mountains from places like Kansas City and New Orleans. Her father's initial investment in a Texas herd had paid off richly nearly right away, for he'd found a lucrative market for his beef in nearby mining camps and boomtowns.

Arliss had been happy here. For her first fifteen years, anyway . . .

The house now stood atop the southern rise, a steep, forested ridge looming behind it — an affront to her fond memory of the place. The house's clapboards and colonnade fronting the veranda badly needed paint. Shutters hung askew. Some were missing altogether. Weeds and brush grew thick inside the picket fence that also needed paint or replacing altogether. Some of the boards, including the entire front gate, looked entirely rotten. They were the color of soiled rags.

Arliss glanced toward the men on the bunkhouse porch. She didn't recognize any of them. They must have all been hired since she'd left here two years ago, married off to the town marshal of Cedar Bend. She wanted to find a familiar face, and ask him what had happened. Was her father dead? But she saw no one she felt inclined to speak with. They all eyed her curiously but also vaguely menacingly. Some had outright lust in their drink-rheumy eyes.

Arliss shook the reins over the gelding's back. The horse pulled the wagon up the rise and onto the cinder-paved drive forming a turnaround before the rotting trellis fronting the picket fence. The trellis was covered with dead vines tufted with dead, dried-up leaves that made dry rasping sounds in the breeze that kicked up dust around the hill.

Arliss set the brake and wrapped the reins around it.

She glanced at the house once more. Apprehension plucked at her. The house not only looked deserted, but haunted. She was half afraid she'd find her father dead inside, moldering, while his hands had been scavenging the place, drinking in the bunkhouse.

She climbed off the wagon and patted the gelding's neck. She looked down the rise toward the bunkhouse. The men were still standing out there, gazing at her. She turned away and pushed her way through the vines choking the trellis, through the front gate, and into the yard. She stopped when she saw a figure move out of the square shadow of the front door, and step out onto the broad veranda.

Arliss stopped with a start, slapping her hand to her chest.

She studied the tall, stoop-shouldered man with wild, thin, curly gray hair growing like a tumbleweed around his long, caved-in face. Mortimer Stanley leaned against one of the veranda's rotting wooden columns as though he needed propping up. He wore a ratty robe over balbriggans. He wore stove-pipe, mule-eared boots, and a gun holstered on his left thigh.

In his right hand, hanging down low by his side, was a bottle.

"Father . . ." Arliss said, a little breathless. He looked as though he'd been ill. He hadn't shaved in days. His skin looked pasty and oily.

"Damn." Stanley lifted the bottle to his lips, taking a drink. Swallowing, he said, "You're purtier'n a speckled pup. I always did say that."

Arliss couldn't bring herself to say anything. She was in shock at the state of the place. At the state of her father. Suddenly, she wished she hadn't come. She felt as though she were living one of those nightmares that occur just before waking, in which you find all the landmarks of your life in ruins, and all is lost. You awaken from such dreams, reeling a bit, but relieved that you'd only been dreaming.

Only now she wasn't dreaming.

Mort Stanley studied her through only vaguely familiar eyes, and when she didn't say something, he glanced at the wagon and said, "Who you got there?"

Arliss cleared her throat. Her tongue felt thick. She suddenly didn't feel the gloating satisfaction she'd felt on her way up here with the body of the brother whose life her father had ruined.

"Your son."

"What?"

Arliss glanced slowly back at the wagon, then turned to her father once more. His eyes came alive with concern as he pushed away from the column. He set the bottle down on the veranda floor, got his boots set beneath him, and, looking at Arliss with a suspicious, troubled expression, came down the steps heavily, shamble-footed, and strode uncertainly down the stone walk.

He brushed past Arliss, pushed through the vines threatening to seal up the trellis, and walked over to the wagon. He looked down at the coffin for a time, his hands on the wagon's side panels.

Arliss watched his shoulders rise and fall as he breathed, staring down in dread at the sanded pine box.

Finally, he glanced over his shoulder at Arliss once more, then walked around to the end of the wagon. He climbed inside, grunting and sighing, his face flushing with the effort. He stood over the casket, facing Arliss, his back to the ranch yard and the men watching from the bunkhouse.

He dropped to his knees. He was breathing even harder than before. His face was red-splotched and swollen, and his lips were parted. He dug his fingers under the edge of the lid, pried up the cover, and tossed it aside. It thudded loudly to the floor of the wagon.

Mortimer Stanley stared down at the body of his son glaring up at him.

"Oh," Stanley said, throwing his arms up and out from his sides in a weird pantomime of a slow hug. "Oh," he said again, his voice pinching and his lips pooching out as sobs overcame him. "Oh . . . oh, god!"

Mortimer Stanley lowered his arms and

lifted Johnny's torso out of the coffin. He hugged his son tight to his chest, pressing his left cheek against the side of Johnny's head, and bawled. His dead son hung slack in his arms, Johnny's open eyes glaring into space over his father's left shoulder.

From where Arliss stood in the yard, she could look out over the ranch yard below. Her father's men were all standing in front of the bunkhouse now, staring this way.

Stanley sobbed and howled over his dead boy's slack body.

Finally, he dropped the body back into the coffin. He drew a deep breath, snot and saliva dribbling off his nose and lips. He squeezed his eyes closed, shook his head, said, "Oh, god!" and then crouched over the coffin once more.

He drew Johnny out of the pine box and, crouching uncertainly, pulled the body up over his right shoulder. Arliss wasn't sure how he managed it — she felt certain he'd topple over the side of the wagon and break his neck — but he climbed out of the back of the wagon with Johnny hanging slack over his right shoulder.

Stanley must have been stronger than he looked, though as he passed Arliss on the cracked stone walk, he staggered badly, sobbing, his breath rasping in and out of his tired, old lungs. Arliss watched him negotiate the broad veranda steps and then disappear into the dark house that stood like a specter of its former self.

Arliss stood there on the walk, wanting to give her father some time alone with Johnny. She felt hollowed out and dull and very, very alone. This day had been a shock to her mind, though of course it had really started yesterday when Roy had raped her on their kitchen table. What was happening now seemed like the natural, dark progression of the bad time that had started twenty-four hours ago. Or maybe it had started even earlier.

Maybe it had really started two nights ago, when the stranger had rescued her from the lake and they'd coupled like wild wolves on that stony ledge above the dark water . . .

The raucous patter of off-key piano chords jerked Arliss out of her reverie. They caromed out the front door like the volleys of some strange-sounding pistol, reverberating gratingly. The notes softened slightly, and her father's voice sang:

"Sowing in the morning,
Sowing seeds of kindness,
Waiting for the harvest and the time of reaping,

We shall come rejoicing, bringing in the sheaves."

Arliss glowered through the half-open front door. As her father continued singing the old song, starting the refrain, she walked up the veranda's moldering steps and continued through the front door.

"Bringing in the sheaves, bringing in the sheaves,
We shall come rejoicing, bringing in the sheaves . . ."

Arliss followed the unruly piano hammering and the loud, flat, drunken singing through the broad foyer. The parlor opened to the right, through a set of open French doors. She noted that two of the panes in one of the doors had been broken out, and the glass was still on the floor. Another pane was cracked diagonally. She moved slowly, tentatively, through the opening and into the carpeted foyer with its heavy leather furniture and bookshelves.

The grand piano sat in the room's far corner, just beyond the cold stone hearth of the large fireplace. The Confederate flag was still draped over the top of the piano, as it had been all the years Arliss had grown up here in this too-grand house.

Now her brother's body lay atop the flag, atop the piano, glaring up at the ceiling.

Johnny's arms were flung out to each side. His boots hung down over the piano's near edge. His legs bobbed a little as Mortimer Stanley continued to whack violently at the piano keys, leaning forward and singing loudly, crazily, and with obvious emotion, tears rolling down his sallow cheeks.

"Sowing in the sunshine, sowing in the shadows,
Fearing neither clouds nor winter's chilling breeze,
By and by the harvest, and the labor ended,
We shall come rejoicing, bringing in the sheaves."

Arliss moved slowly into the room and sat on the edge of the overstuffed leather couch angled before the cold, stone fireplace. She placed her hands in her lap and tucked her feet close together beneath her. She stared with solemn incredulity at the drunken ghost of a man her father had become, wishing she could feel more satisfaction at the wicked turn his life had taken.

Stanley had just started the refrain again

when he stopped, then hammered the keys violently, the notes thundering out of the piano and making Johnny's lifeless head wag from side to side. Stanley dropped his head and sobbed for a long time. Finally, he lifted his head, ran his hands through his hair, and then turned his wet gaze to his daughter.

He didn't say anything. He just stared through those tear-flooded eyes, his face a mask of terrible agony. It was as though he were silently imploring her for an antidote to his malaise. Again, Arliss wished she could take some satisfaction in his pain, after all the pain that he had caused his family. But she could not. All she could feel now for the man she hated even more than Roy Coates was befuddlement at his unexpected turn, and pity.

She looked around the dusty, cluttered room, then shuttled her gaze back to her father and shook her head slowly, uncomprehendingly. "What the hell has happened here, Father? What have you become?" She lifted her chin toward a front window. "Who are those men out there, and why aren't they out on the range, working your cattle?"

Stanley drew a long breath, swept first the back of one hand across his face, wiping away tears, then the other one. "I need 'em here. The range is infested with rustlers. Mostly from other ranchers pushin' their way in. These mountains are crawlin' with men wantin' to take me down."

"Really?" Arliss found that hard to believe. She knew her father had once had some trouble with rustlers, but most ranchers in these mountains had respected her father's prominence as the first stockman here, and steered clear of the Circle S. "What about Early and the other man — your men — I saw hanging from a tree down on the main trail?"

Stanley shrugged. "Rustlers, both. Stealin' my cows. A few at a time. Harder to miss 'em that way, the beef." He gave a shrewd wink. "They were buildin' their own herd — their own *stolen* herd, *my* herd — to start their own spread or to sell to the railroad, or maybe the Ute reserve."

"Lyle Early?" Arliss found that even harder to believe than the notion that other men were crowding her father. "He was on your roll a long time. Why would he suddenly — ?"

"That's just it." Stanley rose, glanced down at his dead son adorning the piano, then walked over to a liquor cabinet resting beneath a trophy elk head that had turned gray with dust. Cobwebs clung to its horns.

"He figured I trusted him. That's how it always works. The ones you trust most" — facing the wall, he threw back a shot of brandy, then turned slowly to face his daughter — "are the ones you gotta watch."

"Like Mother."

Stanley narrowed his eyes at his daughter, then lifted his mouth corners a little.

"A shrewd, cunning wench — eh, Father?" Arliss curled her upper lip. Her eyes blazed. "Looking for any advantage over you. Took the first opportunity that presented itself to step out on you."

Still, Stanley said nothing. He stood there staring at her with that bizarre half-grin on his wasted face.

Arliss shook her head. "She had no intention of doing what she did. I know she didn't. She couldn't help herself. You were . . . are . . . a cold, cold man. Your ranch always came first. And you were rough on her. Too rough. She wasn't like you. She was a sweet Southern belle. I'm more like you. I can take life a little rougher. But Mother was a romantic. She needed love. Tender love from a man who genuinely loved her."

"I loved her," Stanley said stubbornly.

"You don't know the meaning of the word."

Crimson smudged Stanley's cheeks. "Don't you talk to me that way!" He canted his head toward the piano. "Who killed your brother? That's all I want to hear out of your mouth. Then you can ride on back to town."

"No." Arliss shook her head with her father's own kind of stubborn. "I want you to hear this, because I've been wanting to get it off of my chest for a long time."

CHAPTER 9

"Say it, then," Stanley barked at his daughter. "Say it, if it means so goddamn much to you to beat a man when he's down! Your own father! Go ahead!"

His angry, bellowing voice echoed throughout the house.

Arliss's heart had quickened against the familiar attack — the burning eyes and thundering voice. She swallowed, welcomed the burn of anger once more radiating out from the base of her spine, but kept the wave of emotion under control.

She said, "He was a man to her — Richard Neeley. He was a good, kind man to her. I saw the moment they fell in love. It was just after Neeley had moved to the mountains and established his own ranch — in partnership with you, of course — at the base of Dead Man's Forge. He and his foreman had come for Christmas dinner. It was Neeley's sixth or seventh visit. It was that night — the one I'm talking about — when I suddenly realized he hadn't come to talk business with *you.* It was to see *her.* I saw the way they looked at one another. They'd fallen in love!"

Stanley stood glaring at his daughter, lips bunched, a vein bulging in his left temple. He was squeezing his empty goblet in his right hand, down low by his right thigh.

Arliss continued: "I came upon them that spring. They'd met in a glade by Roberts Creek. I was horrified, of course. I'd never seen such a thing — let alone my own mother with another man. In that way."

Stanley's eyes widened. "You saw them?"

Arliss smiled, nodding. "I was horrified at first." Her smile broadened. "And then I was happy for her. Finally, she had found love."

"You bitch! You knew and you didn't tell me! You *bitch*!"

Arliss clenched her hands into fists beside her on the couch, steeling herself against his wrath, and said, "I was terrified when I realized you suspected something about Mother's frequent rides into the countryside, not returning for several hours. I prayed god would not let you follow her, but that day that you did . . . I followed *you* as you followed *them.*"

Arliss felt her lips quiver as the dam of her emotions began to rupture.

"I wanted so badly to get around you and to find her . . . *them* . . . before you did . . . but you were too far ahead . . . and you were riding too fast. You rode right up to that little woodcutter's shack they'd been meeting in."

Arliss closed her eyes as tears oozed from them. *She didn't want to remember any more about that day, but the images flowed across her mind until she was there, in the woods by the little stream that muttered around the south side of the ancient woodcutter's cabin, long abandoned, that had become her mother's and Richard Neeley's meeting place.*

She crossed the stream and stopped her horse. She stared in shock as her father dismounted his cream stallion about thirty yards from the cabin's front door, and dropped the reins.

Stanley jerked up the flap of his coat, unsheathed his revolver, and strode toward the shack. His shoulders were tight, his stride resolute, angry.

"No!" Arliss wanted to scream. "No, Father. No!"

But it seemed as though her vocal cords had dissolved in her throat.

Just then she heard a woman's loud groan-

ing laugh seep out between the unchinked logs of the shack. Arliss hadn't yet made love at that point in her life, but she knew instinctively what that sound had been — her mother's love cry.

Her father stopped abruptly. He stared as though stricken at the shack.

"No, Father!" Arliss had tried to scream, sitting frozen to her saddle. "No, Father. No, no, no, no!"

Stanley continued forward. He kicked in the dilapidated door, ducked through the low opening, and disappeared into the shack's deep shadows.

A woman screamed.

Neeley shouted, "My god — nooo!"

A gun popped twice. Then a third time. A fourth, a fifth . . . a sixth.

Arliss had sat her horse so tensely, her bones ached. Her eyes were squeezed shut. She jerked with each hollow-sounding blast erupting inside the shack.

There were garbled choking sounds.

Arliss opened her eyes just as her father ducked his head to walk out of the shack. He strode over to where his cream stallion stood, whickering nervously. Mort Stanley did not look toward Arliss, who sat her horse about forty yards from him, her figure no doubt obscured by trees and branches. He seemed in a trance as he grabbed his reins and swung into the leather.

He guided his horse around to ride back the way he'd come. Only then did he see his daughter staring in wide-eyed terror at the cabin. He stopped the stallion, jerking back on the reins and regarding Arliss in shock, his face flushed crimson. He sat his prancing stallion for nearly a full minute before, apparently finding no words, he kicked the cream into a gallop.

Horse and rider dashed past Arliss, crossed the stream, and hammered back in the direction of the Circle S.

Moans and sobs rose from inside the shack. There were scuffing sounds, as well. Arliss's mother appeared in the doorway. Naked and bloody, she crouched under the weight of Richard Neeley, whom she seemed to be trying to help exit the shack. She was holding Neeley's right arm around her neck. Her own left arm was around the bloody man's waist. Neeley's head was down. Blood dribbled from his mouth and onto the shack's earthen floor.

The skin of both appeared parchment white behind the blood that seemed to cover them nearly entirely.

"Help!" Arliss's mother cried, sobbing. "Someone . . . please, help us!"

She managed to make it outside with Rich-

ard Neeley, but then Neeley collapsed and Arliss's mother collapsed on top of him. They lay groaning and sobbing together for what seemed a long time, but must have been only a minute or two.

Neeley fell still. A few seconds later, Arliss's mother fell still, as well.

They lay entangled in each other's arms — two dead lovers, their blood mixing in the dirt and pine needles beneath them.

Arliss stared in shock. It was as though her heart had stopped and she was staring back at the world from a place just this side of death. A voice inside her head spoke to her. It told her to go to her mother. But she could not.

Her mother lay naked in death with Richard Neeley. The fact that she was naked and dead and lying in the arms of her dead lover so repelled the fifteen-year-old Arliss that when she regained some semblance of consciousness, she swung her horse around and galloped back across the stream, back in the same direction her father had gone as he fled the scene of his horrific crime.

Arliss looked up from her lap now to stare at her father, who stood, his arms hanging slack, staring at the floor in front of him. He looked as though he were in a daze.

"Neither one of us ever mentioned that

day," Arliss said, brushing the tears from her cheeks. "All these years . . . we never said a word about it. It was a secret I helped you keep. Why?"

She shook her head. "I have no idea. Maybe because I was a coward. Maybe because I had no one to tell. Not even Johnny. I couldn't tell him what his father had done. I couldn't tell anyone. I couldn't even confront you with it . . . or leave here, which is what I should have done. Instead, I lived here with you, sharing your secret. Betraying the mother I loved. All I could do was hate you as you hated me for the secret you knew I was keeping, reminding you each day of the horrible thing you did.

"Finally, two years later, you found a way to get rid of me. You shipped me off to Roy Coates in return for his everlasting loyalty to you in town."

Arliss rose and walked over to stare down at her dead brother. She placed a hand on the side of Johnny's cold, pasty cheek.

"I'm as much to blame for his death as you are, Father. Johnny loved Mother more than either of us. His never knowing who killed her was sheer torture. All he ever knew was that she and Richard Neeley were found together, just as you left them. So he erupted with a violence he inherited from you. He gathered the roughest of your men and did exactly what you'd wanted him to do when you'd showed him their bodies, as if you were coming across them for the first time. He and those toughnuts rode over to Neeley's ranch, killed all of Neeley's men, and burned his headquarters to the ground."

Arliss turned to her father still staring at the floor. "You got Neeley's range in the bargain. I suppose you figured you deserved it." She looked at Johnny again. "Well, I hope you're proud of what you turned your son into. A man without a conscience. A frustrated bandit and killer out to murder the whole world as though he could kill his demons along with it. The joke was on him, though — wasn't it, Father? The real demon was you."

Stanley turned to Arliss. He blinked, staring at her dully. "Who killed my son? Tell me that and then leave. Get the fuck out of my house and don't you ever come back, you filthy bitch."

Arliss smiled. She wasn't sure why, but suddenly her father's words no longer hurt her. Her bitterness caused her to want to taunt him, to stick the knife in a little deeper and twist it. "That, dear Father, is something you're going to have to find out for your —"

"Gideon Hawk." The unexpected man's voice caused Arliss to jerk with a start.

She darted her gaze to the French doors and saw a man standing just outside them — a medium tall, deeply tanned man with a drooping mustache, floppy-brimmed canvas hat, corduroy breeches, and knee-high leather boots. He wore a black vest over a pinstriped shirt trimmed with a string tie. A pistol was thonged on his right leg, *pistolero*-style.

He stared into the parlor, slid his gaze between Arliss and her father, and then doffed his hat with an unctuous air.

He cleared his throat. "The man's name is Gideon Hawk, Mister Stanley."

Stanley scowled at the newcomer.

The man stepped into the room, holding his hat down low in front of him. "I'm John Donnan, Mister Stanley."

"I know who you are. Avril Donnan's brother."

"My brother died with your son, Mister Stanley. Hawk killed Dave Yonkers, as well."

"Hawk, you say?" Stanley's expression had turned incredulous.

"Gideon Hawk. Known by newspaper scribblers as 'the Rogue Lawman.' "

Donnan smiled with satisfaction. He had

seedy, dark-brown eyes drawn up at the corners. Large, dark-brown freckles spotted his leathery cheeks. Arliss had seen him around town from time to time, sometimes with Johnny. She figured that, like most of those her brother had ridden with, he probably worked as little as possible.

Otherwise, he rode with Johnny, holding up stages, rustling cattle for outlaw syndicates, or getting involved in one small but bloody range war or another up north or down south.

There was always a squalid, seamy air about John Donnan. That air hung heavy on him today, here in the dilapidated parlor of the once regal Stanley house.

"The Rogue Lawman," Stanley said.

Arliss's heartbeat quickened anxiously as she studied her father, knowing what was to come.

"The Rogue Lawman," Stanley said again, musingly. "Why that handle?"

"The man was a deputy United States marshal over in Nebraska Territory. Then some gang led by 'Three Fingers' Ned Meade hanged his son. They was gettin' even for Hawk havin' run Meade's outlaw brother down. Same day as Hawk's boy's funeral, Hawk's wife hanged herself from a tree in their backyard."

Donnan apparently felt comfortable enough to have a seat on the same sofa on which Arliss had been sitting a few minutes earlier. He set his hat on his knee, leaned back, and placed his left arm on the sofa back, casually, as though he were an equal here.

He continued: "Some crooked prosecutor got Meade off, saved him from hangin'. Turned him loose. After that, Hawk went off his nut. He hunted the prosecutor down. Hanged him. Hunted the rest of Meade's gang down, killed 'em. Hunted Meade down. Hanged him. After that, he started wearin' his badge upside down. Now, he rides for his own brand of justice."

"Why did he kill my son?"

Arliss answered this one. "Johnny and Mister Donnan's brother and Yonkers were trying to hold up the Arkansas River Saloon."

Donnan said, "What I heard was Johnny tried to shake down Hawk. Apparently, Johnny didn't know the brand of man he was dealin' with."

Stanley turned to Arliss. "Where was your husband when all this was going on?"

"He was there." Arliss gave a sardonic snort. "He tried to arrest this Mister Hawk . . . and is now sporting about five broken ribs and a face that looks like freshly ground beef. He's in bed. Drunk."

"Where's Hawk?" her father asked, angrily.

Arliss said, "He left town."

At the same time, Donnan said, "He's still there." He glanced at Arliss, dubious. Switching his gaze back to Stanley, he said, "Johnny winged him. He'll likely be holed up till tomorrow mornin', at least. Last I heard, the doc sewed him up."

Stanley looked at Arliss. His eyes were hard, questioning, accusing. She held his gaze with a stern, accusing, mocking one of her own.

"What do you want, Mister Donnan?" he asked out of the side of his mouth.

Donnan gave a sheepish half-grin, hiking a shoulder. "Well . . . I know how much you value information on the doin's in town, Mister Stanley. Especially when it concerns you."

"Money?"

Donnan hiked his shoulder again, then smiled again, awkwardly.

Stanley turned to the liquor cabinet and refilled his goblet. He took a sip of the brandy and then walked over to the piano. He stood beside his daughter and stared down at his dead son glaring up from the

Confederate flag.

"You want money for helping me better understand the circumstances of my boy's death." It wasn't a question.

Donnan's face darkened with a flush. He winced a little, shifting his head around on his shoulders, uncomfortably.

"I know you, Donnan. I know your family."

Donnan didn't say anything. Stanley threw back the entire goblet of brandy. Then he slammed the goblet down on the piano and swung around to face Donnan. He slid his revolver from his holster and clicked the hammer back.

"You're all Yankee trash. Always have been, always will be. And now you . . . you, common gutter trash . . . have the gall to ride out here in the aftermath of my boy's murder and seek to exchange information on the circumstances of his death for *money*!"

"No!" Donnan threw his hands up in terror. "Mister Stanley — hold on!"

"Yankee vermin!"

The gun slammed its report against Arliss's ears.

She jerked with a start, blinked, and stumbled back against the piano. She stared in shock at Donnan, who sagged back against the couch with a quarter-sized hole in the middle of his forehead. Arliss closed a hand over her mouth as though to stifle a scream that did not come. Befuddlement nearly overcame her. Her knees threatened to buckle.

She looked at her father, who grinned with satisfaction at Donnan, who now sat back against the couch, jerking wildly as he died, blood bubbling out of the hole in his forehead.

Stanley saw his daughter's horrified, incriminating gaze. He raised his pistol again, and aimed it at Arliss's head.

"Get out," he said through gritted teeth. "Go on back to your worthless husband. Tell him if he can't take care of the man who killed my boy, he's fired!"

Arliss stared at the maw of the revolver in her father's fist. It was only about three feet from her head. She was not surprised that she felt no fear at all. It had been a while now since she'd last cared if she lived or died. The way her life had gone since her father had killed her mother and Richard Neeley was like a nightmare she'd been living day by day, with no end in sight. Since it hadn't ended in the lake, it might as well end here as anywhere else.

Slowly, Arliss shook her head. "Who are

you, Father? Do you know? Have you ever known?"

"I told you to get out."

"You started out well. Now, look around you." Arliss glanced at her dead brother atop the piano. She looked around the dusty room, cobwebs hanging like thin curtains from the ceiling corners, dead leaves on the rug. "All you had was ambition. That was all you ever had. You had no heart and no soul. Now, look what you've become. A lonely, raging, obsessed lunatic believing the world is closing in on him. Have you taken a good look at your men lately?"

Arliss arched a brow and looked at Donnan, who had now stopped quivering and was sagging against the couch as though napping.

"They're all the same trash as Mister Donnan there."

"I told you to get out," Stanley said. "I won't tell you again."

"You won't need to."

Arliss glanced once more at Johnny and then walked across the room and out the door.

She climbed into the undertakers' wagon and started down the trail to Cedar Bend. She hadn't ridden far when five riders overtook her from behind, and galloped past her. It was late in the afternoon. Copper sunlight winked off the guns the riders wore strapped around their waists or jutting from rifle scabbards.

They swept her with their lusty gazes as they passed, laughing. They galloped on ahead and disappeared.

Her father had sent them, Arliss knew. He'd sent them to Cedar Bend to avenge her brother.

Arliss shook the reins over the back of her horse. "Hy-yahh, boy. Hy-*yahhhh*!"

Chapter 10

A knock sounded on the door of room nine in the Colorado Hotel.

Hawk was sitting in a chair by the window, hoping the glass of whiskey he was sipping would soon kill the pain in his arm. After the doctor had sewn and wrapped the wound, Hawk had taken a long nap. The pain had awakened him a half hour ago.

When the single knock had come, he'd been leaning forward in the chair, laying out a game of solitaire on the upholstered ottoman before him. Now he reached for one of his two holstered pistols, cocked it, and looked at the door, frowning.

"It's me," a young woman's voice said on the door's other side.

Hawk rose, wincing at the gnawing pain in his left arm. He wore only his balbriggan top, unbuttoned. He glanced at his shirt on the bed, then gave a wry chuff. She'd seen him in far less than his underwear. Keeping the cocked Russian in his right hand, because he wasn't one to take chances, he walked to the door, twisted the key in the lock, and turned the knob.

The young woman whose name Hawk had learned from the sawbones was Arliss Coates, the former Arliss Stanley, sister of dearly departed Johnny Stanley, stood in the hall, staring at him. Her cheeks were newly sunburned. Several locks of her dark-brown hair had pulled loose of the horse tail she'd gathered them in, and curled down against the sides of her face.

Her eyes were wide and bright.

She placed her hand on his chest, just above the open button V that exposed the inside slabs of his exposed pectorals. "You have to leave here!"

Hawk looked at her hand on his chest. She looked at it, too. Her cheeks flushed slightly. She removed her hand and then looked both ways along the hall. A half-dressed, middle-aged man with a bulbous paunch stood in a half-open doorway, holding a half-eaten sandwich. He stared at Arliss and Hawk dubiously, chewing.

Hawk stepped back into the room, drawing the door wide.

Arliss came in, and Hawk closed the door.

Arliss moved in close to stare up at him,

her eyes anxious. "You have to leave here, Gideon. My father has sent men. They're in town. I just came from the undertakers' place, and I didn't see them on the street, but I know they're —"

She stopped when Hawk placed two fingers on her lips. "Drink?"

She frowned. More color rose in her cheeks. "What?"

Hawk walked to the dresser, grabbed his bottle, and held it up. "You look like you could use a drink."

She studied him incredulously. Then she looked at the bottle, and shrugged. "Why not?"

Hawk poured whiskey into a water glass on the dresser and took it over to her. "Ride a long way today, did you?"

She accepted the drink. "I took my brother home."

"Oh?"

Hawk sat back down in his chair and leaned forward, resting his elbows on his knees. "Have a seat."

Arliss strode past Hawk to stand beside the window flanking him. She slid the curtain back from the window and peered out, looking cautiously up and down the street. She turned to Hawk, sipped the whiskey, swallowed, and made a face.

When the rye had mellowed inside her, she said, "My father is a powerful man in these parts, Gideon. My brother cut a wide swath. Most folks let him cut it because my father usually made up for it, somehow."

"Is that a fact?"

"My brother once killed a shotgun guard on the local stagecoach. He was a young man with aging parents. My father built the guard's parents a new house and gave them a thousand dollars. Nothing more was said about the killing, and my brother was allowed to run free."

"Tidy."

"I am married to the man you beat the hell out of."

"The town marshal. I gathered that."

"My father forced me to marry Coates in return for Coates's loyalty to my father."

"Is that why you walked into the lake?"

Arliss didn't seem to know how to answer that. She gazed at her glass. She took another sip, glanced carefully out the window once more, then sat down near Hawk, on the end of the bed. "I don't think you understand. My father has fifteen, maybe twenty men. They're gunmen. My father believes someone's crowding him. He's sent five of those gunmen here. He can send more." She leaned forward, placing a hand on his knee. "You have to leave here, Gideon."

"I don't run, Arliss."

She studied him closely, her eyes probing his. After a time, a knowing smile shaped itself on her pretty lips, and she tapped the nail of her right index finger against the rim of her glass. "You don't care, do you? You don't care what happens. You don't care if you live or die."

Hawk shrugged and sipped his own rye.

"I heard what happened," Arliss said. "To your boy . . . your wife."

Hawk just stared back at her, stone-faced, the hand holding his drink resting on his right knee.

Finally, Arliss took another sip of her drink and then she rose and, holding the drink low in her left hand, walked over to him. She used her foot to slide the ottoman out of her path, and stood between his spread knees, crouching over him. She placed her right hand on his cheek. "All right, then. If anyone understands you, it's me. You've been warned. Tomorrow you'll likely be dead. Just know one thing. That night . . . by the lake . . ." She shook her head slowly. "I've never felt so alive."

Hawk took her hand in his, slid it to his mouth, and pressed his lips to it gently.

She drew a breath, tucked her bottom lip under her upper front teeth, then removed her hand from his and turned away. She walked to the door. She took too long opening it. By the time she started to slowly turn the knob, Hawk had crossed the room to her. He reached in front of her and turned the key in the lock, locking the door. She turned to face him.

Hawk sandwiched her face in his big hands and tipped her head back. She parted her lips for him, and he kissed her. She wrapped her arms around his neck and returned the kiss, hungrily, mashing her mouth against his and groaning deep in her throat.

Hawk felt his blood rise. He could feel Arliss's heart beating against his own. Her breasts swelled, pushing against his chest.

He kissed her with more and more passion, more and more hunger, before he drew his head back from hers, leaving her breathless and staring up at him, her eyes smoldering, lips parted. Hawk drew her over to the bed, gently pushed her down on it, then not so gently began removing her dress.

She let him do all the work himself, staring up at him, doe-eyed, her chest rising and falling sharply.

When he had her out of her clothes, she

stood, naked, and pushed him down on the bed. She pulled off his boots, tossing them away with dull thuds on the carpeted floor. She lay down beside him and, kissing him intermittently, playfully, unbuckled his cartridge belt. He pushed up on his elbows, arching his back, so she could slide the belt and the guns out from under him. Hawk tossed the guns up near the head of the bed, within reach if he needed them.

Even in the throes of carnal passion, Hawk was a cautious man . . .

Arliss kissed and nibbled his lips again for a time, raking her impassioned hands across his chest, kneading his pectorals through his longhandle top. She reached down and pressed her hand against his swollen crotch. Holding her mouth against his, she stretched her lips back from her teeth, giving a lusty smile, staring into his eyes, mesmerizing him.

She continued kissing him while her hands worked below his belly, unbuttoning his trousers. When she had them open, she scuttled down around his knees and grunted and groaned with the effort of sliding the trousers down his legs.

She tossed them away and then scuttled back up the long length of him and began sliding his longhandle top down his arms and chest. Her pale, tender breasts sloped toward his belly, jostling as she worked. Hawk reached out to fondle them, plying the burgeoning nipples.

She peeled the wash-worn cotton down his legs and over his feet and dropped the duds to the floor. She glanced up at him, tucked her hair behind one ear, smiled at him coquettishly, and took his throbbing member in one hand. Using her other hand to hold her hair back, she lowered her head to his crotch. She closed her lips over the head of his mast.

She slid her warm, wet lips down the length of him, teasing him with her tongue.

Hawk groaned as she plied him; he ground the backs of his heels and his fists into the bed.

When she'd toyed with him for almost longer than he could stand, she straddled him. He reached up and took her beautiful breasts in his hands, kneading them gently. She reached down below Hawk's belly, grabbed his mast, and lowered her bottom until he felt himself sliding inside her.

Deeper, deeper . . .

Hawk freed a held, heavy breath through his teeth.

"Oh, yes," Arliss whispered, breathless, her hair raking lightly across his chest. "Oh, yes." She straightened her back and squared her shoulders as she slowly rose and fell on her knees, closing her eyes, pressing her hands against his chest. "Oh, yes. Oh, god," she said. "I can die now . . . just any ole time. . . ."

They made love for most of the night.

Finally, they slept, Arliss resting her head on Hawk's chest.

Hawk rose before dawn. While Arliss continued to sleep deeply, curled into a ball in the middle of the bed, beneath the covers, he dressed, hooked his wounded arm in the sling the doctor had given him, left the hotel, and took a slow walk around the town, getting the lay of it, scouting for predators. The only other people he saw out and about at that early hour were a couple of shopkeepers either sweeping the boardwalks fronting their stores or splitting wood in the alleys behind them.

He bought a stone jug of coffee from a café, then returned to the hotel. The sleepy-eyed hotelier, Whitehall, was trimming the leaves of a potted palm in his lobby. Hawk asked the man to deliver a tub of hot water to his room, and the man delivered the tub a few minutes later, pushing through the door Hawk had left partway open. Hawk sat in the upholstered chair near the window, sipping a cup of coffee while Arliss continued to sleep deeply, the bedcovers rising and falling with her luxurious slumber.

Hawk pressed two fingers to his lips, shushing the hotelier, who turned to regard the sleeping woman incredulously, puffing his cheeks out and shuttling his incriminating gaze to Hawk. The rogue lawman grinned at the man, shrugging a shoulder.

Wagging his head disdainfully, the hotelier went out and came back several more times, pouring hot water into the tub. He came up a final time with a bucket of cold water, which he set down beside the steaming copper tub.

Arliss had roused while the hotel man had fetched the cold water. Now she lay with her head propped on her hand, her hair a lovely mess around her head and face. Her eyes glittering with sexual fulfillment, she smiled, blinking sleepily, at the hotelier, and said, "Mister Whitehall, have you ever felt as though you'd just died and gone to heaven?"

She thrust an arm and a clenched fist out, stretching.

Whitehall chuffed his disdain, puffed his cheeks out, and said, "What is your husband going to say about this?" He pointed at the rogue lawman.

"Mister Whitehall," Arliss said, resting her head on the heel of her hand again, "I just really couldn't give a good goddamn."

"I'm sure *he* could," Whitehall said, heading for the door.

A man's hoarse, bellowing cry rose from below. *"Arr-lisssss?"*

Whitehall stopped and turned to the sleepy young woman in Hawk's bed. "Ah, Jesus — you're about to find out!"

"I reckon we will," Arliss said.

Coates bellowed his wife's name again so loudly that Hawk could feel the reverberation through the soles of his boots.

Whitehall went out, slammed the door, and stomped off down the hall. Two sets of boots pounded on the stairs. Coates was halfway through another bellowing yell when he cut himself off abruptly. Hawk could hear him and Whitehall talking on the stairs. Boots thudded again — angry, hammering thunder.

Coates came stomping down the hall.

"Arliss?"

She sat up in bed, holding the sheet over her breasts. She slid her gaze to Hawk. He shrugged, then reached across his belly to slide his Russian .44 from the cross-draw holster on his left hip. He rested that elbow on the arm of his chair and casually hiked his right boot onto his left knee.

Arliss smiled. "In here, Roy!"

She let the sheet drop down below her breasts.

Coates's boots thundered in the hall. They stopped just outside the door.

Arliss's eyes brightened with expectation and excitement as they darted between Hawk and the door.

"Arliss, I know you're in there — you cheatin', fuckin' bitch!" With "bitch," Coates kicked in the door. The door hammered against the wall. As Coates bounded into the room, the door bounced off the wall and into Coates's right shoulder. He'd been carrying two pistols, but he dropped the one in his right hand with a yelp as he staggered to his left and dropped to a knee, groaning.

He tried to lift the pistol in his left hand, but it was as though the gun weighed twenty pounds. The man was obviously in pain. His face was badly swollen. Both eyes looked like pink eggs. His cheeks and lips were crusted with fresh scabs.

Hawk said, "No need to hurt yourself, Roy. The door was open."

Coates was panting. He stretched his lips back from his teeth as he cast his enraged, humiliated gaze from his bare-breasted wife sitting up in the bed before him, to the rogue lawman aiming his cocked .44 at him. Coates turned to Arliss again and bellowed, "You cheatin', filthy, back-alley bitch!"

Arliss laughed, showing her husband her love-chaffed breasts. "That's no way to talk, Roy." Now she hardened her voice, and, while her smile still quirked her lips, it had turned as brittle as January ice. "No way at all to talk to the back-alley bitch you raped on your kitchen table."

She looked at Hawk. "Meet the man who saved my life the other evening, Roy. I'd thought my life was over. I tried to drown myself in Pine Lake. He saved me." Her smile turned soft and sweet again, albeit it vaguely mocking, as well. She cupped her tender breasts in her hands. "In more ways than one."

Roy stared at her, panting as though he'd ridden a long way, spittle spraying through his gritted teeth. He started to turn his Remington toward her.

"Uh-uh, Roy," Hawk said aiming his own cocked Russian over his raised right knee, clicking back the hammer. "Drop the smoke wagon."

Coates turned to Hawk. "Fuck you!"

Hawk narrowed one eye as he aimed down

the Russian's barrel.

Coates's eyes widened and brightened with fear. He depressed the Remy's hammer, leaned forward, and set the piece on the floor.

Hawk kept the Russian aimed at Coates's head. "Now, the badge."

"What?"

"The badge." Hawk wagged his gun barrel at the five-pointed star pinned to Coates's wool shirt. "Set it down beside the gun. I'm takin' over. I'm takin' your woman and your badge. Your entire town, matter of fact."

Coates just stared at him, his face a battered, puffy mask of speechless rage.

"Go ahead, Roy," Arliss said. "He's got your woman. Best give him your badge, too. Your badge and your wife or your life, Roy." She smiled.

Coates looked at her, silently snarling. He peered at Hawk staring down the barrel of his Russian at him. Coates gazed down at the star on his shirt. Cursing under his breath, he removed the badge and threw it down beside his gun.

It bounced and rolled and came to a rest on the floor near Hawk's chair.

"There, now," Hawk said. "That wasn't so hard — was it?"

"Who the fuck *are* you?"

Hawk just stared at him, expressionless.

"Take your leave, now, Roy," Arliss said. "We're going to take a bath."

Coates jerked an exasperated look at his wife. "Fuck you, Arliss!"

"No, Roy," Arliss said, smiling again. "Fuck you."

Coates rose awkwardly, grunting painfully, and staggered out of the room and down the stairs. Hawk got up, closed the door, and locked it.

He got undressed and crawled back into bed.

Chapter 11

Hawk and Arliss spent the first half of the morning in room nine of the Colorado Hotel, enjoying each other's company.

They bathed each other slowly, gently, intimately. Hawk had ridden the hard, bloody trail for a long time. It felt good down deep in his soul and soothing to his mind to spend some time with a woman. Making love to a woman. Getting to know a woman's mind as well as her body. He hadn't realized how much he'd missed that in the years since Linda's death.

When he'd finished bathing in the water Arliss herself had bathed in, she took her time drying him with a towel, lingering over his brawny nakedness, in her own supple, tender nudity, pausing occasionally to press her lips to the sundry scars marking him and that were a road map of his past several years on the hard-bitten frontier.

She'd removed the bandage on his left

arm before they'd bathed, and now she rewrapped it with fresh flannel greased with arnica.

His body clean and dry, Hawk dressed. He forewent the sling for his arm, as he had a feeling he'd need both hands free today. He stood at the window, staring into the street while he drew his shirt on over his balbriggan top, and buttoned the cuffs.

Behind him, Arliss dressed in front of the mirror mounted above the bureau. She spoke to his reflection.

"You know they're waiting for you out there," she said. "Especially now. After Roy . . ."

"Yeah," Hawk said, turning his head to thoroughly peruse the street. "But they're patient, I'll give them that. They're layin' low."

"There's five of them."

"That's what you said." Hawk reached behind him to pluck his vest off the bed; then, shrugging into it, he returned his gaze to the street bathed in golden morning sunlight. Dust rose from the churning wheels of supply wagons. "I reckon they're waiting for me to bring the fight to them." He nodded. "Yep. That's about the size of it."

Arliss turned to him, her expression one

of tempered exasperation. "Why not leave, Gideon? Why stay here? They outnumber you. My father will not stop sending men until you are dead."

Hawk turned to her, reaching for his guns and shell belt hooked over the front bedpost. "Your father an' me got us an issue." He buckled the shell belt around his waist. "I'm gonna stay until the issue's settled."

Hawk donned his hat and walked to the door. "I reckon after what happened here, you'll be less than welcome at home. You'd best stay here until the matter's resolved."

Arliss sat on the edge of the bed, a hairbrush in her hands. "I have nowhere to go. But then, I've grown accustomed to that. I'll be here for you . . . if you need me."

Hawk smiled, pinched his hat brim to her, went out, and walked down the stairs. Whitehall stood on a chair in the lobby, setting a wall clock. He glowered as Hawk walked toward the front door.

As Hawk passed him, he asked, "You seen five Circle S riders in town?"

Whitehall nodded grimly.

"You know where they are now?"

"Arkansas River."

"Obliged."

"Don't mention it." Snootily, Whitehall said, turning his head to follow Hawk to the front door, "You ain't gonna be mentionin' much of *nothin'* ever again once you have a few drinks over there!"

Hawk went out and looked toward the north end of town. Five horses stood tethered to the hitchrack fronting the Arkansas River Saloon, lazily switching their tails. Two stood hipshot.

The sun was bright, and the heat was settling over this high-valley town. Woodsmoke remaining from breakfast fires wisped over the rooftops and false façades.

There wasn't much traffic on the street — only a couple of farm wagons heading for Cruz's Grocery Store or the mercantile. A couple of elegantly attired middle-aged ladies were perusing the front windows of Mrs. Markham's Fineries for Women.

Hawk glanced around him quickly, making sure he wasn't about to step into an ambush, then crossed the street and headed north. The ladies in front of Mrs. Markham's eyed him dubiously as he passed on the canopied boardwalk, pinching his hat brim to each of them. They wrinkled their doughy noses at him. Obviously, word of the scandal at the hotel had made its way around town, as it would around any small town.

The notion amused Hawk. No one could

have been less worried about scandal. At least, where it concerned him. As for Arliss, he didn't think she much cared what anyone around here thought of her anymore, either.

As he approached the saloon, he saw a man standing between the half-open batwings, staring Hawk's way. When Hawk met the man's incredulous gaze, the man's eyed widened in surprise. He pulled his head back into the saloon, and the doors fell into place.

As Hawk mounted the Arkansas's front stoop, he unsnapped the keeper thong from over his Russian's hammer and loosened the gun in its holster. He pushed through the batwings, stopped just beyond them, and cast his gaze quickly around the room.

The little barman with the ostentatious mustache — Joe Pevney — stood in place behind the bar. The riders from the Circle S sat at two separate tables to Hawk's right. Two sat at a small, square table near the front windows. From there they had a good view of the street. The three others sat about halfway between the first two men and the bar.

The three had been playing cards, but none of the five were doing anything now except staring at Hawk.

They looked surprised to see him here, as

though they'd thought they were going to have to root him out of some hole he was cowering in. They'd probably thought they were going to have to drag him kicking and screaming out of the hotel room he'd been sharing with Coates's wife.

Whatever they'd been thinking, they were definitely taken aback to see him here.

Hawk strode straight ahead to the bar. Pevney looked at the badge on Hawk's vest, and said with obvious disdain, "What're you doin' with Coates's star?"

"It's my star now." Hawk tossed his hat down on the bar. "Whiskey."

Pevney scowled as he popped the cork on a bottle and splashed whiskey into a shot glass. "What do you mean, it's your star now?"

"I mean this is my town now." Hawk was keeping an eye on the five Circle S riders in the back bar mirror.

They were shuttling their gazes from him to each other, shifting uncomfortably in their chairs. The leader of the toughnut group seemed to be a blue-eyed man with long, straight blond hair tumbling down from a brown bowler. The man's face, carpeted with a beard and mustache two shades lighter than his hair, was ugly as year-old sin. But his hair was as pretty as a girl's, though it had some seeds and trail dust in it.

The others looked toward this man as though inquiring for the go-ahead to start the dance . . .

The leader just sat back in his chair, staring dull-eyed at Hawk, his mouth forming a slash across the bottom third of his face.

"No better way to start the day than with a shot of whiskey," Hawk said, throwing back the entire shot, then slamming the glass back down on the bar top. He glanced at the five men glaring at him in stony silence. "Ain't that right?"

Hawk grinned and stared at the five Stanley riders, as though genuinely awaiting a response. When he didn't get one, he hardened his jaws, slid his hand across his belly to wrap his fingers around the butt of the Russian, and picked one of the five hired guns out of the group with his angry gaze. His voice thundered in the close confines: "I said there's no better way than to start the day with a shot of whiskey. Ain't that *right*?"

The man he had his eyes on jerked with a start, and said, "Yeah, yeah — that's right. Take it easy!"

Immediately, he flushed with embarrassment. The others looked at him, chuckling softly or sneering. All except the blond-headed gent in the bowler hat. He kept his hard blue eyes on Hawk.

"There," Hawk said with a nod. "That's better." He waved to Pevney. "I'll have one more. Figure it's a special occasion, since I'm starting a new job, an' all."

The ends of the barman's mustache twitched as he tilted the bottle over Hawk's glass. Hawk threw back the shot, slammed the glass down on the counter, and said, "All right — I'm off to my new job, I reckon." He smiled at Pevney. "Ain't you gonna wish me luck?"

Pevney slid his gaze to the silent Circle S riders, then raked out a sheepish, "Good luck."

"Thanks, Mister Pevney. I hope I won't disappoint you." Hawk donned his hat, winked, pinched his hat brim to the five Circle S riders, and strode out through the batwings.

Omar Yates was the blond leader of the five men whom Stanley had sent to town to settle up with the man who had killed his son. Now Yates stared at the tall, broad-shouldered man in the black hat and black vest pushing through the batwings and stepping out onto the porch.

Through a front window, Yates watched Hawk descend the Arkansas's porch steps, swing sharply right, and head north along the main street. He was heading in the direction of Coates's office.

"Let's get after him!" said Phil Price, sitting to Yates's left.

"Oh, now you're ready to sic him," Yates said. "A minute ago I thought you were gonna piss your pants and soil your drawers."

The others snickered caustically.

"Nothin' better than a shot of whiskey to start the day — ain't that right, Phil?" jeered Louis Sidner, a one-quarter Cheyenne gundog from Wyoming. He had one of his three pistols in his dark-brown hand on which he wore a turquoise ring. He was spinning the cylinder, enjoying the crispness of the whine.

"Fuck you fellas. He caught me off-guard." Price was enraged, humiliated. He slammed the heel of his hand onto the table he shared with Yates and said, "Come on, Yates — let's get after him!"

Yates leaned over the table and said slowly, softly, and with wide-eyed mockery, "We're gonna give him a minute, Phil. It's his first day on the job. It's only right we let him get situated."

"Fuck you, Yates!"

Yates's ugly face blossomed into a smile. "I know you been thinkin' about it, Phil. Just as long as you know that's all the further it's gonna go. You stay in your bunk. I'll stay in mine."

He winked.

The others had a good laugh at that. Price sat glaring at Yates, his ears as red as overcooked beets.

Yates rose and adjusted his brown bowler on his head. "All right, killer," he said to Price, throwing his long blond locks behind his shoulders. "Let's sic him."

Adjusting the set of his bowler hat, Yates sauntered toward the batwings. He glanced over at Joe Pevney, who was regarding the five gunmen from over the top of his bar, worrying one upswept wing of his mustache. "Leave our drinks where they are, apron. We'll be back for 'em."

He pushed out through the batwings. The others followed him down the steps and up the street, heading north. The town marshal's office was a block and a half away. Men and women involved in the leisurely act of midweek commerce eyed the single-file striders skeptically from both sides of the street. A couple of doves were sunning themselves on the balcony of one of Cedar

Bends two main-street pleasure parlors. Yates gave the girls a gentlemanly dip of his chin and touched his hat brim.

One of the girls, regarding him with the characteristically dull gaze of an overworked whore just waking up, blew cigarette smoke at him.

Yates slowed his pace when the jailhouse appeared thirty yards ahead. He stopped on the cross street. He looked at three of the men behind him, and said, "You fellas wait here. If you don't hear no shootin' inside of a minute, head to the back. He might try to skin out on us."

"All right, okay," said Sidner, holding his polished Bisley in his right hand and spinning the cylinder with his left. He was sweating, and his eager eyes were darting around in their sockets.

Yates looked at Price. "Come on, killer."

"Fuck you, Yates," Price said.

Curling a corner of his upper lip, Yates turned and continued up to the front of the jailhouse. He took a good hard look at the humble mud-brick place. Nothing looked amiss, though he couldn't see anything through the single dirty window left of the plank board door.

He pulled both of his Remington revolvers, clicked the hammers back, and stepped onto the rotting boardwalk fronting the door and to the right side of which sat a hide-bottom chair, one leg propped on a flat stone. An uncorked bottle, likely belonging to Coates, a known tippler, stood beside the chair.

Yates stepped up to the door. Price stood to his right, both of his own pistols in his hands. Price had his chin down, nostrils flaring, lips pooched out — an angry bulldog eager for a reckoning. Yates gave a dry chuckle, then flipped the door latch and gave the door a light shove.

Hinges whined as the door fell back into the room.

The smell of sweat, whiskey, and pent-up air pushed against Yates, who looked into the shadows.

To his left was Coates's battered desk covered with what looked like common household trash — everything from yellowed papers to cigarette and cigar butts to corks to empty bottles and soiled drinking glasses. The only furnishings in the room were a potbelly stove, a rifle rack holding only one old Winchester on the far wall, a small table beside a dilapidated rocking chair with an Indian blanket draped over its back, and a cot with a rumpled army blanket and a sweat-stained pillow.

Yates moved into the room, glancing cautiously behind the door.

Nothing.

Price entering behind him, Yates walked farther into the room, as though the dingy, stinky shadows might reveal something with closer inspection. They did not.

"Must be back in the cellblock," Price said, standing by the stout cellblock door.

Yates grabbed a key ring off a peg in a ceiling support post, and tossed it to Price. Price tried several of the keys before finding the one that opened the cellblock door. He dropped the keys on the floor, shoved the door open, and stepped into the cellblock.

Yates followed Price down the narrow corridor. It was even darker in here than it had been in Coates's office, only two small, barred windows covered with a fine steel mesh allowing in natural light. There were two cells on each side of the block. All four were empty.

"Come out, come out, wherever you are," Price sang, his low voice echoing off the stone walls.

Following Price, Yates looked over the shorter man's left shoulder to see sunlight showing along the left side of the stout door at the end of the short corridor. The door wasn't latched.

"Must be out back," Yates said. "Hurry up, Price. Check it out."

Price glared over his shoulder at Yates. "Don't push me, damnit!"

Price walked up to the unlatched door. Yates could hear birds piping and weeds rustling in the breeze beyond it.

Price shoved the heavy door open with his right-hand gun barrel. Bright yellow sunlight angled through the narrow opening. Price shoved his left-hand gun through the opening. When he had half of his extended arm through the opening, the door slammed closed on Price's arm.

The doorway turned briefly dark. There was a wicked-sounding crack of breaking bone. Price howled miserably and dropped to a knee.

The door lurched open. A gun blasted. Price fell into the yard just beyond the door. Before Yates could wrap his mind around what had just occurred, half-blinded by the bright outside light being cast into the dark shadows around him, he saw a tall, hatted silhouette extend an arm at him.

It was the last thing he saw before black wings engulfed him.

CHAPTER 12

The blast was still rocketing around inside the cellblock as Yates staggered backward, his lifeless head wobbling on his shoulders. The hole from the .44-caliber round Hawk had just drilled through his forehead filled with dark-red blood.

Hawk lowered the smoking Russian, grabbed Yates by his shirt, and stepped to one side, twisting around as he thrust Yates out the open door and into the yard flanking the jailhouse. Hawk kicked the quivering legs of the first man he'd drilled out the door, then stepped back into the cellblock and closed the door.

Through the door he could hear men shouting and running toward him.

Hawk turned and strode down the cellblock. The cellblock door was partway open. Hawk stepped behind it just as light flooded the block from the rear. Someone had pulled open the back door.

Guns thundered.

Bullets cracked and whined and screeched around the cellblock, clanking off bars. Several punched into the cellblock door behind which Hawk crouched, a grim smile twisting his mustached mouth.

"Die, you fucker!" one of the gunmen yelled beneath the near-deafening din.

One by one, the revolvers stopped blasting. Gun hammers clicked benignly onto firing pins.

Silence.

There was the metallic clicking of loading gates being opened and the tinny clatter of spent cartridges being dumped onto the stone floor.

Hawk's ears rang. Beneath the ringing, he heard a man say in a tight, apprehensive voice, "You think we got the son of a bitch?"

Hawk shoved the cellblock door away from him and stepped forward. "Nope."

Three man-shaped silhouettes stood in the sunlit doorway at the end of the cellblock, twenty feet away. All three were reloading. All three jerked their heads up and stiffened.

Hawk slid his Colt from its holster and then went to work with both the Colt and the Russian.

When he was done, all three man-shaped silhouettes had danced out the open back door. The only movement in the cellblock was the lazy buffeting of gun smoke touched with the lemon hues of the morning sun.

A boot scuff came faintly to Hawk's ears.

He jerked the cellblock door open. As he did, a gun flashed and roared from inside the jailhouse office. A bullet seared across Hawk's right cheek. He winced, raised his Russian, and fired three times at a shadow moving inside the office.

"Damn!"

There was a thud as the shooter, who'd fallen across Coates's desk, dropped to the floor. Hawk went in, kicked the fallen pistol away from the writhing figure of Roy Coates, and aimed the cocked Russian straight down at Coates's swollen face. One of Hawk's bullets had clipped the man's right arm. Another had drawn a blood-red line across the outside of his neck. There didn't appear to be any mortal wounds, but those two on top of the beating Hawk had given the former marshal earlier left him howling and kicking like a trapped wolf.

"Don't you die, you son of a bitch?" Coates railed up at Hawk.

"I'm beginnin' to ask myself the same question. Get up."

"I can't get up. I'm injured."

Hawk aimed down the Russian's barrel at

Coates's head.

"Ah, shit," Coates said. "All right, all right, though where in the hell I got to go, I got no idea. My home is wrecked, thank you. And you have my badge."

"Shut up."

"Oh, fuck you!' That last was bellowed on the jailhouse's front boardwalk, for Hawk had shoved the former town marshal of Cedar Bend out the door.

Hawk pushed the man in the direction of the Arkansas River Saloon. As they slanted across the street, heading south, the undertaker, Charles McCauley, stepped out of his furniture store. Wiping his hands on a rag, he gazed at Hawk.

"Got some more for me?" the undertaker asked, eyes brightly expectant.

Hawk jerked his head back to indicate Coates's office. "Behind the jailhouse."

McCauley winked and nodded. "Thanks!"

Hawk gave the slow-moving Coates another hard shove.

As he and the former town marshal continued toward the saloon, Hawk heard McCauley yell back into his store, "Buster, hitch up the mare!"

"Where the hell we goin'?" Coates asked, glancing over his shoulder at Hawk. "You mean to tell me you intend to buy me a drink? Thanks, but —"

Hawk pushed the man against one of the five horses standing at the hitchrack fronting the saloon. The horse gave a start, and Coates would have fallen if Hawk hadn't grabbed him again.

Joe Pevney came out of the saloon to stand before his sputtering batwings, both brows arched anxiously. The barman twisted an end of his mustache.

Hawk said, "Get up there."

"Huh?" Coates said, getting his feet settled beneath him again. "Get up where?"

Hawk glanced at the saddle. Coates followed his gaze, and his face crumpled with incredulity. "I can't ride!"

"Well, you're *gonna* ride." Hawk grabbed Coates's collar again, half-dragged and half-led him around to the left side of the horse while the four others whickered and sidestepped and pulled at their reins. "Get up there!"

"Where am I goin'?" Coates nearly screamed.

"Just let these Circle S mounts worry about that."

Hawk not so gently "helped" Coates onto the horse — a bright-eyed coyote dun that didn't particularly care for the strange maneuver nor the grunts and groans of the man being settled onto its back. When Hawk had Coates in the saddle, the rogue lawman cut the coiled *riata* hanging from over the horn into three two-foot lengths and used each of those lengths to tightly bind Coates's hands to his saddle horn and each foot to its corresponding stirrup.

"You're gonna kill me, you bastard!" Coates bellowed.

Folks had come out of the stores on both sides of the street to look on warily, muttering amongst themselves.

"When you get to the Stanley ranch," Hawk said, untying the horses from the hitchrack, "tell Stanley the local undertaker appreciates his business."

"My ribs are broken. Ridin's gonna drive one of 'em into a lung, and *you're gonna kill me!*"

Coates hadn't gotten that last out before Hawk fired both his pistols into the air over the horses.

The coyote dun and the other four mounts lunged off their rear hooves and broke into instant gallops, heading south toward their home in the mountains.

Coates's screams could be heard for nearly a whole five minutes before they finally dwindled to silence.

Hawk looked around. Townsfolk were staring at him from various positions along the street, muttering amongst themselves.

"Chaos, eh?"

Hawk turned to Joe Pevney, still standing before the batwings, scowling at Hawk.

"Is that what you're all about, Mister Hawk? Yes, I know who you are. I overheard them five hammerheads talkin' in here earlier."

"All right," Hawk said. "You know. So what?"

"What are your intentions here? You've just run off our marshal after beating holy hell out of him. He might not have been much, but Coates was all we had. Lawmen are hard to find. Without the law around here, this place goes south real fast. Fills up with bad men of every stripe on the run from the law in other places. I see you're still wearing Coates's badge. Do you intend to stay here, to enforce our laws?"

Pevney shook his head. "I doubt that. A man like you can't stay in one place very long, though the argument is probably moot since Stanley won't rest until you're dead. That shouldn't take too long."

"I didn't start this fight, Pevney. Johnny Stanley did. He tried to rob you, you damn fool."

"A few years ago, when the Utes still ran

amok in these parts, we said that we could afford to give up a cow or a horse or two to their braves, as long as that's all they took and didn't attack the town. Same with wolves. Allow them a calf or two in the spring, as long as they don't mess with the whole herd. Johnny Stanley was like that. We let him rob a saloon or a shop once or twice a year. Hell, it was sport for him. His father settled the debt, anyway. At least, sometimes he did."

"That's no way to run a town, Pevney. That's no way for a man to live his life — truckling to no-accounts like Johnny Stanley."

"Maybe you see things as black or white, Mister Hawk. That ain't no way for a man to live life, neither, because that ain't how life is."

"Johnny Stanley wasn't no Ute brave, Pevney. And he wasn't no wolf, either. He was a kid who hadn't been said no to nearly enough. I said no to him. As far as Coates goes, your marshal tried to arrest the wrong man." Hawk started walking toward the hotel, angling across the deserted street.

A hush had fallen over the town.

"What I'm tryin' to say, Mister Hawk," Pevney called to his back, his effeminate voice quaking a little with trepidation, "is thanks just the same, but we'll get along fine without your help!"

Hawk stopped and looked back at the barman. "No, you won't. Not if you don't stand up to bullies, Pevney. Even if they are the law. Even if they are rich and powerful. As soon as I'm gone, you can go back to hiding behind your counter and givin' away your money to men you're afraid of. Me? I'm gonna stay here and I'm gonna settle up with Stanley. Then and only then will I be on my way . . . if I'm not toe-down. Till then, you're stuck with me."

Hawk continued to the hotel. Whitehall was standing in the lobby, staring out the window. He gave Hawk a constipated look and moved his lips as though he were trying to say something.

Hawk stopped, then looked at the man. "What's the matter, Mister Whitehall? Cat got your tongue?"

Hawk headed up the stairs. He knocked on his door, opened it, and stopped. Arliss stood before him. She wore her hat and the wool coat she'd worn when she'd first come to his room. She stood just inside the door, as though she'd been on the way out.

"Where are you going?" Hawk said.

"I'm going home to pack a few bags. A stage will pull through here tomorrow. I intend to be on it. I have an aunt, my mother's sister, in Denver."

Hawk studied her. Then he nodded. "That's probably wise."

Arliss walked up to him, placing a hand on his cheek. "Come with me, Gid?"

Hawk frowned at her, and placed his hand on hers, atop his cheek. He'd been about to say no, but he found himself hesitating, if only briefly. The hesitation surprised him. He'd never thought he'd ever settle down again. With anyone. The loss of his wife and son had left a hole in him that he'd thought no one else could ever fill.

Had he envisioned, however vaguely, Arliss filling it?

She seemed to sense that he had.

"Please," she urged. "We could travel far from here, start another life."

Hawk took her hand in his and pressed it to his lips, kissing it. He shook his head. The faintest of grim smiles pulled at the corners of his mouth.

"It's too late."

"It's not, Gideon." Arliss implored him with her eyes as well as her words. "It's never too late. We could leave here . . . together. I know you're a wanted man, but you could change your name. We could marry, start a life together in a town where no one knows either of us."

"And do what?" Hawk said. "Buy a business? Run a mercantile? A livery barn? Maybe become farmers?"

"Or ranchers. I know the ranching business inside and out."

"Then that's what you should do," Hawk said. "Me?" He shook his head and pursed his lips.

Arliss swallowed, glancing at the floor between them. "If you stay, you'll die here. I don't want to be here to watch my father's men kill you. I can't." She looked up at him again. "We've known each other only a couple of days, but I feel like I know you almost as well as I know myself. You feel the way I feel, Gideon. We share a similar darkness. We can help each other."

"There's help for you, Arliss. There's no help for me. Outside of a gun, that is."

"Your guns will not bring your family back."

"I know that." Hawk frowned. "But . . . only half of me knows that. The other half thinks . . . that if I kill enough bastards who need killin' . . . they'll at least rest a little easier — Linda and Jubal."

Arliss shook her hair back from her eyes. Then she rose up onto her toes and pressed her lips to Hawk's. "Goodbye, then, Gideon."

"Goodbye, Arliss."

"Oh, I forgot." She walked over to the dresser, plucked something off of it, and held her hand out to him. "I found this on the floor on your side of the bed. It must have fallen out of your coat pocket."

Hawk took the wooden horse out of her hand. It was the bucking black stallion that was the only thing he had left to remind him of his son. He ran his thumb across the deftly crafted mane and sleek neck. The horse looked real enough to gallop right out of Hawk's hand and into the next world.

"Thanks."

Arliss smiled, stepped around him, and moved out into the hall. She stopped and glanced back over her shoulder. "If you reconsider, I'll be in Roy's house till nine tomorrow morning. That's when the stage pulls out."

"All right."

"Goodbye."

"Goodbye, Arliss."

And then she was gone, and Hawk felt a sharp stab of the loneliness he'd thought he'd become inured to.

CHAPTER 13

A raucous coughing/strangling sound woke Mortimer Stanley out of a dead sleep in his chair on the porch of his once impressive ranch house.

The rancher jerked his head up off his shoulder and kicked out with both mule-eared boots, gasping. He saw a crow staring at him through pellet-sized black eyes from its perch on the porch rail before him.

"You blasted vermin!" Stanley tried to shout, but the words came out sounding more like the bird's own raspy caw. "I was dead asleep, an' . . . an' you woke me . . . like to give me a heart stroke!" He leaned forward and coughed. "Mangy critter. Winged viper . . ."

Stanley frowned as he studied the bird, almost as large as some eagles he'd seen, and black as the blackest night. The rancher canted his head to one side, narrowing one eye suspiciously. "Why do you pester me so, crow?"

He'd awakened that morning to find the crow perched atop his son, Johnny, who still lay sprawled belly up on Stanley's piano. (Mortimer intended to get his son in the ground soon, but at the moment he just couldn't part with the child. The grave just seemed so *final . . .*) The wretched, carrion-eating bird had been dipping its beak into the corner of Johnny's right eye, pulling up some clear, jelly-like substance. Horrified, Stanley had run to fetch his double-barrel shotgun.

By the time the rancher had returned to the parlor with his gun in hand, the crow was gone.

That wasn't the first time the crow had appeared to Stanley. It had been showing up for weeks, intermittently. Lately, those visits had been growing more and more frequent. It was as though the crow was a warlock sent by some hoodoo witch to haunt him and taunt him for his past transgressions.

A few days back, he'd been dreaming of his beloved Caroline — yes, he'd loved his beautiful wife despite their wretched daughter having accused him of being incapable of love! — and just after she'd come to him in a diaphanous gown that had billowed out around her like angel's wings, only to have her turn to dust in his embrace, he'd awakened to find the crow perched atop his bureau.

The bird had been staring at him as it studied him now, its little, black, pebbly eyes strangely opaque but also accusing, jeering.

"What do you want with me?" Stanley asked the bird through gritted teeth. "Out with it, bird! Cat got your tongue?" He gave a weak chuckle at that. "What is it? Who sent you here?"

The bird gave another caw that resounded wickedly inside Stanley's tender, whiskey-sodden brain, then lifted one wing and probed with its stiletto-like beak for mites.

The sound of drumming hoofbeats drew Stanley's attention beyond the bird and down the long hill toward the bunkhouse and other outlying ranch buildings and corrals. Several horses were just then galloping into the yard.

When Stanley had fallen asleep in his chair, he'd been bathed in the warm, lemony hues of a midafternoon sun. But now only a coppery, late-afternoon light remained, and cool shadows were descending from the high peaks that hemmed in Stanley's once-vibrant mountain stronghold.

The dust the horses pulled into the yard glistened like newly minted pennies. The horses ran up to the stable, where the barn shadow all but concealed them from the rancher's probing gaze. Before they'd disappeared, however, he'd thought he'd seen something on the back of one of the mounts.

Stanley scowled down the hill, puzzled, his alcohol-drenched brain working sluggishly, but a dull apprehension began to wrap itself around him like a cold, wet cape.

"Five horses," he muttered to himself, running his thumb and index finger down his jaw. "Five . . . horses . . ."

Then it nudged him like a poke from a sharp stick.

He'd sent five men to town earlier that day. At least, he'd thought it was that day. Wasn't it? Yes, he was sure it was . . .

The wet cape drawing tighter about his already-chilled frame, Stanley rose heavily from his hide-bottom chair and ambled to the porch rail. The crow stretched its neck at him, gave two more jeering admonishments, then lifted its wings, rose from the rail, twisted around in the air, and wheeled off down the hill and over the bunkhouse where the mountain shadows, nearly as dark as the bird itself, consumed it.

Stanley saw his men begin to gather

around the five horses. He could hear them muttering incredulously amongst themselves. Sweat glistened silver on the horses' withers.

The man whom Stanley considered his foreman — a big, sullen but capable three-quarter Indian named Wilfred Red Wolf — turned toward Stanley. The rancher could always pick Red Wolf out of his small crowd of ranch hands down there. Red Wolf was a six-foot-six mountain of a man who wore a low-crowned, snuff-brown sombrero ornamented with the teeth of several U.S. soldiers his father had killed when he'd fought with Custer at the Greasy Grass.

He wore a long bull-hide duster and two cartridge bandoliers around his broad waist. Now in the shadows around the horses, the cartridges flashed like sequins on a debutante's ball gown.

Stanley threw his arm up and beckoned.

He watched the shadowy mass of men and horses mill in the salmon-touched copper light until one horse and Red Wolf separated from the crowd. Standing nearly as tall as the horse's head, Red Wolf led the horse up the hill in his slow, dogged, trudging way. As the foreman and the horse came to within fifty yards of the house, into the dull saffron sunlight still bathing the hill, Stanley could see a man sat astraddle the mount.

Actually, he hung half down the right side of the beast.

Red Wolf stopped the horse in the yard. The big foreman stared in silence at Stanley, who was now walking carefully down the veranda steps. He crossed the small yard and pushed through the arched trellis tangled with dead vines and looked from the broad, expressionless face of Red Wolf to the man hanging from the horse.

"What the hell . . . ?" Stanley said.

He walked over to stare down at Roy Coates, whose feet were tied to his stirrups. Coates's bound wrists were tied to his saddle horn. He was slumped against the horse's right wither. He didn't appear to be conscious. Maybe not even alive. Stanley couldn't tell if he was breathing.

"Go around there and cut his foot out of that stirrup, Red Wolf."

When the big Indian foreman walked to the other side of the horse, Stanley used his own folding Barlow knife to cut Coates's right boot free of its stirrup. Together, he and Red Wolf cut the ropes binding the town marshal's hands to the saddle horn. When the final strands broke, Stanley stepped back quickly as Coates tumbled out of the saddle to hit the ground with a dull thud and a faint groan.

He lay on his side, stretching his lips back from his blood-frothed teeth.

Stanley kicked the man onto his back. "What in tarnation . . . ?"

Coates's face was a bloated mess. It looked like a cut of meat that had been left outside to rot in the sun and be nibbled on by predators. The marshal opened his eyes, and blinked.

"Coates?" Stanley said. "You worthless piece of shit."

Coates stared up at him for a time. Then Stanley wasn't sure if it was a pain spasm or a slight grin that tugged at the man's battered, swollen lips, but he had a feeling it was a grin. Coates swallowed, tipping his head back a little. It was a gesture for Stanley to bend an ear.

The rancher got down on one knee and lowered his head to within a foot of the marshal's mouth. "What is it? Get on with it. You don't got much longer on this side of the sod, Roy."

Coates opened his mouth, but spoke too softly and gravelly for Stanley to understand.

"What? Speak up, goddamnit," the rancher intoned. "I can't hear you!"

Coates made some more sounds. Stanley

cursed and lowered his ear to within six inches of the man's mouth.

Coates raked raspily out: "She's fuckin' him. Arliss is . . ."

Stanley jerked his head with a start, turning to glare down at the marshal smiling up at him. Coates blinked slowly. A little more loudly, he said, "He said to tell ya . . . you're makin' McCauley a happy man."

"Oh, he did, did he?" Stanley said, pushing with a grunt off one knee, straightening. "Roy, you're a worthless mound of dog dung — you know that?"

Coates only smiled up at him, in a dreamy near-death state.

Stanley pulled his pistol, clicked back the hammer, aimed at Coates's head, and blasted a hole through the man's left temple. With the pistol's roar, the horse whickered loudly, leaped off all four hooves, turned, and galloped off down the hill toward the corral.

Stanley clicked his Colt's hammer back and shot the town marshal again. Coates's head turned sharply, as though he were obstinately disagreeing with Stanley's assessment of things. More frothy blood sputtered on his lips, like hot butter in a skillet, and then he gave a couple of feeble death jerks and lay still.

Stanley turned to Red Wolf standing beside him. "Send every last man I got. Tell them if they don't kill that man in town . . . that Gideon Hawk, the rogue lawman character . . . to not bother comin' back here. They will not be given their final paychecks."

Red Wolf gave a single, resolute nod, then started retracing his steps back down the hill.

"Hey?"

The foreman stopped, then glanced back over his shoulder at Stanley.

"You stay here. In case he gets around 'em."

Red Wolf gave that purposeful nod again, then continued down the hill.

Hawk rose the next morning feeling refreshed. He was surprised to find that his arm, which had been aching devilishly since Coates had shot him, no longer hurt. He'd slept deeply. He didn't think he'd even been stirred by dreams, which was odd. Ever since he'd laid his family to rest, his slumber had been haunted.

He sat on the edge of the bed, staring into the misty shadows of the early dawn, blinking, wondering why he felt so light and awake and energetic, his mind already sharp.

So alive.

Then, he knew. There was a good chance that by the end of this morning, he would be joining his flower, his beloved Linda and that rascal son of his, Jubal. Joining them in heaven, if the stories were true. Or in the earth, if they were not. Wherever he ended up, he was certain to join his wife and son.

He pushed up from the bed, humming an old song he and Jubal used to sing when they'd walked out to the creek with their fishing poles. Drawing only a blanket around his shoulders, and not bothering with his boots, he walked downstairs in his stockings, found Whitehall sweeping dust and tumbleweeds off his veranda, and ordered a bath.

"Never seen a man take so many damn baths!" the hotelier complained, blowing smoke out around the quirley dangling from between his lips.

"It's a special day, Whitehall," Hawk said, and turned away.

"Special, huh? Yeah, I reckon it's special," the hotelier groused to Hawk's retreating back. "It's the day you're gonna die, unless you pull foot out of here while you still can!"

Hawk merely threw an arm up in acknowledgment as well as in dismissal of the man's advice. Hawk sat smoking a stogie he'd been saving for a special occasion, in the upholstered chair by the window, when Whitehall came up with two buckets of steaming water. The hotelier looked at the rogue lawman incredulously, shaking his head, as he poured the water into the tub.

After he'd added the last bucket of hot water and set a bucket of cold down next to the tub, Whitehall scowled at Hawk, breathing hard, fists on his broad hips. "I don't understand you. You must have something wrong in your head. Why don't you just ride out away from here?"

"My reasons are none of your business, Whitehall."

"All right, all right." Whitehall turned to the door. When he got to it, he stopped and turned half around to regard Hawk once more. "It's just that I hate to see a decent man die so needlessly. Whatever they say about you, and despite your dalliance with Miss Arliss, you do seem decent. You could make a good mark if you put your mind to it."

Hawk gazed back at him flatly, casually puffing his cigar.

"The problem with you," Whitehall said, pointing an accusing finger, "is you make too many enemies."

Hawk pulled the fat cigar out of his mouth

and blew smoke rings in the air before him. "Thanks for the water."

"All right, all right," Whitehall repeated, throwing his arms into the air.

He left the room and drew the door closed behind him.

Hawk rose, tossed away his blanket, stripped out of his balbriggans, and stepped into the bath. He sat in the steaming tub for a long time, smoking, leaning back with a dreamy smile on his rough-hewn but handsome face, studying the ceiling. Finally, he lathered himself from head to toe, scrubbed himself raw, then climbed out of the tub, toweled off, and dressed slowly, carefully, taking special care with his appearance.

After all, it might be the last time he dressed himself. Not that he needed to look good for the undertaker, but he'd been anticipating this day for a long time. It felt good and right to heed details this day. After all, it was a special day indeed.

Hawk combed his hair in front of the mirror above the bureau, and raked a hand across his jaws. He frowned at the stubble pricking his palm. He needed a shave.

To that end, he finished dressing, put on his hat, carefully adjusting the angle in the mirror, then grabbed his rifle, and left the room. He looked around the street. Seeing no sign of Stanley's men — there would likely be more today than yesterday — he headed over to Albright's Barbershop. He had to wait a few minutes for an old-timer to get a trim, then stepped up into the chair.

"Shave," he told the barber, Alvin Albright — a thick-waisted, bald man with swept-back brown muttonchops and a mustache nearly as wild as Joe Pevney's.

"Hair's gettin' a little long," Albright said to Hawk in his mirror, arching both brows and giving a salesman's roguish, slightly sheepish grin. "You're a good two inches over the collar."

"I am at that," Hawk said, canting his head this way and that in the mirror. "Take a little off the back forty, will you? And let's give my ears a little sun."

"Why not?"

Albright chuckled as he drew the pin-striped cape around Hawk's shoulders and snapped the paper collar into place around his neck.

"Funny," the barber mused, as he combed and snipped at the back of Hawk's head.

"What's funny?" Hawk asked, holding his chin down and regarding the man in the mirror.

"Mort Stanley is likely emptying out his

bunkhouse right now, sendin' all hands this way to take you down. And you . . ." Albright gave his head a single, puzzled wag. "You don't seem one bit het up about it, when most men would be long gone or pissin' down their legs." He frowned at Hawk in the mirror. "You actually think you can *take* all them?"

He stopped cutting for a moment.

Hawk gave the barber's reflection a patient look in the mirror. "If you don't mind, Albright, I'd rather you worked more and talked less."

"All right, all right," the barber said, his clippers starting to clip away again. "Just curious, is all."

"This town has a bad case of that."

The clippers stopped clicking again when the thunder of many hooves rose and a man's voice sounded, bellowing stridently.

Automatically, Hawk tensed in the chair. He was about to rise and head over to where his Henry leaned against the papered wall, when Albright, who'd gone over to one of the front windows to peer out, said, "The mornin' stage from Carthage."

Hawk got out of the chair and stepped through the door Albright had propped open with a rock. He looked up the street to his left, where the Wells Fargo office sat across from the town marshal's office. Hawk knew a moment's prickling regret when he saw Arliss standing there in a cream traveling suit and matching plumed picture hat. Several smaller bags stood near her feet on the boardwalk fronting the office, abutting a large steamer trunk.

Arliss stood gazing up at the station while two passengers climbed out of the carriage and two hostlers hurried up from a broad break between buildings, leading a fresh team from the relay barn. Arliss dipped her chin suddenly and then, as though she'd sensed Hawk's stare, turned her head slightly toward him.

Her eyes met his. She held his gaze for a moment with an oblique one of her own. Then she turned her mouth corners down and looked away.

"Mrs. Coates," the barber said. "She must be pullin' foot . . . now that her husband ain't in such good health no more."

Hawk turned to Albright, whose face flushed sheepishly. Then the barber slid his eyes beyond Hawk to the stage again, and said in a philosophical tone, "I don't know what it is, but I've always admired to see the stage come and go. You know — bringin' people in, movin' 'em out. I guess it talks to my own wanderlust."

Hawk moved back into the shop and retook his perch in the chair.

The barber followed him in and went back to work, the clippers clipping away.

Fifteen minutes later, when Albright had finished Hawk's hair trim and was half done with his shave, Hawk heard a bellowing cry. He started to tense again automatically. But then there was the pop of a blacksnake over the backs of the fresh stage team.

Hooves rumbled. A horse whinnied shrilly, indignantly.

Hawk shoved the barber's hand away from his face and tripped the wooden lever that righted the chair, so he sat level with the front window.

He peered out as the team whipped into view, in a full gallop, heads down, ears pinned back. The coach jounced along behind. Arliss sat on the coach's near side, facing forward. She was looking out the window toward Hawk. She and the coach passed in a jostling blur, but just before she was gone, she lifted her right, white-gloved hand in a parting wave.

Albright gave a crude snort.

Hawk glanced at him. Again, the barber flushed, sheepish.

Hawk tripped the lever again, and the chair fell back.

It just so happened that at the same moment Albright was scraping the last of the rogue lawman's beard from his right cheek, Hawk again heard the thundering drum of many hooves. He did not tense this time as he'd tensed before. He was ready for them now, having expected them for the past couple of hours.

The drumming grew louder and louder until it was joined by the jangle of bridle chains and the squawking of leather tack.

Hawk winced when Albright's right hand, which had been rock steady until now, quivered slightly, and the razor pricked him.

"Oh!" Albright grunted, lifting the blade to see the snowy, rippled mound of lather touched with dark-red blood.

"That's all right." Hawk shoved the man's hand aside with his arm, then grabbed the towel off the barber's shoulder, and swabbed it across his face. "You did good, Albright."

"Ah, shit," the barber said, scowling at the nick on Hawk's cheek. "Sorry about that. I pride myself on —"

"Think nothing of it."

Hawk patted his cheek until he stopped seeing blood on the towel. Then he tossed the towel back over the barber's shoulder and smiled. "See there? It's already clotted."

The drumming of horse hooves had stopped. It was followed by an eerie silence. Wisps of sunlit dust moved along the street fronting the barbershop, drifting there from the south.

The barber drew a deep breath and then wiped the razor on the towel.

Hawk rose from the chair, ripped off the cape, and tossed it over a chair arm. He reached into a pocket of his whipcord trousers. "How much?"

"On the house," Albright said, waving a hand.

"Normally I'd appreciate that," Hawk said. "But under the circumstances . . ." He stuffed a half-eagle coin into the barber's shirt pocket. "McCauley's made enough money off of me."

He gave the barber a wink, then grabbed his hat from a peg and picked up his rifle.

Outside, in the direction of the hotel, a man shouted, "Hawk!"

Albright gasped and jerked a look out into the street. "That's them. They're here for you."

"What?" Hawk said, adjusting the angle of his hat. "You think they wouldn't come?"

Chapter 14

Hawk shouldered his rifle and stepped out through the door. Stopping on the boardwalk fronting the shop, he looked to his right up the broad main street. The hotel stood a block and a half away. A dozen or so horseback riders sat in front of it, staring toward the hotel.

One of them cupped his hands around his mouth and shouted, "Hawk! Gideon Hawk! Mortimer Stanley's got a bone to pick with you, Hawk!"

Hawk smiled. He started to step into the street but stopped when he saw two people staring at him from an alley mouth between a ladies' hat shop and a feed store. Hawk's heart hiccupped, then quickened.

His wife and son, Linda and Jubal, stood there in their Sunday finest, smiling at him expectantly. Linda's blond hair curled onto her shoulders. She held young Jubal's hand as he stood beside her in his knickers and long, wool socks. They each appeared just the way they had when Hawk had last seen them, before he'd laid them to rest only one day apart.

Hawk's eyes brightened beneath the broad brim of his black hat. "Soon," he whispered. "Soon . . ."

Linda's smile broadened, as did Jubal's. Then they turned and walked off down the break between buildings, and disappeared.

Hawk felt a sob well up in his throat. His eyes stung.

"Hey!"

Hawk glanced at the hotel. One of the Stanley riders was pointing toward Hawk. The others swung their heads toward him now. Hawk swallowed the knot in his throat, reached into his right vest pocket, and pulled out Jubal's horse. He held it before him, smiling down at it, then lifted it to his lips and kissed it.

"Soon, Jube," he whispered to the carving. "Soon."

In the periphery of his vision, he could see the Stanley men dismounting and shucking their rifles from saddle scabbards. Hawk replaced the carving in his pocket, took the Henry in his right hand, and stepped down off the boardwalk. He rested the repeater on his shoulder as he walked into the street.

The Stanley riders were all walking toward him now in a steadily loosening clump, spreading out around and behind one man — the apparent leader of the pack. He was maybe thirty — tan and pockmarked and with a thick mustache that angled down wide of his chin. He wore three pistols, and he had a Winchester carbine in both gloved hands. A big Bowie jutted from his right boot well.

He stopped about forty yards from Hawk, the morning breeze tugging at the old, dark-blue, sun-faded army jacket he wore over a buckskin shirt. The eyes beneath his hat brim were cornflower blue. They were the eyes of a pretty girl set in the deep sockets of a Missouri outlaw's sneering face.

T. J. "Cord" Jessup.

The name popped off some wanted dodger and into Hawk's head. Due to his lawman's training, he had a memory for names he'd spied on wanted circulars. He thought he could probably fit names to the raggedy-heeled, unshaven, hard-eyed lot flanking Jessup as well, if he wanted to. But there was no point. He'd take down a few of the twelve facing him now — as many as he could before the law of averages did him in — and call it a life.

Hawk faced the bunch, opening and closing his hand around the neck of the Henry riding his shoulder.

"You Hawk?" Jessup called.

"That's right."

Jessup blinked, lifting his chin slightly, with acknowledgment. He canted his head to one side and half-smiled as he said, "Our boss, Mister Mortimer Stanley, would like a word."

A couple of the men around him chuckled at that.

"Why don't you just relay a message for me?" Hawk said.

"What message is that?"

Hawk kept his flinty, jade gaze on Jessup's cornflower blues for about seven seconds. Jessup's eyes began to flicker a little with acknowledgment of Hawk's intentions. They darted full wide as Hawk jerked the Henry off his shoulder, thumbed the hammer back as he snapped the stock's brass plate to his shoulder, aimed down the barrel, situating the sites on Jessup's chest, and fired.

Jessup had timed his own move a quarter-second too slow.

Just as he leveled his own rifle on Hawk, the rogue lawman's bullet shattered his breastbone and shredded his heart, punching him backward, tripping over his heels and triggering his rifle into the street before him. He didn't scream, but only hardened his jaws and blinked his wide eyes in exasperation at his mistake — believing that he was the one calling the shots, that he was the one who would have the honors of starting the dance.

Hawk dropped two more but then the lead started flying his way, screeching through the air around him. One seared a hot line across the side of his left knee. He thought he could drop one, maybe two more before they . . .

But then one fell that Hawk hadn't shot.

Another screamed and twisted around, then, blood oozing from his lower left side, cast an enraged glare to Hawk's right, where the little barman from the Arkansas River Saloon, Joe Pevney, was down on a knee behind a rain barrel, triggering two pistols over the barrel and into the jostling crowd of Stanley shooters.

Before the man Pevney had shot could return fire at him, Pevney triggered one of his two mismatched revolvers once more, and the wounded man bought another round — this one to his forehead.

Hawk had been distracted only one fleeting second by Pevney's unexpected display. Now he dropped to one knee and continued firing, accounting for two more screaming, dancing Stanley riders but not the one he just now saw drop to the street clutching his right knee. Grimacing and clamping a hand over his bloody leg, the Stanley rider turned to Hawk's left, shouting, "Whitehall, what the fuck you think you're doin', you son of a bitch?"

Hawk glanced over to where the hotelier, Chester Whitehall, wearing a floppy-brimmed canvas hat and a holstered pistol, was triggering an old Sharps carbine at the Stanley riders, wincing and flinching as return fire drilled bullets into the feed store behind him.

Hawk racked another round into the Henry's action, and sited down the barrel.

There were only three or four riders left standing, dancing around and dodging bullets while looking exasperated and trying to trigger their own rifles. A Stanley man was down on one knee, tossing his rifle away and reaching for the two pistols on his hips. Before Hawk could shoot him, either Pevney or Whitehall took the honors. The man slumped backward, dropping one pistol to clamp his hand over the blood-geysering hole in his neck.

Hawk swung his Henry's barrel to his right as one of the few still-kicking Stanley riders turned to run toward the right side of the street, loudly bellowing curses. Hawk shot him between his shoulder blades and the man flew forward off his boots, landing on a boardwalk and then colliding violently against the front wall of the Miller Family Drug Emporium.

Another man ran off the street's left side, kicked open the door of a shoe store, and disappeared inside.

Whitehall cackled a wild laugh and, clutching his own bloody left leg, yelled, "Look at him run!" He laughed again. "I ain't had that much fun since the last Ute attack damn near ten years ago!"

Hawk looked at the Stanley men. They were all down. Most were unmoving. Two were moaning and writhing.

Hawk turned to Whitehall and said, "What the hell are you doin'?"

"You was right," Pevney said, rising from behind the barrel on the opposite side of the street from Whitehall. "It was time we took town matters into our own hands — since it is *our town,* an' all!"

"And since you're only one man against a whole horde," Whitehall said, grinning, proud of himself despite the bloody leg. "Hell, me and Joe fought Injuns together before we settled down here. I reckon we forgot we got it in us to hold the wolves at bay — eh, Joe?"

"You got it, Ches!" Pevney said, grinning and twisting an end of his mustache. "Did you see how I gutshot that consarned Donny Houston. There he is there — the pile of beef in the red shirt!"

"Good one, Joe!"

There was the tinkle of breaking glass. A gun popped from the direction of the shoe store. The bullet plunked into the rain barrel near Pevney.

Hawk shouted, "Get down, you crazy bastards!"

A girl's scream followed the pistol's blast out of the shoe store.

"Oh, no," said Whitehall, hunkered behind a square-hewn awning support post. "That's Janey Ryan. She's in the shoe shop alone today, as her pop took sick over the weekend!"

"Stay here and keep your heads down." Hawk raked a round into the Henry's action, then jogged through a narrow alley on the street's left side. At the end of the alley, he turned to his right and ran behind several buildings until he came to the rear of the shoe shop.

He pulled the door open and found himself behind the shop's rear business counter, staring at shelves of displayed or boxed shoes extending beyond, toward the front of the store, which he couldn't see from his vantage. A schoolbook lay open on the counter near Hawk, a pencil resting in the crease between pages, a lined note tablet peeking out from under the book, above a wood stool over which was draped a knitted blue sweater.

From somewhere near the front of the store, a girl's frightened, quavering voice said, "Pl-please don't hurt me. Please . . . please, don't hurt me!" She broke down in sobs.

"Shut up, goddamnit!" a man's voice thundered. "I told you to shut up or I'd drill a hole through your purty head!"

Hawk moved into the store and stepped through a break in the counter. From the front of the shop came the clanging rattle of a cowbell. The girl continued sobbing. Hawk moved to his left in front of the counter and stopped to gaze up a dark aisle toward the front.

The Stanley rider was sidestepping through the open front door, holding a young, long-legged girl in a checked gingham dress and with dark-blond hair in front of him. He pressed the barrel of a cocked, long-barreled revolver to the girl's right temple. The girl's lips were fluttering as she sobbed.

Hawk raised his rifle and aimed up the aisle, but then the Stanley rider pushed on outside, and the door closed behind him and the girl, obscuring Hawk's shot. When the Stanley man and the girl had dropped down the shop's front porch steps, Hawk hurried to the front of the store and stared through the door's window.

The Stanley rider — tall and dark and with a broad, fleshy face carpeted in ratty patches of a cinnamon beard — stepped out into the street, shoving the girl ahead of his with his body, keeping the revolver's barrel pressed to her head. He was staring up the deserted street to Hawk's right.

"Where are you, Hawk?" the man shouted. "You come out where's I can see you! I'm gonna kill this girl less'n you don't give me free passage back to my hoss! Understand?"

He looked around, swinging his head from left to right as he continued to shuffle up the street near where the other Stanley men lay dead. "You hear me, Hawk?" he shouted shrilly, his voice echoing off the false façades around him. "You come out where I can see you, or I *will* drill a bullet through this girl's *head*!"

Hawk took one step back from the door.

He pressed his Henry's rear butt plate against his shoulder, and aimed through the door's window, clicking the hammer back with his thumb. He lined up the beads on the Stanley rider's head and was about to squeeze the trigger when the man turned abruptly, half-facing Hawk. Now the girl's head obscured the Stanley man's.

Hawk pulled his head away from his rifle, scowling.

"Hawk, goddamn you!" the Stanley rider shouted. "This ain't no game, now. If you don't show yourself in three seconds, I'm gonna blow this purty li'l gal's brains out!"

"No!" the girl sobbed, her face a mask of terror.

"One . . ." the Henry rider shouted, turning slowly back to stare up toward where Hawk had faced the gang.

"Two . . ."

The rider pressed his pistol more firmly against the girl's head.

The girl screamed.

"Thr—"

The Henry jerked against Hawk's shoulder. A quarter-sized hole appeared in the glass of the door's upper panel. The outlaw stood in the street, now facing the opposite direction from Hawk. He and the girl stood stock-still. For a second, Hawk thought he'd missed his shot.

But then the Stanley rider's arm dropped. He triggered his pistol into the dirt in front of him and the girl. The pistol fell into the dust.

The girl screamed.

The Stanley rider took one stumbling step forward before his legs buckled. He dropped to his knees in the street and then fell forward without trying to break his fall. He lay belly down, kissing the dirt from which he'd come and to which he had so unceremoniously and quickly returned.

The girl staggered away from the dead man, screeching.

Hawk opened the door and stepped out onto the shop's front boardwalk. He looked around, planting the smoking Henry's rear stock to his right hip. Joe Pevney ran out from behind the rain barrel, glanced at Hawk, and then made a beeline to the howling blonde, who kept screaming horrifically as she stared down at the man who'd abducted her.

As Pevney drew the girl to him, hugging her, cooing to her, calming her, Hawk stepped into the street. He scowled at Pevney as the girl sobbed in the barman's arms. He looked at the dead men lying strewn around him, then back to Pevney.

Exasperation burned through the rogue lawman. He'd been prepared to die. His wife and son were waiting for him. But in the same way he'd saved Arliss Coates from the frigid mountain lake, he'd been saved from Stanley's men by Pevney and Whitehall, who'd been emboldened by what they'd perceived as Hawk's own bravery but which had, in fact, been merely a private wish to die.

"Shit," he said now, out loud, as he looked at the dozen men lying twisted and bloody around him.

He couldn't help seeing the irony in the situation, however. A laugh raked up out of his chest. Then another. Then he was walking around, directionless, laughing as though at the funniest joke he'd ever heard.

He saw the doctor walking across the street from his office to where Whitehall sat on the boardwalk beyond Pevney and the still-sobbing girl. The sawbones and Whitehall, as well as the barman and the girl, now stared curiously, apprehensively at the rogue lawman stumbling around in the street near the strewn bodies, guffawing, occasionally tipping his head back to send his bizarre laughter at the blue, sunlit sky.

After a time, Hawk's laughter dwindled to

chuckles, which, in turn, dwindled to silence.

The humor was gone.

Now he just felt hollowed out and beaten down.

Hawk sighed, poking his hat brim back off his forehead with his Henry's barrel. He spat into the street and stood, pondering, with a fist on his hip, the Henry resting on his shoulder. Apparently, today hadn't been his day to leave this dung-heap world. And since he had one last loose end to tie up here in Cedar Bend before moving on to his cabin in the mountains, he might as well get to the tying.

He walked over to the livery barn, and saddled his grullo.

He rode to the hotel and loaded his gear onto his horse. Mounting up, he drew his hat brim down over his eyes and galloped west.

Joe Pevney was helping the doctor get Chester Whitehall across the street to his office. A few people were filtering back onto the street after the shooting. A working girl from one of the brothels had taken young Janey Ryan under her wing, and was pouring the understandably distraught child a brandy in the whore's parlor house. The undertakers — both McCauleys — had already pulled their wagon into the street and were busily loading up the bodies, the elder McCauley whistling as he worked.

Pevney stared beyond the undertakers toward Hawk, whose broad-shouldered figure dwindled quickly as he rode out of town, toward the mountains looming beyond.

"What in the hell do you suppose is the matter with him?" the barman asked Whitehall.

"Who knows?" Whitehall said through a pained grunt. "Some people are just naturally colicky, I reckon."

Chapter 15

Hawk had no trouble backtracking the now-dead Stanley men to the Circle S headquarters. There were few well-traveled trails in the mountains, and the dozen riders had left plenty of fresh sign.

As he rode into the high-mountain clearing in which the headquarters was located, he stopped just beyond the wooden ranch portal and looked around. It was high noon, and the headquarters buildings looked washed out and surreal in the harsh, high-altitude sun. The bunkhouse and other outbuildings sat at the base of a rise from the main house, which was impressive.

At least, it had been impressive once.

Now it looked as though it had been abandoned five or six years ago. The rest of the place looked similarly neglected despite the stamp of horse hooves indicating men had lived and worked here. An eerie silence hung heavy. It was relieved by only the whispering breeze and the twittering of birds in the pines surrounding the place.

Hawk touched spurs to the grullo's flanks and rode under the wooden ranch portal bearing the Stanley brand burned into the overhead crossbar, and into the yard.

He glanced around warily, his Henry resting across his saddlebow, as he crossed a corner of the yard and started up the trail climbing the hill to the main house. As he rode, he studied the house carefully. It was awash in brassy sunlight, but the windows resembled the dark, empty eye sockets in a dead man's skull.

Hawk followed the trail's curve up into the driveway, and stopped in front of the shabby picket fence surrounding a yard that had become overgrown before all the transplanted trees, shrubs, and vines had died and turned brown.

The loud banging of a piano assailed Hawk's ears from inside the house. The boisterous clanging had started so abruptly that Hawk's heart quickened, and his fingertips tingled as he tightened his right hand around his Henry's neck.

A man's raspy, off-key voice began singing loudly in accompaniment of the piano's harangue:

"On the banks of the Roses,
My love and I sat down,
And I took out my violin
To play my love a tune,
In the middle of the tune,
Oh, she sighed and she said,
O-ro, Johnny, lovely Johnny,
Would you leave me?"

Hawk racked a cartridge into the Henry's action and off-cocked the hammer. Again, his gaze swept the sunlit house. The singing — if you could call it singing and not some mad hybrid of a wail and a howl — continued as he swung down from the grullo's back, dropped the reins in the dust, and pushed through the trellis cluttered with dead vines.

The wailing grew louder as Hawk approached the house via the chipped and cracked stone walk, the broad, once-grand veranda widening before him.

"Oh, when I was a young man
I heard my father say,
That he'd rather see me dead
And buried in the clay,
Sooner than be married
To any runaway,
By the lovely sweet Banks of the Roses."

Extending his Henry from his right hip, his gloved thumb on the hammer, Hawk walked up wooden steps badly in need of fresh paint. He glanced cautiously through the door, which had been propped half-open with a brick. Beyond lay a broad foyer in thick shadow. Dead leaves and dirt littered the wooden floor. Sour air pushed against Hawk as his gaze probed the shadows.

He looked up the stairs that ran up the foyer's right wall.

"Oh, then I am no runaway
And soon I'll let them know,
I can take a good glass
Or can leave it alone;
And the man that does not like me
He can keep his daughter at home
And young Johnny will go roving with
another."

Seeing no one, no movement, Hawk clicked the Henry's hammer back to full cock, and walked into the house. A tall, thick shadow slid out of the darkness behind the stairs. A gun flashed and thundered. The bullet plowed into Hawk's lower right side. He winced as he squeezed his Henry's trigger.

The two reports were like near-simultaneous thunder.

Hawk stumbled backward and hit the floor near the door's threshold. The man-shaped silhouette before him staggered back into the shadows beyond the staircase. Hawk heard a man grunt. The rogue lawman quickly pumped another cartridge into the Henry's action, and fired.

The man-shaped shadow jerked violently backward and fell with a thundering boom as the big man hit the floor.

"And if ever I get married
'Twill be in the month of May —"

The singing as well as the piano-banging stopped abruptly.

Hawk's right side burned. He placed his left hand over the hole. It came away bloody. Grunting, he gained his feet, staggering a little, trying to suppress the pain of the wound. Gritting his teeth, he loudly racked a round into the Henry's chamber.

The piano-banging and singing resumed:

"When the leaves they are green
And the meadows they are gay . . ."

Hawk followed the wailing and wild piano-hammering through a broken French door and into a large parlor filled with the cloying odor of death. On the parlor's far side, a man with a tumbleweed of curly gray hair growing atop his lean and weathered head banged away at a grand piano on which a man lay belly up, atop what appeared a Confederate flag.

Hawk recognized the stiff figure of Johnny Stanley glaring at the ceiling, knees and boots dangling down the piano's near side.

The old piano player's eyes met Hawk's as he sang:

"And I and my true love
Can sit and sport and play
On the lovely sweet Banks of the Roses."

The man raised his hands from the keys. He stopped singing.

The piano's reverberations dwindled slowly, echoing around the cave-like room.

The man who could only be Mortimer Stanley lifted a bottle to his lips, and took a long drink. He set the bottle down on the piano, smacked his lips, and stared across the room at Hawk, standing just inside the French doors, aiming the Henry at Stanley from his right hip.

"Do you mean to tell me that you have

now killed every one of my men, Mister Hawk?"

Hawk wrinkled his nose with dismay. "I had help."

"Help?" Stanley was incredulous, insulted. He wrinkled his brows angrily. "Who helped you?"

"A couple townsmen couldn't mind their own business."

Hawk moved into the room, sort of dragging his right foot to ease the pressure in that side. Blood dribbled from the wound, over his cartridge belt, and down his right leg. He tossed his rifle onto a leather sofa and walked over to a liquor cabinet between the big fireplace and the piano. He glanced over at Stanley, one brow arched inquisitively.

"Help yourself," the rancher said, flaring a nostril. "I reckon you deserve it."

Hawk lifted a cut glass decanter to his nose, sniffing. He splashed the brandy into a goblet and threw back half. When he'd refilled the glass, he turned to Stanley, wincing with the pain surging through his side and causing his shoulder blades to draw together.

Stanley gave a smile, showing large yellow teeth. "Red Wolf get you?"

"Is that the big man in the foyer?"

Stanley nodded. "He dead?"

"Probably."

Stanley pursed his lips. "You clean up right well, Mister Hawk. But the joke's on you, as well. If you don't get to a sawbones, you're gonna bleed to death." He smiled again, shrewdly. "There ain't no sawbones up here, and I'll be damned if I'll fetch you one."

"That's all right." Hawk grabbed the decanter off the liquor cabinet and, holding the goblet in his other hand, shuffled back over to the sofa. He gave his back to it and sagged gently into it, wincing. "I'll be comfortable right here. Your brandy will kill the pain till it doesn't need killin' anymore."

Stanley looked over his dead son at Hawk, frowning. "Ain't you gonna kill me? Ain't that what you come here for?"

"No." Hawk finished off the brandy in his goblet and awkwardly splashed more into it, slopping some over the side of the glass and onto the sofa. "And yes."

"Explain yourself, sir!" Stanley barked.

Hawk hiked his left shoulder. "I rode out here to kill you, yes." He smiled as he raised the glass to his mouth. "But I've had a change of heart. I'm not going to kill you."

He sipped the brandy, enjoying the soothing burn that washed down inside him, slightly tempering the pain of the bullet wound.

Stanley seemed indignant. "Why not? I tried to kill you. Several times!"

"You're doin' too good a job yourself," Hawk said, and took another, bigger sip of the brandy. He sighed and rested the glass on his right leg. He looked at his wound. Blood continued to flow out of him.

Stanley grabbed the bottle off the piano and rose uncertainly to his feet. He tripped over a leg of the bench as he walked out from behind the piano and turned toward Hawk.

He wore a ratty plaid robe over filthy balbriggans. A pistol hung low on his left leg, on the outside of his robe. His cadaverous cheeks were carpeted in beard stubble the color of metal filings. He stopped and glanced at his son lying dead on the piano to his left. The body was bloating, the cheeks puffing, as though with a held breath.

Stanley glowered at Hawk. "You killed my only boy."

Hawk shook his head. "I only shot him. You killed him a long time ago . . . when you killed your wife and her lover. Maybe your daughter still has a chance. She left here. She's gonna start a new life for herself . . . far away from here. Far away from you, Stanley, you sick bastard."

Tears dribbled down the old rancher's cheeks. "You killed him. You killed my boy." He drew the big Colt revolver from the holster on his leg, and clicked the hammer back. He glanced at Johnny once more. "My boy, my boy . . ."

He jerked his head to Hawk, gritting his teeth, tears continuing to roll down his slack, pasty face. "I'll kill you for that!"

Hawk smiled, raising his drink in one hand. "Don't blame you one damn bit."

Stanley lifted the Colt, aiming down the barrel at Hawk's face.

A gun barked.

Hawk jerked with a start.

He frowned as he stared at Stanley's revolver. There had been no lapping flash of flames from the barrel.

The gun quivered in Stanley's shaky hand. Then the old man's hand opened, and the gun thumped onto the carpeted floor. Stanley staggered backward, eyes wide. He looked down at the hole in his chest from which blood bubbled with each tick of his heart.

Footsteps sounded behind Hawk. A familiar female voice said calmly behind him, "You're right, Gideon. I still have a chance. But when I got to the first relay station, I decided that my chance was here . . . at home. So I rented a horse from the station manager and rode back here to kill you, Father."

She walked up to the sofa, on Hawk's right side. She glanced at Hawk and then at her father, who had stumbled against the piano. She held an old Remington revolver in her right fist. Smoke curled from the barrel.

"I rode back here to kill you and take over, Father. This ranch hasn't been run right in years. But it's going to be run right now . . . with you dead . . . and me in charge. I know this ranch like the back of my hand. I can run it the way a ranch needs to be run."

Slumped backward against his dead son, Stanley stared in exasperation at his daughter. Arliss smiled at him. "Goodbye, Father. Say hello to the devil for me."

Stanley raised his left hand in supplication.

Arliss's pistol popped once, twice. The thunder blasted off the walls. Stanley jerked as each bullet hammered into him. He grunted and gurgled and rolled off the side of the piano to pile up on the floor.

Arliss stared at him for a moment, looking a little shocked herself.

Then she turned quickly to Hawk, set the

smoking pistol down on the floor, and knelt beside him.

"Gideon!" she breathed. "Oh, Gid — I thought for sure they'd killed you!"

"They have," Hawk said. "But it's all right." He smiled at her, brushing his fingers gently across her flushed cheek. "It's all right, Arliss. I'm glad you're here, though. I'm glad you came home. A fresh start . . . here . . . at home. That's good."

"A fresh start," Arliss said, leaning down to examine his wound. "That's right, a fresh start — for both of us. You're going to help me get this place in shape."

Hawk frowned at her, then shook his head. "I'm finished, Arliss."

"Pshaw!" Arliss said. "That's nothin' but a flesh wound. As soon as I've sewn you up and got the blood stopped, you'll be good as new. Why, in two weeks, I'll have you hammering nails and slinging paint all over this place!"

She draped Hawk's right arm around her neck and, grunting, hoisted him to his feet.

"Let's get you upstairs. Then I'll fetch some hot water and get to work on that hole."

As Arliss helped him up the stairs, Hawk laughed.

He laughed lest he should cry.

Bloody Canaan

CHAPTER 1

Jacob Broyles looked abruptly up from the rabbit-skin mittens he was finishing sewing at the kitchen table, and turned toward the window beside him. He cast his pale blind eyes to his older sister. "Trouble, Jennie."

Jennie Broyles turned away from the pot she'd been stirring on the range. "Oh, hell — what now?"

Her younger sister, Mercy, gasped. "Jennie, what has Pa told you about that blue tongue of yours!"

"Pa's in bed, so I'm the one in charge, and you'd best get used to my blue tongue," Jennie said as she made her way around the table. "I'll cuss when I feel like cussin'. If you don't like it, little Miss Mercy, you'd best stuff your ears."

Mercy looked at their brother in shock and sighed. Jacob gave a devilish grin.

"Don't let her pull you down to hell with her!" Mercy scolded her older brother.

Jacob was sixteen. Mercy was thirteen. At nineteen, Jennie was the oldest of the three Broyles siblings. If a girl could be at once radiantly and earthily beautiful, that was Jennie. Which made her salty tongue all the more shocking to most who knew her.

Jennie swept a curtain aside and looked out through the dusty sashed panes, turning her head this way and that as she scoured the yard of the small mountain ranch with her gaze.

"I don't see anything."

"Me, neither," Mercy said. She'd gotten up from her chair at the table to peer over Jennie's left shoulder.

"Riders," Jacob said, staring straight ahead across the table littered with his tanning tools, at the canvas of mountain wildflowers Jennie had painted earlier that summer. He wasn't seeing the painting or anything else. A severe fever had taken his vision when he was five years old.

"Seven, maybe eight horses," Jacob said in a dull monotone. "They're comin' fast."

A chill ran down Jennie's spine. She didn't doubt her brother's judgment about such things. He may have lost his vision, but his other senses had grown keener to compensate. Jennie looked across the ranch yard to the rail corral abutting the barn.

Several horses were looking to the south and twitching their ears. The chestnut gelding Jennie called Whisper pawed nervously at the dirt, arching its tail.

Jennie's heartbeat quickened. Her hands grew clammy.

"Burnett," Jacob whispered, awfully.

"Oh, my god!" Mercy cried, and clapped both hands to her mouth.

"He said he'd come," Jacob said, the dullness in his voice belying his own fear. "So, now he's come." He turned toward Jennie, his blind eyes looking past her to the window. "What're you gonna do, sis?"

Jennie drew a calming breath as she walked over to where her father's Sharps carbine rested on wooden pegs above the fireplace.

"You two get upstairs, and stay there till I tell you to come down." The Sharps was loaded. As Jennie held it in both hands, barrel up, breathing hard now with fear, she gave Mercy a direct look. "For god's sakes, keep Poppa up there — you hear, Mercy? Don't you dare let him get out of bed — no matter what he hears outside."

"What're you gonna do, Jennie?" Mercy's voice was small and trembling as she stared at the rifle in her sister's arms. "What're you gonna do?"

"Just do as I say, dammit, Mercy!"

"I'll try," Mercy said, fear showing in her own wide eyes as she looked out the window, staring at the horses. She slid that glassy gaze to her older sister. "Do you . . . do you really think it's Burnett? He wouldn't, would he? He really wouldn't?"

"He said he'd come," Jacob said, kicking his chair back as he rose a little unsteadily from the table. "He thinks he can do anything. He thinks he owns the whole range, and . . . all the folks on it. All the women on it. So . . . he's come. Who else would be comin' at this time of day, bringing all those riders? We knew he'd come . . . sooner or later. He said he would, and he always follows through on his threats, Burnett does."

Jennie shot her brother and sister a sharp, commanding look. "Would you two stop your gassin' and get the hell upstairs?"

"Come on, Jacob," Mercy said in that little girl's trembling voice again, taking her brother's hand and leading him up the stairs to the cabin's second story.

No lamps had been lit yet in the cabin, so the interior was all shadows and misty edges. Brassy late-afternoon light shone briefly in Mercy's blond hair as she led Jacob up the stairs, past Jacob's furs and hides stretched from nails in the log wall.

The staircase squawked beneath his and his little sister's weight.

When they left the stairs, Jennie could hear them hurrying down the narrow hall up there. Then a door shut with a squawk of hinges, and the bolt was thrown with a metallic thud.

"What's goin' on?" came the phlegmy voice of Angus Broyles from his room on the second story. "It ain't nighttime yet, is it?" A brief pause. "Why, no — it's still light out. Jennie, what's goin' — ?"

"Never mind, Pa," Jennie cut her father off. "Just stay up there and keep quiet. They'll be gone in a minute."

"*Who* will?"

Jennie looked out the window once more, then walked to the door. As she wrapped her hand around the doorknob, she drew a deep, calming breath — which didn't really calm her much at all — and then drew the door quickly open and stepped onto the stoop.

"You can go to hell, Quentin Burnett," she muttered to herself, trying to bring up as much anger as the fear she felt. She had every right to be angry. To be furious, in fact. Burnett's demands were not only unreasonable but illegal. However, it was mostly fear Jennie was feeling now. "You can go to *hell,* Quentin Burnett," she said again as she turned her gaze to the south.

The wooden ranch portal straddling the two-track trail at the edge of the ranch yard almost perfectly framed the group of riders galloping toward her, dust rising behind them touched with the salmons and burnt oranges of the mountain sunset.

The hoof thuds grew louder as the men rode under the portal and continued into the yard.

Jennie's hands turned cold when she saw the group was led by the notorious Texas gunfighter, Vance Dodge, who was Quentin Burnett's first lieutenant. Dodge ramrodded all the beating, killing, and hanging Burnett inflicted on those he considered illegally nesting on government range — free range that Burnett wrongfully, illegally, considered his own.

Jennie's gaze fluttered across the dusty riders drawing up in the yard before her, about twenty feet away. Quentin Burnett himself was not among them.

Vance Dodge was leading the group alone.

Dodge's eyes were cold and dark beneath the brim of his dark gray Stetson. He was a rangy, bearded man with long, dark-brown hair curling onto the collar of his duster. He wore a silver hoop ring in his right ear, and he had a scar in the shape of a large fish-hook on his left cheek. Without the scar and the cruelty in his small eyes, he would have been a man whom Jennie might call handsome.

His double shell belts bristled with three big Colt pistols.

The rest of Burnett's group of hard-tailed riders rode behind Dodge.

Jennie recognized all of them, as would most of the other nesters who called this high mountain valley home, and whom Burnett frequently harassed, and whose beef he often stole. A few weeks ago, a "nester" named Emory had been found hanging from a tree on his own range.

Most of the men facing Jennie now had reputations that stretched beyond this remote mountain range. There was the burly Chick Holt and the one-eyed Frank Sunday and the cow-eyed Hacksaw Campbell, who was known more as a tracker than a gun-slinger, though Jennie, who kept her ear to the rails, so to speak, had heard he'd killed several men in Kansas.

There was O.B. "Antelope" Warner who wore a bowler hat and a three-piece suit with checked trousers as well as dark-tinted spectacles. He looked more like a carnival barker than a gunman, but he'd been known for his bloody work in several range wars in Wyoming and Colorado.

The last two riders were the Miller brothers from Oklahoma, whom Jennie had heard had killed the renowned Deputy U.S. Marshal Bill Ruth over in Dakota Territory, after they'd robbed a train. They'd walked into Ruth's house on a little farm outside of Bismarck in the middle of the night, and they'd shot both Ruth and his wife while they'd slept before raping and killing both Ruth daughters.

The story going around the mountains was that the Millers were the only two men Jesse James had ever declined to fight, for both wild-eyed, blood-hungry young men were known to be several cards short of a full deck. Apparently, the folly in their eyes had turned even Jesse James's blood to ice.

The riders spread out in front of the Broyles's log cabin in a broad semicircle, facing Jennie. Their dust caught up to them, billowing this way and that in the yard lit in tones of the early mountain dusk. The men stared dully at Jennie.

Except the Millers, that was. The Miller brothers had greedy, covetous looks in their eyes as they feasted their gazes on the well-set-up young woman before them.

Jennie's eyes flicked to the top of her

dress. It had been a hot day, so she'd worn a plain cambric sleeveless affair with a relatively low neckline, which exposed the high slopes of her breasts. Her bosom rose and fell heavily as she breathed against the fear ripping through her body like cold tar.

A cool bead of sweat trickled down her cleavage.

Vance Dodge abruptly removed his hat and held it against his chest. "Good afternoon, Miss Broyles. And how are you today? If you don't mind me sayin' so, you're lookin' splendid."

Antelope Warner turned a sneer on Dodge. "Splendid?"

"Yeah, splendid," Dodge said, defensively. "That was Burnett's word for her. Splendid. He said the very word when he saw her in town a few months back. Splendid. I reckon he couldn't get such a splendid-lookin' creature out of his head. Smitten, the old boy is, sure enough. And that's why we're here, Miss Broyles. But then you already know that — don't you?"

"You can go to hell, Dodge," Jennie said, trying to keep her voice from trembling. "And you can tell Burnett he can go to hell, too!"

"Splendid, is what he called you," Dodge said, smiling, as though he hadn't heard what she'd said. "He said to me today around noon, 'Vance, you take the boys and ride on out to the Broyles ranch and bring me that splendid creature. That Jennie Broyles. I'm gonna marry her."

Dodge spread his gloved hands two feet apart. "His smile was that wide!"

Jennie moved to the edge of the porch. She held the Sharps in both hands across her heaving chest. "I'm not goin' anywhere, Dodge. You tell him that. I'd rather marry a diamondback than marry Quentin Burnett."

"No, no, no," Dodge said, grinning and shaking his head. "You don't want me to tell him that. Look, I understand. He's old. He's fat. And he probably has a dick the size of my little finger — and that's fully erect!"

The other men snickered and chuckled.

"But he's the most powerful man in this county. Maybe even in the whole damn territory," Dodge continued. "Why, the governor of Idaho is ridin' to New Canaan tomorrow to go huntin' with the old bastard! Burnett thinks he owns the entire mountain range. Now, we know he don't — it's government range — but you know what happens when you try tellin' him that. In his mind, you see, this is all his range" — he swept his arm out in a broad arc — "includin' your ranch here. Includin' *you* yourself, Miss Broyles. So he's gonna marry you. I'm sorry — it's a real pickle. I know it is. And I'm sorry. But when Burnett says he's gonna do somethin', that's that!"

Chapter 2

"I told Burnett no!" Jennie fairly screamed, aiming the Sharps at Dodge, the rifle quivering in her trembling hands. "When he rode out here and told my pa he was gonna marry me, I told him in no uncertain terms to go to hell!"

"I know ya did," Dodge said. "I was right here where I am now — remember? But he gave you two weeks to ride to town on your own, or he was gonna send us, and he also said you weren't gonna like it if you forced his hand like that. I think it sort of embarrassed him — you not comin' in willin' like. He doesn't like how you're makin' him look in front of the whole town. So he sent us."

Dodge's voice dipped darkly. "He sent us, and, unfortunately, a whole passel of trouble. I'm sorry it's come to this. I truly am."

"This is crazy," Jennie said. "He can't force a girl to marry him. No man can. Not even Quentin Burnett!"

"Now, why don't you go on inside and pack a bag for yourself? You're comin' to town whether you want to or not. Whether it's *right* or not. You'd best get your family out of the house, as well, because me an' the boys here have been ordered to burn it to the ground. That's your punishment, see? I don't think you want them in there when we put the torch to it."

Jennie's heart kicked like a mule in her chest.

She loudly cocked the Sharps, hardened her jaws, and shook her long dark-brown hair back away from her cheeks. "You go to hell, you son of a bitch. I may not be able to get all of you, but I can get you, Dodge. If you take one step toward this cabin, I'll blow you out of your saddle!"

Dodge's face turned red with anger. "Did you hear a word I just said?"

Jennie did not respond to that. She aimed down the Sharps's barrel at Dodge. The other men were grinning now. The Miller brothers chuckled and looked at each other. Delvin Miller ducked his head and turned it to one side — a nervous twitch of sorts — while his brother, C.P., squirmed around lustily in his saddle.

"Go on inside and pack a bag," Dodge commanded, raising his voice. "Tell your family to evacuate the premises. This ranch now belongs to Mr. Quentin Burnett, as you yourself do, Miss Broyles. We mean your family no harm, but we have our orders." He rose slightly in his saddle as he raised his voice even louder. "Now, vamoose, damnit — I ain't gonna tell you again!"

From upstairs in the cabin, Mercy cried, "Poppa, no!"

Hard thuds of someone tramping around up there hit the air.

"Unhand me, damnit!" came the angry voice of Angus Broyles.

"Poppa, you can't go down there!" Mercy screamed.

Jennie glanced at the cabin's open door behind her. "Pa, stay upstairs!"

She returned her nervous gaze to Dodge. The gunman pointed a finger at her in warning. "If that old man comes out here with a gun, he's dead."

As if to demonstrate he meant what he'd said, Dodge shucked one of his Colts from its holster, and clicked the hammer back.

Jennie turned back to the cabin's open door. Mercy and Jacob were both yelling at their father now. Angus Broyles was coming down the stairs. He wore only his pajamas, a ratty blue robe open at the waist, and gray socks. His long, thin, tangled gray hair danced about his shoulders. His blue eyes were wild.

He clutched in both hands the old Colt Navy he'd used in the war and which he'd converted to metallic cartridges afterwards. He kept the weapon in a drawer of his nightstand.

"Pa, goddamnit!" Jennie ran back into the cabin. She set the Sharps on the table and raced to meet her father, grabbing his arm and trying to stop his progression toward the stoop. "They'll kill you, you old fool. You're not going out there with that gun!"

Mercy and Jacob stood on the stairs, Jacob near the top, Mercy in the middle. They were both yelling at their father.

"Unhand me, daughter!" Angus Broyles shouted, red-faced with fury. "No one is kidnapping my daughter or burning my cabin!"

"Pa!"

Jennie grabbed her father's arm once more. But the tall, stoop-shouldered sixty-three-year-old man was still strong despite the heart stroke he'd suffered a week ago and which had likely been caused in no small part by Burnett's demand for Jennie's hand in marriage.

He violently jerked his arm from Jennie's grip. The force of the pull sent Jennie sprawling over a kitchen chair. She and the chair went down. Her head slammed hard against the floor puncheons.

"Poppa," she cried, trying to push herself up off the floor, her head swimming. She watched in horror as her father hurried around the table to the open door, holding the old Colt in his arthritic right hand, his thumb on the hammer.

As Angus Broyles walked through the doorway onto the stoop, he shouted, "Dodge, you tell Burnett he can take a fast ride down a steep — !"

A gun barked in the yard, cutting Broyles abruptly off.

Jennie swung a horrified look at the doorway. Her father had stopped in his tracks. Now he just stood there, unmoving. His right hand fell against his side. It opened. The Colt thumped to the floor.

There was another pistol blast in the yard.

Angus Broyles gasped and stumbled backward.

Another blast.

Another . . . and another . . . and Jennie watched in horror as blood spewed from the holes opening in her father's broad back as the bullets tore through his body, knocking him backwards into the cabin.

There were two more blasts, and then Angus Broyles twisted around with a ragged sigh and hit the kitchen floor, belly down, near Jennie with a thunderous boom.

"Poppa!" Jennie screamed.

Mercy and Jacob were screaming and bawling now, as well. Mercy ran down the stairs.

Jennie pushed up onto her hands and knees and crawled over to her father. Angus Broyles turned his big, gray head toward her. He opened his mouth to speak, but only blood oozed out from between his lips to flow over the warts on his chin.

He looked at his daughter, his eyes bright with shock.

"Pa!" Jennie sobbed.

Then Mercy and Jacob were down on their hands and knees beside her, screaming and bawling and leaning down to hug their dying father. The light left Angus Broyles's washed-out blue eyes, and his body trembled as life left him.

Outside, men were laughing.

Fury roared like a tidal wave through Jennie.

She shrugged off her dizziness from the fall, heaved herself to her feet, and grabbed the Sharps off the table. She cocked the rifle loudly as she stepped onto the porch.

"Goddamn you sons o'bitches!" she

screamed as she raised the rifle to her shoulder, aiming into the yard.

But just as she saw that Vance Dodge was no longer where she'd last seen him, the man gave a chuckle and stepped up on her right. He grabbed the rifle. Jennie's finger snagged the trigger. The Sharps thundered.

Jennie screamed in rage as Dodge ripped the rifle from her hands.

She cursed again as she tried to punch Dodge, but he merely grabbed her wrist, twisted her around, and pushed her down the porch steps. She fell in the yard at the feet of the other men.

"Hold her while we fire the cabin," Dodge ordered as Mercy and Jacob continued to yell and bawl over their father's body.

"I'll do it," said C.P. Miller. "Not a problem. I'd call it a rare treat to hold Miss Jennie!"

As Jennie tried to climb to her feet, Miller grabbed her from behind and lifted her back off her feet. She was Miller's height, her head even with his. He kissed her cheek.

"Go fuck yourself, you limp-dicked little weasel!"

"What a tongue you got on you, girl!" Miller cried. "My dick ain't limp. Wanna see?"

His brother, Delvin, laughed.

Jennie reached for one of C.P.'s holstered

pistols. Miller pulled the pistol out of her hand, stuffed it back down into its holster, and then grabbed both her arms, holding her as she struggled against him.

Meanwhile, Dodge stepped into the cabin, yelling, "You two get on outside less'n you wanna roast alive in here with that old rascal. Go on, now. Go on — *git*!"

Mercy was bawling hysterically. So was Jacob. They were both calling for their dead father.

"You can't!" Jennie screamed, still writhing against C.P. Miller. His brother was right there, too, laughing and pawing at Jennie's breasts with one hand, at her crotch with his other, while his brother held her from behind. "You can't burn us out! You bastards got no right!"

But then the Millers dragged Jennie back off toward the corral, a good distance from the cabin. They slammed her to the ground.

Holding her face down, one cheek mashed into the dirt and ground horseshit, both men pawed her now — grabbing her breasts and her bottom, running their hands up her skirt to brusquely caress her legs with their gloved hands.

One of them managed to stick a thick finger inside her.

"Gahh!" Jennie cried at the violation,

squeezing her eyes closed against the raking pain.

A hand grabbed at her pantaloons. The pantaloons were being ripped down her legs.

"Let her go!"

It was Jacob's voice. Jennie opened her eyes to see her brother run, stumbling toward her, holding his arms out in front of him, swinging his hands as though searching for something or someone to grab.

Delvin Miller rose from where he'd been nuzzling Jennie's neck and punched Jacob in the face. Jacob wheeled and hit the ground in a shuddering pile.

"No!" Mercy cried as, running out of the cabin, she saw the blind boy on the ground.

C.P. Miller was squirming around on Jennie's backside. "See there, now?" he yelled, laughing. "That dick ain't one bit limp!"

He pressed it into the crack between Jennie's buttocks.

"Is it, you little bitch?"

As he tried to force the head of his dick into her anus, Jennie gave a guttural, bellowing cry, twisted partway around, and raked her fingernails down C.P.'s face, drawing a bloody line starting from just above his right eye to his jawline. It was a deep, ragged, bloody gash.

Miller screamed girlishly, clutching his

face with both hands. His pale, erect shaft bobbed up against his belly.

"Why, you little bitch!" barked Delvin Miller, glaring down at her.

He began unbuttoning his own fly.

"You're gonna choke on this, you little whore!"

His back was to the cabin now, from which smoke billowed. There was the crackling of oxygen-fed flames. Dodge and the other men walked up behind Delvin Miller. Miller couldn't hear their footsteps for the roaring of the flames.

Just as Miller pulled his erect manhood out of his fly, grinning proudly as he wagged it at Jennie, Dodge grabbed him from behind, spun him around, and punched him in the face.

Miller screamed and stumbled backward. He tripped over Jennie and fell just beyond her, near where C.P. knelt, clutching his face in his hands.

"Burnett don't want her soiled, you damn fool!" Dodge railed, pointing an accusing finger at Delvin Miller. "That there is his wife — you understand? You're messin' with Burnett's *wife,* now! You think he'd appreciate one of you back-alley curs stickin' his filthy dick in her?"

Snarling like an enraged bobcat, Delvin

Miller reached for one of his holstered pistols. Dodge stepped forward and kicked it out of his hand.

"Ow!" Delvin cried, grabbing his right wrist. "You bastard!"

"You try anything like that again, Miller," Dodge shouted, "I'll blow your head off. I'm Burnett's first lieutenant — you understand?" He punched his right index finger against Miller's chest. "That's me. I am. When Burnett's not around, I'm in charge. And right now I'm about that far from givin' you two dumbasses your walkin' papers."

He held up his thumb and index finger with a half an inch gap between them.

Delvin just stared at him. C.P. Miller pulled his hands away from his bloody face to glare down at Jennie. Blood dribbled from above his brow into the corner of his right eye. That eye was still in its socket, Jennie was sorry to see. She'd wanted to pluck it out.

She turned away from C.P. Miller to look at the cabin. She sobbed when she saw the smoke billowing out the cabin's windows. Her father had built the cabin with his own hands, with the help of his three children and their now-deceased mother. Now that cabin burned around the body of old Angus

Broyles, whose gray-stockinged feet stuck out the front door, the toes facing downward.

The rest of his body was hidden by thickly churning gray smoke.

Jennie turned to where Mercy knelt beside their brother. Jacob sat with his legs stretched out before him. Blood trickled from his split lips. He appeared to be staring at the cabin, his round face drawn and pale with shock.

Mercy knelt beside him, grabbing at the ground and sobbing as she watched the cabin burn.

Dodge turned to Antelope Warner. "Well, ain't this been fun?" He jerked his head at Jennie. "I want her on my horse. Set her up there. Haze all them horses out of the corral, and let's get the hell out of here."

"What about those two, Vance?" asked Frank Sunday, glancing at Mercy and Jacob.

"Leave 'em," Dodge said. "They're scrubs. If they survive out here on their own, maybe we'll round 'em up with the rest of the scrubs in the fall gather."

Dodge swatted his hat against his thigh as he headed for his horse.

CHAPTER 3

"Dodge, look!"

Vance Dodge turned to where Chick Holt was galloping off Dodge's right stirrup. Holt tossed his head to indicate a horseback rider sitting at the edge of a line of trees west of the trail, facing the galloping gang.

Dodge stopped his horse at the head of the pack, and the other riders followed suit. Jennie, riding behind Dodge, on Dodge's horse, with her hands cuffed around her kidnapper's waist to further humiliate her, cast her own gaze toward where Holt had indicated.

A man wearing a low-crowned, flat-brimmed black hat sat a mouse-colored horse at the edge of the pine forest spilling down from the western ridge, about a hundred yards away. Horse and rider sat seemingly staring toward Dodge's men, the horse idly switching its dark tail. Jennie recognized the man's longish dark-brown hair and the dark mustache folding down over his mouth. He was tall and broad, with thick shoulders.

Jennie also recognized the handsome, broad-barreled grullo the man straddled.

The man was George Hollis, a severe-looking, green-eyed man in his early thirties, possibly with some Indian blood — a relative newcomer to the mountains who'd taken over the claim of old Warren Van Hootin, a prospector, about four miles north of the Broyles place. Van Hootin had recently succumbed to a long illness, probably cancer.

A couple of months ago, Mr. Hollis had stopped by the Broyles cabin to introduce himself. He'd been polite and friendly, but there was something sad and brooding in him; his striking jade eyes set against the Indian russet of his chiseled face had seemed to be staring at something far away. He'd said nothing about himself except that he hailed from Nebraska, where the Broyles themselves were from, and that Van Hootin, a friend, had turned his claim over to him.

His reserved demeanor and the two big pistols he carried in addition to the Henry rifle in his saddle boot had told Jennie he might be a gunman. One who was on the run from the law.

She had never suspected he was one of Burnett's men. He carried himself with a singular, solitary air. Oddly, he'd seemed at once menacing and comforting, as though when a woman was in the presence of such a man, he would protect her at all costs. You did not, however, want to tangle with him.

He was alone, and there was something about him that said he would always be alone . . . forever and ever . . . in this life and beyond . . .

Now Jennie's heart fluttered in fear for the man. He was only one man, after all. If these seven men knew that he, too, had nested on range Quentin Burnett considered his own . . .

Just ride away, a voice inside her head urged the solitary stranger. *Just ride away. There's nothing you can do here except get yourself killed. Even if you're good with your guns, you're outnumbered by some of the savviest killers on the frontier.*

"Who the hell is that?" Dodge asked no one in particular.

"Hell if I know," said Holt.

"Another nester, most like." Antelope Warren spat distastefully to one side. "They're getting thick as goddamn rats in these mountains."

Dodge shuttled his gaze from where Hollis

sat staring at him, at where the smoke from the cabin unspooled against the sky. The cabin was too far away to see, but the smoke was clear. Jennie knew what Dodge was thinking.

The stranger had seen the smoke and was on his way to investigate.

Jennie's heart thudded.

"Maybe it's time to do a little more herd-thinnin'." Dodge turned to the Miller brothers. "Why don't you two make yourselves useful for a change?" He canted his head toward the rider on the mouse-brown horse. He said nothing more.

The Millers' cold grins meant they understood what they'd been ordered to do.

"No!" Jennie blurted. "You've done enough killing here today, Dodge. Leave him alone!"

Dodge craned his neck sharply to scowl at his prisoner. "Who is that?"

"I don't know," Jennie said. "He's probably just drifting through. No more killing, Dodge. *Please.* All right?"

Dodge studied her darkly, then smiled just as darkly, his gaze dropping to her breasts. "You're even purtier when you're beggin' — you know that? If you wasn't Burnett's woman, I'd ask you what you'd do in exchange for leavin' that fella alone. But

Burnett's done staked his claim on you, gall-blastit."

He looked at the Millers.

"No!" Jennie pleaded.

"No problem," said C.P. Miller, glaring at Jennie.

Jennie stared in dread as the two Millers galloped off toward the dark stranger, who continued to sit the grullo, facing them, almost as though he were waiting for them. Beckoning them, even . . .

Ride away, Jennie silently urged him. *Just ride away!*

"Let's get movin'!" Dodge called to the others.

They moved out. Jennie glanced back over her shoulder as the Millers approached Mr. Hollis, who continued to sit his horse, facing them.

He had no idea what he was in for.

Jesse James had walked away from a fight with the Millers.

Ten minutes later, two shots rang out, the second one on the heels of the first. Their echoes rolled skyward, dwindling gradually.

Jennie jerked with a start, as though the bullets had been meant for her. She stared straight ahead. She felt like sobbing, but she was all sobbed out.

Dodge glanced at Chick Holt riding beside

him. The men shared brief, satisfied smiles.

Gideon Hawk unsnapped the keeper thong from over the hammer of the big, top-break Russian .44 holstered for the cross-draw on his left hip. Then he unsnapped the keeper thong from over the Colt Peacemaker thonged on his right thigh, which was clad in black whipcord.

He sat straight-backed, grim-faced in his saddle, watching the two riders gallop toward him, their horses sort of hop-skipping over the low, spidery wolf willows. As the men drew nearer, their horses snorting, Hawk saw that the pair shared familial features — namely, pinched-up, stupid, mean-looking eyes and weak chins. One had dark-brown hair while the other was sandy-headed and taller.

The smaller, darker rider had a nasty fresh gash down the right side of his face.

He'd been scratched. Badly scratched . . . no doubt by a girl fighting him.

Likely, the same girl whom Hawk had seen riding on the back of the horse of the gang's lead rider and who'd turned her head to stare in his direction until she and the rest of the gang had galloped out of sight.

The riders — both in their early twenties and filled to their tinhorn brims with piss and rattlesnake venom — pulled back on their reins, stopping their horses about fifty feet away from Gideon Henry Hawk.

The two firebrands sat for a time, keeping their horses' heads raised, studying the dark stranger while he stared back at them, his calm expression belying the anxiety he felt for the fate of the girl the gang had taken away.

The girl he'd met once a few weeks ago and whose name, he remembered, was Jennie.

Jennie Broyles.

You didn't find many girls like her in this remote place. You didn't find many girls like her anywhere. He remembered her because you didn't forget girls like her — beautiful in an offhand, unconscious way, and with a spirited, devilish light dancing like sunlit diamonds in her brown eyes. Those eyes and the light, effortless way she'd moved had reminded Hawk of his dead wife, Linda.

That would be her cabin burning to the east. Hawk had ridden down from his own mountain shack to investigate the smoke, though he'd known that by the time he reached the cabin, it would be too late for him to do anything about the fire.

"What the hell you lookin' at?" asked the dark young man with the bloody scratch on his face.

"I'm lookin' at you," Hawk said. "And you're lookin' at me. Now that we got that important ground covered, who the hell are you and where are you taking the young lady? *Against her will.*"

"What the hell is that to you?" asked the taller, sandy-haired rider, slitting his eyes beneath his hat brim upon which the sun laid a thin pool of glowing salmon light. The sun shone copper in his muddy brown eyes.

"Oh, I don't know. I reckon it's up to any man to be concerned when a girl is being hauled away from her burning cabin . . . obviously against her will."

"Why, you plug-headed fool," said the shorter, darker brother. "Don't you know it ain't healthy for folks not to mind their own business? What's your name?"

"Gideon Hawk." He'd been going by the name of George Hollis to avoid trouble, for he had a sizable bounty on his head. But it didn't matter if these two knew his real name. He doubted they'd be alive much longer.

"You live around here, Hawk?"

"I do."

"Where?"

"I took over the Van Hootin claim."

The two brothers glanced at each other,

then turned back to Hawk.

"Now, why in hell would you do a fool thing like that?" asked the darker of the two.

"I reckon I didn't see it as a fool thing."

The darker brother gave a caustic snort, as though he were dealing with a hoopleheaded tinhorn. "This land belongs to one Mr. Quentin Burnett, you damn fool. He's about the biggest stick in the woods around here. And he don't like nesters. There's already enough nesters on Burnett's range the way it is, and if you think he's gonna sit still while another one gets himself all burrowed in, you got another think comin'."

The sandy-haired brother said, "Especially one so nosy."

"And especially a half-breed," added the darker brother. "You might wear the clothes of a white man, but you're just as Injun as Geronimo, as far as any *white* man is concerned. Shit!"

"Maybe I better go down and talk to this big stick myself," Hawk said. "If Burnett thinks he owns this range, he's got it wrong. Maybe someone better set him straight before he brings a passel of trouble down on himself and earns himself a wooden overcoat."

The darker brother laughed. "Who's gonna earn him that overcoat? *You?*"

Hawk blinked slowly.

"Well, now, ain't that — !"

"Hey, C.P.," interrupted the lighter brother.

"What?"

The sandy-haired brother was staring somewhat incredulously at Hawk. He opened his mouth a full ten seconds before he spoke. "I think . . . I think I seen this fella's face on a handbill . . . time or two before."

"Wouldn't doubt it a bit, Del," said C.P., hiking a shoulder. "Reckon he don't wear them big pistols 'cause he thinks they look purty on his person. Doubt he's a man of the Lord. But that don't mean —"

"Gideon Hawk," Del said, his voice pitched with awe. "The rogue lawman."

C.P. stared appraisingly at Hawk, his gaze raking the big, green-eyed man up and down — from the crown of his black hat down past his black, wool-lined vest and blue plaid shirt to his guns to the cuffs of his whipcord trousers shoved into the mule-eared tops of his low-heeled cavalry boots.

C.P. returned his gaze to Hawk's eyes now. C.P. looked edgy. Deep lines cut into the skin above the bridge of his nose. He watched in silent horror as a grim smile began to pull very slowly at the corners of

Gideon Hawk's broad mouth, beneath the dark-brown mustache curving down around it.

Del stared at Hawk, as well. Both young men looked like two boys who had been poking a stick at a snake only to just now discover said snake was poisonous and as mean as the meanest demon-viper in the bowels of the devil's own hell.

Del's eyes snapped wide as he reached for one of his pistols, shouting, "Let's take him, C.P.!"

He didn't get his revolver even half out of its leather before Hawk jerked up the Russian and blew C.P. out of his saddle.

C.P. had not yet disappeared, rolling backward off the rear end of his coyote dun, before Del joined him in the same violent manner, blood lapping from the .44-caliber-sized hole in his chest. Del triggered his own Smith & Wesson wild just before he hit the ground with a crunching thud.

Hawk held his grullo's reins taut in his left hand as his victims' two mounts whinnied, wheeled, and ran off in the direction from which they'd come, their bridle reins bouncing over the wolf willows. Hawk looked at the pair of doomed shooters.

Del lay the farthest away from Hawk, on his side, his back facing his killer.

He lay sort of curled up, arms crossed on his chest, shivering.

C.P. lay a little nearer, belly up. He stared up at the sky, spread-eagled, in glassy-eyed shock. He flapped his arms and legs as though he were trying to become airborne.

"Oh," he said, flopping his arms and legs again as frothy blood spilled from the hole in his upper right chest. "Oh, shit . . ." He lifted his head with effort and looked at the hole, then let his head flop back down against the ground. "Lung shot!"

Hawk swung down from the grullo's back. Holding his Russian straight down along his right leg, he walked over and stood staring down at C.P., who stared up at him, moving his lips and making gurgling sounds in his throat.

"Oh, shit," C.P. said. Raw horror widened his eyes. "I . . . I can't die! I've done bad things! I can't die! I can't go there! Please . . . help me!"

This last came out in a voice pinched with sorrow mixed with terror. Tears oozed from his eyes. "I can't die! I can't die, ya see, Mr. Hawk!"

"You've come to that realization a mite late in the game, boy," Hawk said, aiming his Russian at C.P. He cocked the pistol and narrowed one eye as he stared down the barrel. "Where are they taking the girl?"

"Wha . . . huh?"

"Where are they taking the girl?"

C.P.'s lips were quivering in horror. Then his eyes turned mean and defiant. He tried to spit at Hawk, but only bloody saliva dribbled over his lower lip. "You go to hell," he said in a phlegmy voice. "Fuck you! You done killed me! Fuck you!"

Hawk slid the Russian lower on C.P.'s body. He aimed at C.P.'s right knee. He blew a hole through it.

C.P. screamed and convulsed, flopping madly in place.

Hawk aimed at his other knee.

"No!" C.P. screamed shrilly. "They're takin' her to Burnett. In New Canaan! Taking her to Burnett for marryin'!"

Hawk frowned at C.P., who was shuddering and sobbing now, quivering on the ground as though he were being struck over and over by lightning.

"What did you say? *Marryin' . . .*"

"Burnett's gonna marry that wildcat! Oh, Christ . . . I'm in pain here . . . and I'm gonna die and swim forever more in a burnin' lake of liquid fire!"

"Yes, you are." Hawk aimed the Russian at C.P.'s head. C.P. stared up at him, his eyes crossing and widening as he realized what was about to happen. He raised his hands as though to shield his face from the bullet. Hawk fired through the shooter's right hand and into his forehead.

C.P.'s arms flopped to the ground for the last time.

"Time you shut up about it," Hawk said. "I'm tired of listening to such nonsense. A boy like you was born to burn in hell." He turned to Del.

Hawk walked over and saw that Del was still breathing, though he wasn't moving much. Del looked up at him in exasperation. "You're faster'n us? No one's faster'n us, goddamnit."

"Ain't that the way it goes?" Hawk said, clicking the Russian's hammer back. "You never know when and from which direction it's gonna come. It's always a surprise. No more surprises for you, my friend."

"Ah, hell," Del said, staring at the Russian bearing down on him.

Hawk shot Del through the kid's left eye, then holstered the smoking Russian. He stood staring along the trail to New Canaan for a time, planning his next course of action.

He turned to where the smoke from the Broyles cabin continued to furl up beyond the pines. The old man would be there. And the blind boy and the little girl. What was her name?

Mercy?

Hawk would help them first. If there was anything left to help, that was.

Then he'd see to their sister.

"Odd way to ask for a girl's hand," Hawk muttered as he swung up onto the grullo's back and galloped toward the cabin.

Chapter 4

The town of New Canaan sat in a lush valley surrounded by jagged mountain peaks still streaked with snow even this late in the summer.

The valley was like the setting for a jewel, and the town of New Canaan was the jewel. But only if said jewel was about the unloveliest chunk of rock a poor, raggedy-heeled groom could get his hands on.

The valley was a large slice of heaven complete with an alpine stream wending its way down its middle. The town was a smoky fetid hell, a collection of motley log shacks and tumbledown rail corrals and privies and trash heaps and scorched tents and whores' cribs scattered willy-nilly around the business district.

In nearly every muddy alley you could find a man or even a woman sleeping off a long bender. Maybe a cur or two sniffing at them to see if they were a viable food source.

One or two of those men or women might be dead from a knife in the belly or a bullet in the back, and a cur or a wolf that had sneaked in from the mountains might be trying to tear a limb off.

The crown jewel of the business district was the New Canaan Inn owned by Quentin Burnett. Named after Mount Canaan, the tallest peak in the chain of mountains surrounding the town, the New Canaan Inn appeared about as out of place here as would a princess in white gloves and a satin gown. It was the one building in New Canaan that would have looked right at home in the heart of Denver or Dodge City or Tombstone or even Leadville.

The ambitious structure was sprawling and gaudy, with ornate painted scrollwork and with balconies off all three floors. A large sign announcing itself stretched across the top of the third story. The sign was so large, it could be read by riders — any rider who could read, that was (and those were damn few in this remote section of Idaho) — riding down out of the mountains looking for a bowl of elk stew, a mattress dance with a cheap whore, and a bottle of busthead to ease the aches and pains that were part and parcel of ranching or prospecting or running trap lines or capturing and breaking wild horses, which were the primary means of sustainment in this neck of the frontier outback.

The legitimate means, that was. There was plenty of outlawry, as well.

Jennie had taught herself to read, if only rudimentarily so, so she'd been able to read the NEW CANAAN INN sign as she'd ridden down out of the mountains, her hands cuffed around Vance Dodge. The light was failing, but a few stray rays of the setting sun glittered upon the sign as though to mock the captive girl.

The sign had made her sick. But she didn't let on. She kept her expression stoic. On the ride down out of the mountains, leaving her burning cabin and dead father and bereaved siblings behind her, she'd tried very hard to turn her mind to stone.

The only thought she allowed in was that of sticking a knife or anything else sharp into the belly of the man who'd murdered her father, burned her out, and kidnapped her to rape her. That's essentially what Burnett's plan was. He called it marriage. It was rape.

A knife, Jennie thought as she and the gang members rode into town. *I have to get my hands on a knife.*

As Dodge, Jennie, and the rest of Burnett's

men entered the heart of the fetid business district, the tents, log cabins, and stock corrals giving way to a few false-fronted buildings including the New Canaan, one of the men at the rear of the pack called, "Hey, Dodge!"

Dodge stopped and turned his horse with a sigh. "What is it this time, Sunday?"

Frank Sunday canted his head to indicate the two horses galloping toward them. Both wore saddles but no riders. Their bridle reins trailed along the ground behind them.

"What in Sam Hill . . . ?" Dodge said.

Chick Holt booted his own horse back toward the two riderless horses, both of which stopped near the group's rear and stood blowing and shaking their heads. They were sweat-lathered and owl-eyed. They'd galloped far and hard to catch up to the gang.

Jennie could tell they were also frightened. She'd seen similar looks in her own horses' eyes after violent mountain thunderstorms.

Holt rode around both horses, scrutinizing them closely, and then galloped back up to Dodge, scowling with incredulity.

"Them's the Miller boys' hosses," he said. "There's blood on their saddles."

Dodge blinked dully, uncomprehendingly. "Shit, you say!"

"There's blood on both saddles, all right," said Frank Sunday, who was now scrutinizing the horses himself. He looked toward Dodge, brows furled with befuddlement. "Satan himself couldn't have outgunned those two hog-wallopin' sons of bitches!"

Jennie looked back at the steep ridge they'd just ridden down. Despite the stone she'd tried to turn herself into, as she stared at those forest-clad, snow-mantled peaks behind her, she felt a faint smile pull weakly at the corners of her mouth.

Dodge stared at the horses. He looked off toward the ridge, as though he half-expected to see the Millers walking down out of the mountains. Then, obviously unable to fathom what had caused the Millers' horses to be missing their riders, he gave a disgruntled snort, swung his own horse around, and booted it on up the street.

New Canaan was bustling with early evening foot and horse traffic. Shadows were lengthening and the lamps in windows on both sides of the street were brightening. Piano and fiddle music emanated from several saloons. Judging by the boisterous male laughter also coming from those saloons and from the town's several brothels, men had come down out of the mountains to stomp with their tails up.

Smoke from chimneys and cookfires hung thick in the air. That and the stench from overfilled latrines set Jennie's eyes to watering.

Dodge pulled his horse up in front of the New Canaan. Jennie's heart skipped several beats when she saw Quentin Burnett himself sitting on the broad front porch with several other men in similar fancy attire, complete with bowler hats and polished boots.

Burnett and the others were smoking large cigars and drinking liquor from fancy glasses.

One of Burnett's brethren had a girl straddling his knee — obviously a working girl, for she displayed more skin than flimsy gown, and green and pink feathers danced in her hair.

"Mr. Burnett," Dodge called.

Burnett was so absorbed in conversation with the other men that he hadn't heard Dodge or seen his riders ride up. Finally, when Dodge called again, louder, Burnett stopped talking and turned to him, as did the other men around him as well as the whore, who slid a strap of her skimpy dress up onto her shoulder, covering her breasts.

The man whose knee she was sitting on, facing him, had been playing with the girl's breasts and laughing seedily.

Burnett scowled, peeved at the interruption. Then, seeing the group of gunslingers on the street before him, he arched his eyebrows expectantly, and rose from his chair — a big, portly man in his late fifties, with a beet-red face sandwiched by thick, curly muttonchop whiskers.

Small, round, steel-framed spectacles sat up high on his broad wedge of a nose. He squinted through the glasses, canting his head a little to one side to scrutinize the young woman riding behind Dodge.

"Ahh, there she is," said Burnett through his large, white, false teeth. "Gentlemen, the Queen of New Canaan has arrived!"

The eight or so other men sitting with Burnett all rose with interest, including the gent who'd been holding the whore. He'd risen so quickly that the whore had plopped to her butt on the porch floor with a clipped yowl. The girl quickly regained her feet and dashed off, barefoot and indignant, into the saloon.

The men, most of whom appeared around Burnett's age — late fifties, early sixties — muttered amongst themselves as they cast their pointed gazes toward Jennie, still sitting behind Dodge, her arms wrapped around his waist. Burnett clutched the lapels of his long, green wool coat as he made his way down the porch steps. His hat and coat were green while his vest and pants were brown, his shirt white, his tie black.

As he approached, Jennie felt her insides shrivel.

Burnett came over to stand beside Dodge's horse, smiling up at Jennie. His eyes were large and blue behind the spectacles. They raked Jennie up and down.

"She'll do," Burnett said, grinning. "Oh, she'll do very well indeed." He leveled his gaze on Jennie herself. "I've admired you from afar, young lady. When I saw you in town with your father, I knew I had to have you. You're mine now. You might as well get used to it. In time, you're even going to enjoy it. I'll lavish you with gifts!"

Jennie worked up a mouthful of saliva, leaned out away from Dodge's horse, and spat in Burnett's face. Part of the spray splattered his glasses.

Burnett jerked backwards, closing his eyes, shaking his head, and removing his spectacles from his nose.

The men on the porch gasped and muttered their reproof.

"Why, you little — !" Dodge said, snapping an angry look at Jennie.

"No, no," Burnett said, holding a hand up.

He raised his glasses, and, grinning, turned to the men standing on the porch. He drew the glasses close to his face, stuck out his fat little pink tongue, and licked the spittle off the right lens.

The men on the porch all laughed and clapped.

Fury exploded inside of Jennie, who leaned out again from the side of Dodge's horse, and shouted, "*Murderer!* You killed my father and burned our barn! When my neighbors learn about what happened, you can rest assured the U.S. marshals will be called in. You're going to hang, Burnett!"

"Oh," Burnett said, setting his glasses back down on his nose. "Do you think so?" He turned once more to the porch, and beckoned. "Henry, would you mind coming down here and introducing yourself to my lovely bride?"

The man on whose lap the whore had been sitting stepped away from his chair and descended the porch steps. He was of medium height, compact, lean and grain-haired, with a neat gray mustache. He wore a gray suit with a gray bowler hat. His eyes were small and steely, his deeply suntanned nose straight and long. His previous dalliance with the whore notwithstanding, he wore about him the righteous, intimidating air of a man of the cloth.

He came to stand beside Burnett, smiling up at Jennie. "Hello, Mrs. Burnett," he said, grinning. "I'm Henry Blackwell, Chief Marshal of the Northwestern Territories."

He slid his left lapel back to reveal the moon-and-star badge pinned to his vest.

Jennie felt her lower jaw sag in shock.

The men on the porch all laughed.

Chapter 5

Hawk galloped along the mountain trail toward where smoke from the burning Broyles cabin rose beyond a fringe of pines that were nearly black now in the deepening twilight. When the grullo galloped around a bend in the trail, the cabin appeared.

Or what was left of the cabin.

Mostly, there were only dark-gray smoke and orange flames. Cinders shone in the column of billowing smoke, winking like fireflies. The smoke rose high to fade against the darkening sky.

Hawk halted his horse just beyond the ranch portal and cast his gaze around the yard. He saw two people in the yard fronting the cabin, closer to the unpeeled pine rail corral, whose gate was drawn wide. The corral was empty.

One of the two people Hawk could see through the smoke was down on both knees, staring forlornly at the burning cabin.

The other one — the Broyles boy, it appeared — was wandering in slow circles around the girl on the ground. Hawk could see that the girl was sobbing, her shoulders jerking.

Hawk booted the grullo ahead and steered it in a broad circle around the cabin and dancing cinders. The heat from the fire pressed hard against him, causing the darkening air to shiver. As he approached the girl and the boy, the girl jerked her head toward him suddenly and lurched to her feet, stumbling backward.

The boy had already stopped walking aimlessly. He faced Hawk, his blind eyes wide as though staring at Hawk, though he appeared to be blindly gazing a little beyond the newcomer. The boy tipped his head this way and that, listening.

"Who is it?" the boy called, his voice brittle with fear. "Who's there?"

"It's George Hollis," Hawk called, reining his horse to a stop before the girl, who stood staring up at him, her eyes glazed with shock. "I'm George Hollis, from the Van Hootin cabin. I stopped by a few weeks back." There was no point in confusing the boy and the girl about the alias.

Hawk swung down from the leather. The boy and the girl stood facing him, the girl continuing to weep, her face a tortured mask of bitter tears. The boy, too, had been crying, his eyes puffy, cheeks red and wet. Their cheeks were muddy with the soot from the fire.

"Poppa's inside," the girl sobbed, convulsing and turning to slowly lift her arm and point her index finger at the cabin. "Poppa's inside! He's inside!" She looked at Hawk, her body wracked with grief. "Can you help him?"

Hawk turned to the cabin. Part of the roof had already fallen in. Through the gaps in the burned-out walls and through the windows he could see that the inside of the cabin was like a fully stoked stove. Anyone inside was burned to a crisp.

"Christ," he said, feeling his heart twist in his chest. He walked heavily forward, dropping to a knee before the girl. "I don't think there's anything I can do for your pa, child. I'm sorry."

Hawk placed his hand on the girl's arm, and gently squeezed it.

Oh, such sorrow. Such bitter sorrow. When will it ever end?

"He's inside the cabin!" the girl cried.

"They killed him," the young man said. Hawk remembered that his name was Jacob. The little girl was Mercy. "They killed him and took our sister. It was Quentin Burnett, though Burnett wasn't here. It was Dodge. Dodge and six others."

"I know, boy," Hawk said. "I saw them ridin' off with your sister. Don't you worry about her. I'm gonna get her back for you."

Neither child reacted to what he'd said. If they'd been able to understand him, they'd likely not believed him. It was well known in these parts that no one messed with Quentin Burnett and lived to tell the tale.

These two young Broyles siblings were in shock, their minds numb. Hawk knew how they felt. He'd felt the same way when he'd seen his beloved child, Jubal Hawk, hanging from that cottonwood branch in a raging prairie rainstorm — the branch from which the vile "Three Fingers" Ned Meade had hung the boy to get even with Hawk's having brought Meade's child-killing brother to justice.

Hawk had felt that same overpowering fog of numbness when he'd found that his wife, Linda, had hung herself from the cottonwood tree in their backyard in Nebraska, out of her unbearable grief at Jubal's fate.

Hawk glanced around to see if any of the Broyles horses had lingered near. He didn't see any. Finally, he turned to the two Broyles children, and said, "I'm gonna get you two up to my cabin. It's not far. There's no point in your staying around here. You'll be safe there. I'll see to it."

"I don't . . . I don't wanna leave Poppa!" the girl cried.

"Mercy, there's nothing you can do for him now. Your poppa's gone. I have to get you out of here. And then I'm gonna get your sister back." Hawk rose and turned to the girl's brother. "Jacob, I'd like you to climb onto my horse. Will you do that?"

Young Broyles just stood looking around as though he were trying to get everything straight in his head. But Hawk knew he wouldn't be able to get anything that had happened here this night straight for a long time. Maybe he never would.

Hawk walked over and touched the boy's arm. Jacob flinched and pulled back, looking frightened. He was a strong, good-looking boy though his eyes were pale and a little off-putting. Hawk knew the boy was good with a skinning knife. The outside of the Broyles cabin had been decorated with skins and furs young Jacob had tanned.

"It's all right, Jacob. I know you don't want to leave here. But there's nothing for you here anymore. I'd like to take you up to my cabin. You and your sister can ride my horse and I'll walk. Okay? Can you understand what I'm telling you, son?"

Jacob drew a deep, ragged breath. He looked around. More tears slithered down his cheeks. They glistened orange in the firelight. He turned toward the cabin, and said, "I reckon . . . that'd be best. Mercy, come on, honey. We're gonna go with Mr. Hollis."

"Are you going, Jacob?" the girl asked.

"Yeah, I'm going. No point in staying here."

"What about Poppa?"

"He's gone, Mercy. We gotta think about getting Jennie back now."

Mercy was staring at the cabin. The fire was gradually losing its intensity. As another portion of the roof collapsed into the leaping flames, Mercy walked over to Hawk's horse.

She extended her hand to Hawk, and he lifted her up onto his saddle. She was so light, she seemed almost like nothing in his hands. For some reason, that gave his heart another twist and a pull.

Then he helped Jacob up into the leather, as well.

"Goodbye, Poppa," Mercy sobbed as Hawk began leading the grullo out through the ranch portal, the cabin's flames dying behind him, the mountain's dense, dark night tumbling down around him.

Hawk led the horse and its two riders wide around the two men he'd killed, and then found the mouth of the trail that wound up the side of the ridge toward his cabin nestled in the next valley.

The sky turned from green to black, but the stars were sharp at this altitude, offering enough light to keep Hawk on the tan strip of trail switchbacking up the ridge through the dark pines. As he walked, the horse clomping along behind him, Mercy broke into strings of intermittent sobs. The smoke from the Broyles's burning cabin occasionally touched his nose as the breeze blew up from the valley below.

When he was halfway up the ridge, Hawk stopped suddenly. The horse stopped behind, the bit rattling in its teeth. The horse gave an incredulous blow.

Hawk had heard something.

He stepped wide of the horse to stare along his back trail.

The short hairs bristled across the back of his neck.

"What is it?" Jacob said, his quiet, worried voice sounding loud in the quiet night. "Why are we stopping?"

"Shh," Hawk said. "Prob'ly nothin', but I'm gonna check it out just the same." He slid his sixteen-shot repeating Henry rifle from the scabbard strapped to his saddle.

"What is it, Mr. Hollis?" Mercy said, her voice trembling.

"I don't think it's anything at all, honey," Hawk said, placing a reassuring hand on the girl's thigh. "Probably just a deer or a nightbird or some-such. I'm gonna take a little walk back along our trail to be sure."

Hawk gave Mercy his horse's bridle reins. "You take these. Hold 'em loose. The grullo knows his way back to the cabin, and, it bein' past his suppertime, he'll likely head right there. When you get there, go on inside and make yourselves to home. Should be some lamps lit. You'll find a blond-headed woman there. That's my wife. My boy, Jubal, is there, too. Linda's likely fixin' supper. She'll make you feel right to home. I'll be along shortly."

"A blond-headed woman?" Mercy said.

"That'll be my wife. She's very accommodating. She'll make you feel right to home."

In his mind, Hawk was seeing his house back in Nebraska, not the little prospector's shack old Van Hootin had built at the bottom of the next valley, along a creek he'd named after himself and along which he had several gold diggings. Things were getting mixed up in Hawk's mind, though he didn't realize it. It was almost like he'd fallen half-asleep and was dreaming, reality infused with the smoke and shadows of fancy.

"Oh," Mercy said, uncertainly. She brushed the heel of her hand across her wet nose, sniffing. "All right."

Hawk slapped the grullo's rump, and the horse thumped on up the trail. As the horse and its riders made the turn onto another switchback, Hawk heard Mercy faintly say to her brother, "I didn't even know Mr. Hollis was married . . ."

Hawk felt his mouth corners rise slightly at that, his belly filled with the warm feeling that thinking about his family always gave him. Now, holding the Henry in both hands across his chest, he made his way slowly down the trail. When he'd walked roughly ten yards, a vague shadow moved between two trees off the trail to his left.

"Hold it," Hawk said in a low voice, pulling back behind a near tree and sliding his gaze out around the side of it. "I saw you. Name yourself!"

No response.

In the far distance, a lone wolf howled.

Hawk held his position, heart quickening slightly as he awaited the blast of a rifle.

When none came, he slid another cautious

glance out around the side of the fir tree. "Who are you? Name yourself." He paused, running his tongue along his bottom lip. "Luke?" He waited. "That you, Luke?"

Nothing.

Hawk said, "I told you, ole buddy, that if you tried to hunt me down, I'd kill you. Now, I don't want to do that, but you give me no choice."

A loud thud from maybe twenty yards downslope.

Hawk stepped out around the tree, racked a cartridge into the Henry's breech, and snapped the rifle's butt against his shoulder.

Another hard thud, and another.

Hawk began to squeeze the Henry' trigger but then eased the tension in his finger when he saw the silhouette of the deer bounding at a slant down the slope. The beast bounded straight up in the air again, lifting all four feet off the ground, to hurtle over a deadfall.

It landed with another thud as all four hooves hit the ground at the same time, and then disappeared over the shoulder of the slope.

Hawk lowered the Henry and scowled off down the ridge. He looked around, ears pricked.

"Luke?" he said quietly.

Why did he have this overwhelming feeling that the kid he'd taken under his wing, oh so long ago, Deputy U.S. Marshal Luke Morgan, was following him? The sense that Morgan was indeed on his trail was nonetheless powerful despite a vague region of Hawk's brain remembering that he'd killed the young lawman — by accident — several years ago.

He'd hoped Morgan would kill him, Hawk, and put him out of his infernal misery. But Hawk had been surprised to see the shooter bearing down on him, and, reacting instinctively, he'd shot the young lawman he'd only a few months before considered his understudy. His younger brother.

And whom he'd later hoped would be his executioner.

But Hawk had shot him dead.

Add another misery to Hawk's trail . . .

Still, a large, increasingly irrational portion of his conscious mind told him that Morgan was back there. Somewhere.

Dogging him . . .

Trying to stop his vigilante run, to stop him from wiping out evil across the frontier. He couldn't let that happen now. He'd become too good at this. Killing bad men had become his irrefutable, irresistible calling. Every man he killed was one more bell being tolled for his dead wife, his dead son.

He might have just now spooked a deer, not stumbled on Morgan. Still, Morgan was back there. Hawk knew he was, despite Morgan being dead. That's the way Hawk's brain was working these days. Or not working. Chief Marshal Henry Clay had sent Morgan. The younker was lying back, waiting for his chance to snuff Hawk's wick.

Hawk looked around again slowly, carefully. His hearing had become so keen that he thought he could hear aphids growing on distant tree limbs. Sometimes he thought he could hear the ocean waves lapping upon a distant shore, or the muffled roar of a fire igniting a distant star.

But hearing nothing nearby now that could be construed as a human stalker, Hawk shouldered his rifle and continued on up the slope. Linda would likely have the coffee pot on the range, waiting for him.

Jubal would likely be sitting at the table, waiting for supper to be served, carving another wooden horse he loved so much to carve, putting his folding Barlow knife down occasionally to gallop the lifelike horse along the edge of the table, making galloping sounds with his lips.

Another bucking bronco.

Hawk smiled, adjusted the angle of his hat, and increased his pace. He had to get home to his family.

CHAPTER 6

Jennie Broyles had sat so long in the bathtub, the water had gone cold. For the past hour or so, she'd been sitting in the cooling water, staring out the tiny window at the peak of the gable ten feet above her, in a large, unfinished attic room of the New Canaan Inn.

Hearing the raucous voices in the street below the room, and smelling the woodsmoke from the town's many fires, Jennie gave a shiver. She looked down at the water.

The bubbles from the scented lye soap she'd been given had disappeared. The water had turned the color of cast iron. Her knees, which she hugged against her breasts, had turned fish-belly white and were as wrinkled as any old woman's.

"You need a hand out of there?" Dixie asked from where she lounged on the red velvet fainting couch behind Jennie.

Dixie was the woman whom Burnett had ordered Dodge to turn Jennie over to for tending. By "tending," he'd obviously meant locking her up in the sparsely furnished attic room that functioned as a bedroom, and forcing her to take a bath.

Two other whores had filled the tub and scrubbed Jennie down with brushes and sponges. They'd washed her hair and held her head underwater longer than necessary, rinsing her. She'd heard them chuckling while she'd held her breath and felt the pressure build in her head.

When Jennie was what they'd deemed clean, despite one saying, "There was no getting the cow shit out of a ranch girl's hide," they'd left, leaving only Dixie in the room.

Dixie was obviously a soiled dove. A whore. Judging by the lines around her mouth and eyes, she was considerably older than Jennie and the two other whores who'd bathed her against her will. Dixie had obviously been pretty once, for she sported a delicately boned, evenly featured face and long, dark-red hair that hung in rivulets about her shoulders. The hair had been dyed, Jennie suspected.

Dixie lounged back on the settee now, both feet on the floor. Her body was angled to one side, and she rested her cheek on the heel of her fine-boned hand. She wore pantaloons and a chemise over a corset, and high-heeled, black boots with silver buckles. On each wrist, she wore a ruffled black garter. Her hair was held back from her forehead with a tightly wound black bandanna, the long tail of which fell down the back of her head before curling forward to hang down over her right shoulder, nearly to her lap.

Her lips were thin. Too thin for her, even in her young days, to have had what anyone would have called a pretty mouth. Her nose was short and upturned. She was pale, attesting to her not getting much sunlight. But then, most of the whores Jennie had seen on her forced march to the attic had been as pale as ghosts — except for the black girl and the several Mexicans she'd seen, of course.

Jennie turned to her. "How long are you gonna sit there?"

"For as long as it takes."

"For as long as what takes?"

"For as long as it takes for you to submit to him — Quentin."

Jennie chuffed with exasperation. "I'm never gonna submit to him. You'll die of old age, sitting right there."

"You will eventually. You'll have to. You'll go stir crazy up here. Finally, you'll realize you're better off submitting to Quentin than being locked in this room, whiling away the days. They all do . . . eventually."

"They *all* do? How many have there been?"

"Quentin's wives? There were four before you."

"I am not, nor will I ever be, Burnett's wife."

"All right, then," Dixie said. "He's had four wives up till *now.* There, is that better?"

"What happened to them?"

"Let me see," Dixie said, leaning forward, resting her elbows on her knees, and tapping fingers against her chin. "The first was a traditional marriage that came to an end a long, long time ago. The marriage happened before Quentin got rich. I never knew the lady. Have no idea how she ended up. Don't really want to know. The second was me."

"You."

"Me. And, you see, I got old. At least too old for Burnett. I'm thirty-three. He likes them your age . . . forever and ever. So he kicked me out of his chamber and married a girl called Sweetheart. A gold miner's daughter. Sweetheart submitted right away.

In fact, Sweetheart and her family thought it was the best thing in the world for the girl.

"Sweetheart was the queen of the third floor, which is Burnett's own private residence. Only problem was Sweetheart went soft in the head after she had a child, and ran away. Burnett had her tracked down. What happened to her is anyone's guess, but if I was to guess, I'd say that Sweetheart had her throat cut from ear to ear."

"Oh, Christ!"

"You got a tongue on you. I wonder if he realizes that. He usually likes them quiet and shy."

"Fuck him!"

"Whoa!" Dixie said, leaning back on the fainting couch in surprise. "You got the mouth of a ten-cent dove from Front Street in Dodge City!" She laughed and clapped her hands. "I don't know how that's gonna work out. You'd best clean it up, sweetheart, or you might just end up like Sweetheart. Or . . . maybe he likes it. Change of pace. Maybe he likes the idea of taming a polecat."

"He'll never tame me. If he comes near me, I'll break a glass or a bottle or something, and carve out his liver!"

Again, Dixie laughed. That infuriated Jennie. She looked at the door flanking Dixie, and asked, "Who has the key to that door?"

"I do. And if you think you're going to get it off me, you'd better think again. You might be tough, Miss Jennie From the Mountains, but I'm tougher. Besides, if you somehow made it out of this room, out of the building, Quentin would have you run down long, long before you could make it a block away. Even if you made it out of town, which you wouldn't, there'd be nowhere for you to hide from Quentin Burnett."

Jennie stared at the door, then, deciding she'd have to take her time to plan a means of escape, her thoughts returned to the three other girls who'd been in her position. "What happened to Sweetheart's baby?"

"Burnett gave it away. Just like that. He didn't bat an eye. Just told me to get rid of it, so I found a poor couple in town who said they'd take the child."

"What happened to the next wife? Surely she didn't have time to grow old."

"Oh, no — she wasn't as old as you . . . when she killed herself."

Jennie had turned her gaze to the gable window, but now she jerked her startled eyes back to Dixie.

"That's right," Dixie said, answering the unasked question. "Quentin can be . . .

um . . . difficult . . . and you just have to accept that. The next girl, a lovely Mexican from a nice family in New Mexico, was bought and paid for. Burnett had been invited to the family's house in Las Vegas on a business trip, and he offered the girl's father a thousand dollars for her. But apparently she'd loved another. She could never get that boy out of her head. She told me all about him. Countless times. She wanted nothing more than to get back to him. When she realized that that was impossible, she hung herself from Burnett's third-floor balcony."

"I can understand that," Jennie said. "I'll do the same thing if he forces me to marry him . . . or to share his bed. I'll kill myself."

"That's why I'm here," Dixie said. "To make sure that doesn't happen."

"Trust me," Jennie said, rising from the cold water. "That would be a last resort. I don't intend to let him win. I intend to get out of here. My sister and brother need me. What Burnett's doing is illegal. I don't care if the U.S. marshal is in cahoots with him. Not all the law can be. Kidnapping and murder is illegal, and I'm gonna see he pays the price."

She glanced toward the bed. "Hand me the towel."

"He sure picked a wildcat in you," Dixie said, rising from the fainting couch and reaching for the towel. Her eyes drifted up and down Jennie standing naked and wet in the tub. "What a lovely body you have. He'll enjoy you, rest assured. He enjoyed me for a time."

Jennie thought she detected a vague longing in the older woman's voice.

As she took the towel and held it against her breasts, she said, "You . . . sound . . . like . . . you miss . . . being his *wife.*"

Dixie looked thoughtful for a moment, idly braiding a lock of her long hair with the long tail of the black silk bandanna. "You wouldn't understand anything about me. I didn't come from a family. I didn't come from a good place. I was an orphan. I started working the line when I was all of thirteen. When I was fifteen, Burnett chose me . . . me, of all the girls working for him . . . to come upstairs."

A faint smile pulled at her mouth. "To become his wife . . . his second one. I felt honored. And secure."

"But he was so much older."

"So were most of the men I spread my legs for, darlin' girl," Dixie said, placing a hand on Jennie's cheek. "At least I had money . . . and comforts . . . and security.

Until he got tired of me and brought in another. He'll get tired of you, too, in time."

She slid the towel away from Jennie's breasts, coolly appraising the lithe, buxom girl before her. "Despite the loveliness of your body."

She brushed a thumb across Jennie's left nipple.

Jennie pulled the towel back against her, repelled by the woman's touch.

"Don't worry, pretty girl," Dixie said, making her voice drag with cynicism. "In time your tits will sag. Your face will wrinkle. Your voice will deepen. And then he'll send you back down to the second story, and you'll be spreading your legs for the old salts who can't afford the younger, more expensive girls."

Jennie thought about that. A chill wracked her. As she began drying herself with the towel, she said, "Why did he pick me, anyway? Of all the girls in this place."

Dixie glanced enviously at the long, supple leg Jennie had lifted to dry with the towel, and then turned away and picked up a hand-rolled cigarette off a small, round table by the fainting couch. She struck a match on the wood-paneled wall, touched the flame to the quirley, and blew smoke into the room, toward Jennie.

"He no longer marries the working girls. After he sent me back down to the second floor, he directed his wife-search beyond the confines of the brothel. I remember the day he saw you. He and I were standing in his office, looking out onto the street. You and your father and brother and sister rode into town in your wagon and stopped at the mercantile for supplies. 'There, that's the one,' he said. 'That daughter of Angus Broyles. Look at her. Oh, she's a beauty. And I'll bet she's a virgin. She's the one for me!' "

"That old goat!" Jennie said, tossing the towel onto the bed and grabbing the powder-blue silk drawers from the pile of clothes that Dixie had laid out for her. "He's as old as my father."

Dixie laughed as she sagged back down on the couch. "That's the whole point, dear child."

"Why doesn't he find a woman his own age, maybe someone who loves him back, if that's even possible?"

"It's not possible. You'll find that out soon enough. There's really very little to love about Quentin Burnett."

As Jennie pulled a thin chemise down over her breasts, she glanced again at Dixie, who wore a wistful look. She held her smoldering cigarette in one hand and was braiding her hair again with the other hand.

Jennie scowled in disbelief. "Don't tell me *you* love him!"

Dixie looked at Jennie, and drew on the cigarette.

As she exhaled smoke she said, "It's more complicated than that. Look, why don't you finish dressing and I'll take you to his room? You might as well get that first night over with. No point in dreading it. He's really quite gentle, and he'll make you feel utterly adored. It won't be so bad . . . even if it's your first time." She arched a brow. "It will be your first time, won't it?"

"It would be my first time," Jennie said. "But since it's not going to happen . . ."

"All right, all right." Dixie sighed and dropped a hand to her thigh.

"He killed my father," Jennie said. "He burned my cabin. He turned my brother and my sister out into the mountains." She picked up the low-necked dress Dixie had laid on the bed for her, and held it up in front of her. "And now he wants me to dress like a whore and allow him to savage me. He thinks I'll become his submissive wife. Hah! If I get close to the bastard, I'm gonna murder him."

She tossed the dress onto the bed and

turned back to Dixie. "If he tries to kiss me, I'll rip his tongue out of his mouth with my teeth!"

Dixie laughed and clapped again, flopping back onto the fainting couch.

While Jennie stood glaring at her, her frustration beginning to turn to fear and sorrow, Dixie rose and strode over to her. She stared at Jennie for a time as though probing her deepest thoughts.

She shook her head fatefully. "Don't you see? He doesn't mind your refusal. It excites him. It challenges him. He intends to break you like a horse. Slowly. Savoring every minute. It's when you finally succumb — which you will do — that he'll start to lose interest."

Nodding, Dixie walked back to the fainting couch.

"In time, he'll break you. He'll ride the hell out of you . . . until he's had enough of you."

"Yeah, I know," Jennie said. "Then I'll end up on the second floor."

Clad in only the chemise and drawers, Jennie sat on the edge of the bed. She fought to keep her fear and sorrow down deep inside her. It was a fight she couldn't win. Her father was dead, her home burned, and her brother and sister were likely wandering alone in the mountains, easy prey for bears or mountain lions.

And Jennie had been locked up by a madman in New Canaan.

She lay down on the bed as the dam inside her broke.

She cried uncontrollably.

Chapter 7

Hawk strode along the last curve in the trail dropping into the valley he called home, and stopped.

A puzzled frown carved deep lines across his forehead.

What he saw was not his neat frame house with its white picket fence sitting there at the bottom of the valley, on the other side of Van Hootin Creek. It was a common settler's shack — a brush-roofed log cabin limned in the light of a quarter-moon kiting high above the valley.

Van Hootin's cabin. The one the old man, whom Hawk had befriended when he'd come to this remote valley several months ago to recover from wounds and to take stock of his life, had built nearly twenty years ago.

But of course it was Van Hootin's cabin sitting there. Why had he found himself expecting to find his house in Nebraska sitting here in the moonlight of this high-mountain valley in southern Idaho?

Why was he expecting to find his wife and son here?

Hawk shook his head, blinked, and brushed at his eyes as though to clear his vision. At the same time, a wetness came to his eyes, and a cold fist squeezed his heart. Sadness welled up in his throat. He choked back a sob.

His wife and his son were dead. His house was back in Nebraska. It likely belonged to someone else now. He'd abandoned it soon after he'd put six bullets each into the judge and the county prosecutor who had turned the killer of Jubal free from jail, and then he'd headed west to run down "Three Fingers" Ned Meade himself and hang him from a dead nut tree in Arizona.

Still, Hawk had believed with all his heart and mind that he'd find Linda and Jubal here, despite his knowing he'd buried them both back in Nebraska. His gut constricted. Another sob bubbled up in his throat. He dropped to a knee, scrubbed his hat from his head, letting it tumble off a shoulder, and raked a gloved hand down his face.

Linda and Jubal were not here. They were moldering in their graves, one beside the other.

Despite the certainty that he'd inexplicably felt — or *known* — he'd find them here alive and waiting for him, they were still just as dead as they'd been when he'd left them under mounded rocks back in Nebraska, several long years ago now. The cabin in the valley before him was Van Hootin's old shack, the one the old hermit prospector had turned over to Hawk in payment for Hawk's nursing him through the last few weeks of his struggle with an illness that had seemed to eat him from the inside out.

Hawk wept for a time, his face in his hands, shoulders jerking.

Then a strange incredulity and fear began to rise beneath his sorrow, squeezing it aside.

Why had he been so certain he would find his wife and son here?

Was he going — or had he gone — mad? Had his single-minded determination to kill evildoers like "Three Fingers" Ned Meade, long after Ned Meade himself was dead, ruptured a wall that had stood between sanity and total looniness inside of him?

Had his zealous determination to continue to avenge the deaths of his wife and his boy and thus assuage his own relentless grief turned his brain to mush? Relieving such soul-swallowing grief as Hawk's wasn't any more possible than Linda and Jubal being brought to life again.

Had his devotion to riding the outlaw trails with his deputy U.S. marshal's badge pinned upside down to his vest — an upside-down lawman riding against upside-down laws and killing upside-down outlaws — turned his brain to mush?

Hawk turned to stare up the ridge, at the pale ribbon of trail in the moonlight.

Luke Morgan was dead, as well. He was no longer on Hawk's trail. Hawk had killed the young marshal himself — the young man whom Hawk had tutored in the art of man-tracking and law-enforcing, to whom he'd been as close as an older brother.

Luke was just as dead as Linda and Jubal.

So, who had Hawk sensed shadowing him back there?

Phantoms. Only phantoms . . .

He straightened, composed himself, pulled a handkerchief from his back pocket, and blew his nose. He returned the kerchief to his pocket, returned the Henry to his shoulder, and continued on down the trail.

At the bottom of the valley, he strode across the bridge stretched over the creek. He himself had replaced several of the boards that, because of his illness, old Van

Hootin had let rot. A light burned in the cabin's windows across which the flour sack curtains had been drawn.

Hawk tapped on the door twice, then tripped the steel and leather latch, and shoved the door open. The cabin was the same as he'd left it earlier, after he'd spied the smoke. Only the boy and the girl were there, on the bed built of logs and a skinned pine frame against the wall to Hawk's far left. That had been Van Hootin's bed. The one against the wall to Hawk's right was his own.

The boy sat facing Hawk, tipping his head this way and that, listening.

The girl lay with her head on the boy's lap. She had her eyes open. Now she rose to a sitting position, brushed tears from her cheeks with the backs of her hands, and said haltingly, "We . . . uh . . . we didn't see no blond woman."

She looked around as though to further corroborate her statement.

"Or boy," added her brother.

Hawk felt his face warm with chagrin. He moved on inside the cabin and closed the door. "I had that wrong," was all he could find to say. He leaned the Henry in a corner by the door, pegged his hat, and moved to the shelves housing airtight tins of beans and tomatoes and some jars of Van Hootin's canned elk meat.

"I bet you two are hungry," Hawk said.

"I'm not hungry," Jacob Broyles said, staring straight ahead.

Mercy shook her head, then lay back down on her brother's lap.

"You gotta eat." Hawk glanced at the wood box to the right of the small, sheet-iron stove. The box was empty. He'd stepped outside to fill it earlier when he'd seen the smoke. "I'll get a fire going. Get coffee going, anyways. I think we could all do with a cup of mud, eh?"

He tried a smile. It didn't lighten even his own mood. He was still thinking about Linda and Jubal, feeling the horror of their being taken from him all over again.

He walked outside and started to gather wood from the stack along the cabin's north wall. Then he remembered his horse. He walked around to the small stable and corral out back of the cabin, at the base of the valley's western ridge.

The grullo stood facing the corral, its reins dangling. The horse turned its head to regard its rider, and gave an eager snort.

The horse was ready to be unsaddled and fed.

"All right," Hawk said. "All right, there, fella."

He continued toward the horse. There was the sound of rustling brush behind him. He swung around and dropped a hand to the butt of the Russian. He left the pistol in its holster, however. There was nothing out there. He'd only thought he'd heard something moving around in the brush by the cabin.

Phantoms. Only phantoms . . .

Hawk tended his horse and then brought an armload of wood into the cabin and started a fire.

Mercy didn't eat or drink anything.

When her brother rose from the bed to sit at the table with Hawk, the girl curled up on the bed, beneath the double blankets, for the mountain night was getting cold, and went to sleep. Jacob ate a few bites of the beans and elk meat Hawk had cooked in a pot on the stove, and drank a few sips of the coffee Hawk had brewed, as well.

The boy didn't say anything as he ate. He just stared straight ahead in that stricken way of his. Hawk thought he must know how the boy felt. Jacob really had it worse than Mercy did. Maybe even worse than their sister Jennie did, because he couldn't see. Without vision out here in the mountains, he'd have to depend on others to survive.

Hawk thought there must be no worse feeling in the world than to be nearly totally dependent on other people. He knew how fallible all people were. How fallible he himself was. In Jacob's blind eyes, he thought he could read his hesitation, even his fear, of sharing Hawk's cabin. After all, Hawk had met the family only once and not for long enough for them to get to know him; nor he, them.

And the boy was probably doubly suspicious of strangers, since he couldn't see them and was especially vulnerable to outside threats. In a way, he was like a blind calf on a mountain full of wolves.

Then, again, wasn't everybody?

Hawk didn't know what to say to the boy, so he said nothing. He was somewhat relieved when Jacob cleared his throat and, staring straight ahead across the table and off toward the cabin's far side, opened his mouth to speak.

"Mr. Hollis?"

"We'd best get something cleared up right away," Hawk interrupted the boy. "My name isn't Hollis. It's Hawk."

That didn't seem to surprise the boy in

the least. "You're an outlaw, aren't you?" There was a faint trembling in the young man's voice.

"Some would call me that."

Jacob felt around for his coffee cup, and lifted it to his lips. He sipped the tepid brew, and said, "What would you call yourself?"

"I'd call myself a lawman. One who does things his own way."

"Are . . . are you a lawman?"

"Some would say no. I say yes." Hawk reached for the badge that sat on a shelf near the table. He took the boy's right hand in his own and placed the badge in the boy's palm.

Jacob "read" the badge with his fingers and thumbs, and frowned.

"The moon and star," Jacob said, frowning. "A deputy U.S. marshal?"

"That's right."

"I don't understand. Why would some say you're not?"

"Long story," Hawk said, hooking an arm over the back of his chair and taking a sip of his coffee. "A gang of outlaws murdered my boy. Jubal was only a few years younger than you. He was a special boy. Like you. Not blind. He wasn't much for readin' and writin', but he had a special ability, like you with your skins. He could carve horses from an early age so those horses appeared to run with the wind."

Jacob smiled. "A wood-carver, your boy."

"That's right. The best you've ever se—." Hawk cut himself off.

Jacob shook his head. "That's all right. It happens all the time. What happened to Jubal, Mr. Hawk?"

"The gang led by 'Three Fingers' Ned Meade killed him." Hawk cleared emotion from his throat. "Hanged him. Ned wanted to hurt me because I arrested his brother, who himself was hanged, but rightfully so. He was a child-killer. Ran in the family, looks like. After Jubal was murdered, my wife hung herself out of grief. The same day as Jubal's funeral."

"I'm so sorry."

"I ran Meade down, arrested him, turned him over to the workings of the law. The law let me down. The judge and prosecutor were bought off by Meade. I killed them. Then I went after Meade and the other men in his gang, and I killed them all. I did it my own way, following my own laws."

Hawk tapped the badge Jacob had placed on the table. His fingernail made *ticking* sounds on the badge.

He looked at Jacob. Sober-faced, the boy seemed to be absorbing what he'd been told. Jacob curled one side of his upper lip, and nodded. "Good."

"The reason I told you that, Jacob, is because I wanted you to know what kind of man is going after your sister. She's been taken by evil men. No ordinary lawman would have much chance against such men. I have a much better chance. In fact, I'll go ahead and promise you that if she's still alive when I find her — and you know that part of it can't be guaranteed — I'll avenge you all and I will bring Jennie back to you and your sister. And we'll rebuild what you young'uns and your father built in that valley yonder."

"Yes," Jacob said, nodding his head again, and broadening his smile. "Yes, I see. I see, Mr. Hawk. Thank you."

Hawk rose from his chair. "You take the other bed. I'm gonna go bed down in the stable."

"You don't need to do that, Mr. Hawk."

"Son, I've been sleeping with my horse so long, I tend to miss him when we're not sharin' the same roof. Go ahead and turn down the lamp when you're ready to. . . ." Hawk let his voice trail off, cheeks warming with embarrassment. "Damn!"

"That's all right, Mr. Hawk," Jacob said, smiling as he rose from the table. "You can go ahead and turn down the lamp. I'll manage in the dark. I've been managing in the dark for quite a few years now."

"So have I, son," Hawk muttered as he turned the lamp down, grabbed his rifle, and headed out of the cabin. "So have I . . ."

Chapter 8

The rogue lawman snapped instantly awake and automatically reached for a pistol. The Russian and Colt were snugged into the holsters that hung from a chair back, beside his cot in the lean-to side shed off old Van Hootin's knocked-together stable.

Hawk slid the big, top-break Russian from its holster and clicked the hammer back as light spread out from the lamp on a small table, under the room's only, sashed window cloudy with dust and spiderwebs.

Hawk eased the tension in his trigger finger.

He scowled incredulously as a pretty blonde clad in a dress nearly the same shade of yellow as her hair turned to him. Only she wasn't turning from the table in Van Hootin's crude side shed. She was turning away from the scrolled oak dresser that had appointed the main bedroom in Hawk's house back in Crossroads, Nebraska Territory.

"L-Linda?" Hawk croaked, having to clear his throat as he stared in utter shock, lower jaw dangling. "L-L-Linda . . . ?" he said again as he slowly lowered the Russian in his right hand and raked his left hand down his face, brushing sleep from his eyes. "Is . . . that . . . *you* . . . ?"

"Gideon," Linda said, moving to him from the dresser. "You've been working way too hard, honey. You're not yourself. Look at you. You're all tensed up!" She pulled the revolver out of his hand and slipped it back into its holster.

She sat on the edge of the bed and leaned over him, smiling her gentle, concerned smile.

Hawk's heart thudded as it lightened. He looked around the room.

It really was his and Linda's old bedroom in Crossroads. Right down to the tortoiseshell comb lying on Linda's dressing table, beside the doily on which her pink Tiffany lamp sat. Her nightgown hung from a peg in the bedroom door. Her soft, wool-lined, elk skin slippers that Hawk had given her for Christmas the year after Jubal was born rested where they'd always rested, near the armoire by the door, on the dyed hemp rug

Linda had braided herself one winter, as she'd braided all of the rugs around the Hawk family home.

"Gideon, honey," Linda said, leaning on one arm and placing her other hand against his face. "What on earth is wrong?"

Hawk's heartbeat was increasing. He turned to her, feeling a relieved smile pull at his lips. Relieved? No. Hysterical!

Hawk leaned forward, grabbed both her arms, gazed into her eyes, and then scrutinized her face, her beautiful face with the three tiny moles forming a triangle on her neck, just beneath her jaw. The skin of her neck was the color of nearly ripe peaches.

The first slopes of her breasts shone above the bodice of her yellow, laced-edged dress, the one she usually wore in the summer. There was a faint blemish at the very top of her right breast, nearly as low as the crease between both bosoms.

Hawk ran his hands up and down her arms, over the sleeves of her dress.

"You're alive! Linda, you're really alive, aren't you?" Hawk sandwiched her face in his big, red-brown hands and stared deeply into her eyes again. Indeed, they were her eyes. Linda's eyes. He had every little fleck and swirl in both irises memorized. "You're alive!"

"Yes, Gideon," Linda said, frowning at him a little skeptically but also quirking an amused but cautious smile. "I'm alive. Just like you're alive!"

Hawk placed his head against her bosom, tipping an ear to her chest.

"Gid—"

"Shhh!"

Hawk listened. He could hear the soft thudding of her heart beneath the slow rise and fall of her breasts. Tears came to his eyes. He blinked them away as he lifted his head to gaze into his wife's beautiful face once more.

"Jubal . . . ?" he asked.

"I just put him to bed. Like I told you I would, just before you headed up to bed early. Now, why don't you lie back down . . . ?"

"I have to see." Hawk swept the covers back, dropped his feet to the wooden floor — a floor that seemed so inestimably solid and real beneath his bare feet! — and started toward the door. He took only two steps before, laughing, he swung back around, grabbed Linda around the shoulders, and kissed her hungrily, sucking her lips, tasting her, sliding his tongue into her mouth to feel her tongue against his.

He could smell her and taste her and feel

her in his arms. She smelled and tasted and felt just as she had before.

"You really are alive!"

"Oh, Gid, you must have been having a terrible nightmare!"

"Wait — I'll be right back. I just . . . I just have to go have a look at . . ."

He let his voice trail off as he walked out of his and Linda's room, and stopped outside their son's door. Linda had left it cracked three inches, just like Jubal liked it.

The sensitive boy didn't like sleeping behind a closed door. He didn't want a closed door coming between him and the security of his parents right across the hall.

Hawk nudged open the door. The light from his and Linda's room inched into the darkness to touch the brown-haired head of their child lying in his bed and covered with a tied patchwork quilt of red and blue and white. Jubal had pulled the covers up to his nose, just like he always did. He lay on his side, curled beneath the bedcovers.

On the shelf above him lay seven or eight of his horse carvings. All could have been done by a master craftsman. But, then, they had been done by a master craftsman. Jubal didn't do well at school. His teacher called him "slow," in fact. But he could carve a horse so the horse appeared a living, breathing animal a man could saddle or throw a buggy hitch to.

Jubal's covers rose and fell slightly as the boy breathed.

Hawk went over and knelt beside the bed. He lightly placed his hand on Jubal's head, feeling the silky softness of the boy's hair, which was a compromise between his mother's blond hair and his father's half-breed dark-brown hair, for Hawk was the son of a Ute war chief and a white mother.

"Oh, Jube," Hawk whispered, more tears dribbling down his cheeks. He felt a tightness in his throat. "Oh, Jubal, you're alive! Oh, god, boy — I've missed you so much. You'll never know how much your father missed you!"

Hawk wanted to take the boy in his arms and hug him tightly and forever, but he restrained himself. The boy needed his sleep. Days of school and chores afterward were long and hard for Jubal Hawk, who weathered the storm of life well for one so fragile and sensitive.

Inside, though, he had Hawk's Indian toughness and the stalwart resolve of his mother's Texas pioneer stock.

Hawk lowered his head and very gently planted a kiss on Jubal's left temple.

The boy stirred, moving a little beneath

the blankets and groaning deep in his throat.

"Sleep tight, my son," Hawk whispered, rising. "I love you more than you'll ever know, boy. Tomorrow, after school and chores, I'm gonna take you fishin'."

He stood staring down at his sleeping boy. He looked around at all the horses displayed here and there about the room, and at the several skins that Hawk had helped the boy tan over the past couple of years.

A dream.

All of his misery had been merely a dream.

A nightmare.

"Three Fingers" Ned Meade had not hung Jubal. Linda had not hung herself out of grief after Jubal's funeral. There had been no funeral.

Jubal was alive.

Linda was alive.

They were *both* alive! Their deaths and Hawk's years of wandering homeless, with only his horse and his guns for companions . . . all the years of hunting bad men and killing them — all just a dream.

Knife-Hand Monjosa and the Kilroy/Jones Gang and Estella, the devil's whore — and the crooked sheriff, D.W. Flagg — all just figments of a torturous, seemingly endless nightmare of wandering and loneliness with abrupt explosions of deadly, bloody brutality.

My god, what kind of a mind did Gideon Hawk possess, anyway, to have conjured such a nightmare or *series* of nightmares?

Should maybe talk to a doctor about that.

Then he chuckled, his mind returning to the relief he felt. The last several years had been a dream. A dream of epic proportions, epic agony, to be sure. But a dream just the same.

Had that long, variegated dream replete with so many ghastly chapters all occurred in only the past couple of hours?

But, then, most dreams occurred just after going to sleep and just before waking.

Stifling the jubilant laughter that wanted to bellow up from his chest, Hawk tiptoed back out of Jubal's room, adjusted the boy's door, and then pushed back into his and Linda's bedroom. "Boy, I sure am glad I woke. You have no idea what a nightmare I just . . ."

Hawk let his voice trail off.

Linda stood before him naked. Her dress and undergarments hung from the back of the chair by her dressing table.

"Holy . . ."

Linda tucked her bottom lip into her mouth, and moved slowly up to him, chin down, her eyes flashing with erotic flirtation. "You know what I think you need, Marshal Gideon Hawk?"

"What's that?"

He groaned when she placed her hand on his crotch, which had started coming alive the moment he'd first laid eyes on her, when she'd turned up the light on the dressing table. Her hand was like a lightning strike to his loins.

"I think you need to relax. And you know I know the best way to relax you" — she planted a delicate kiss on his right cheek, her lips feeling warm and silky and pleasantly moist — "don't you, Marshal Hawk?"

"Oh, yeah," Hawk said, trying to remember back.

Odd, how it seemed that they'd last made love so long ago. Years ago. But it couldn't have been more than a day or two, depending on if he'd been out on the outlaw trail recently. For the life of him, he couldn't remember. And he was too relieved to see his wife and son alive — the seemingly endless nightmare over — to worry about that now.

As Linda rose up onto her tiptoes to press her lips very gently on his, she began to unbutton his fly. Her fingers moved across him, vaguely teasing, building up the fire in his loins.

She nibbled his lips and tugged at his mustache with her teeth. She opened his pants and slid her hand into his long-handles. At first her hand felt cold against him, but it quickly turned to fire as she wrapped it around his stiffening manhood.

She pulled it out of his pants, and then she kissed him more passionately as she stroked him and pumped him, pulling his shaft up between them and against her bare belly. Hawk lifted his hands and caressed her tender breasts, rolling his thumbs across the swelling nipples.

"Sit down, Marshal Hawk," Linda whispered.

When he was sitting on the edge of the bed, she knelt between his spread legs, pumped him for a time and then gave him one of her smoky, alluring smiles before shaking her hair back to one side and sliding her head forward and closing her mouth down over his shaft.

She ran her mouth down, down the length of his hard member until she convulsed slightly, gagging quietly, when the head of his manhood met the far back of her throat. He could feel her throat expand and contract as she swallowed. She slid her mouth slowly back out to the end of his shaft and started all over again.

While his wife worked her slow magic between his knees, Hawk moved his hands through her hair, combing his fingers through the silky, yellow strands, then brushing his fingers across the back of her neck and over her ears. He ran them down her cheeks, across her forehead, and down her long, smooth neck.

She was alive. She really was alive. He'd vaguely wondered if *this* — what he was experiencing *now* — were the dream.

But, no.

There was no denying the sensations he was feeling. He could not be dreaming such tactile and erotic ministrations. He could not be dreaming the sensations of his wife's mouth on his penis, her head bobbing slowly up and down over his crotch, between his spread legs.

Linda's mouth was warm and moist and wonderfully familiar, her tongue moist and pliant as she slid it around him, toying with him, teasing him, manipulating him, gently sucking as she slid her mouth up and down on him, slowly increasing the rhythm and zeal of her manipulations, until he could stand it no longer.

Groaning and tensing his shoulders, fighting back the tide of passion threatening to reach a crescendo inside him, he grabbed her arms and pushed her back away from him.

She was reluctant to leave him. When she did, she chuckled throatily and brushed a hand across her moist mouth.

"I aim to please, Marshal Hawk."

"Get into bed."

"Whatever you say, Marshal."

Linda got into bed and rolled toward him, her eyes flashing in the lamplight while she watched him undress. It didn't take him long. He pulled the covers back, crawled under them, shoved his wife onto her back, and kissed her lovingly on the mouth for a long time, caressing her cheeks with his thumbs.

He nibbled her ears, kissed her neck, and ran his tongue through the valley between her breasts. He sucked her nipples and her belly button, and then pressed his face into the silky muff between her legs. She draped her long, pale legs over his shoulders and ground her heels into his back as he pleasured her with his tongue.

After several minutes, she was writhing and chewing her knuckles, having risen to the bittersweet crest of her passion.

"Oh . . . oh, god, Marshal Hawk!" she cried, thrashing around, quivering. "Oh, god

— oh, Jesus Christ, you're killing me!"

Vaguely, Hawk reflected that while theirs had always been a passionate marriage, they'd never been quite this passionate, and Linda's tongue had never been quite that energetic. However, he chuckled in delight at his wife's lost inhibitions, and mounted her, sandwiching her face between his big hands.

He thrust his hips against hers.

They came together in a long, violent spasm of shared bliss.

Then, breathless, Linda rose to turn out the light, and they slept, entangled in each other's arms. He'd never slept so well in his life.

He woke to milky blue dawn light pushing through the dusty window.

He blinked, jerked his head up from his pillow, and looked around.

He was not in his and Linda's bedroom at home. He was back in Van Hootin's stable. The clothes hanging from the back of the near chair were not Linda's. They were light-blue denims, a lacy chemise, a hickory blouse, and a light-tan Stetson hat.

A pair of fancy, pearl-gripped Colts jutted from the holsters attached to the cartridge belt dangling from a near wall peg.

Hawk's heart thudding dreadfully, he

looked down at the naked girl curled against him.

He swept the thick tangle of sun-bleached blond hair away from her plump cheek and her ear from which a large silver hoop dangled. He recoiled in horror when he recognized the face in repose against his chest as belonging to his long-time tormentor, the gorgeous outlaw devil herself, Saradee Jones.

"No," Hawk said aloud. *"No!"*

His heart had turned to a cold stone in his chest.

Saradee groaned, then lifted her head. Blue eyes, heavy with sleep, gazed up at him, blinking. A silver crucifix dangled between the beautiful, full, upturned breasts chafed red from a recent manhandling. She slid her hand across his belly and squeezed his shaft, which, to his own incredulity and against his will, was coming alive again.

"Good morning, Marshal Hawk," she said, teasing him with her words and her hand. "Wanna go again, do you? Good lord — you're gonna kill me!"

Chapter 9

In a dream, Quentin Burnett stared up in horror as a large, heavy pillow was thrust over his face. He tried to lift his hands to fight away the assault, but his arms had turned to lead. They wouldn't budge from the bed.

The pillow was mashed down hard against his face.

He tried to draw a breath, but it wouldn't come. The pillow was pressing down savagely on his nose and mouth. His lungs constricted. Terror overwhelmed him.

He opened his eyes and sat up sharply, gasping, sweating, his chest aching as his heart hammered his ribs. Beside him, last night's girl groaned, rolled over, and went back to sleep.

Burnett brushed a hand across his face. There was no pillow. He looked around his vast, well-appointed bedroom. No danger lurked in the dawn shadows.

Catching his breath, he smacked his lips. Odd, how real that dream always seemed. He'd swear he could taste the pillow on his lips, even feel some residue of feather stuffing on his tongue.

Suffocation. Always, someone was trying to suffocate him.

But, why? Who?

Why was he constantly, night after night, plagued by such dreams?

Slowly, the fear released its grip on him. He turned to the table beside the bed. He wanted a drink of water. There was no water there, only the bourbon he'd been drinking before he'd made love to the girl.

To last night's girl. Whoever she was. He couldn't remember, though he was sure he'd had Dixie examine her to make sure there were no signs of disease, the bane of whores everywhere as well as their jakes and pimps.

Burnett lifted the tumbler and threw back the bourbon. It burned nicely going down. He didn't normally drink before noon, but maybe he should start. The strong liquor soothed the night terror.

He didn't care for that emotion. He'd gotten too big and powerful to feel it. He'd grown up on the streets of New York where boys were terrorized every waking and even every sleeping moment. He'd left the Bowery and Hell's Kitchen with his pockets and a velvet, gold-tasseled pillowcase full of money he'd stolen from a man of power.

The man, Hans Christiansen, had taken him in off the streets under the guise of offering him sanctuary from the mire and violence of the cobbled streets. But in fact Christiansen had badly abused Burnett in ways the boy never could have imagined if he had not been similarly abused in the ghettos. When he'd broken away from Christiansen with Christiansen's money, he'd vowed that he'd use that moneyed devil's wealth to build a life for himself in which he'd never feel terror again.

He'd live a life in which he was the inflictor of terror, not the receiver. That's how the world worked. You either received terror or you were the inflictor of terror.

He'd come a long way, Burnett had. He enjoyed inflicting his own brand of terror. He enjoyed wielding power.

Still, the damned dream . . .

Of course, he knew why he dreamt it. One night, after Christiansen had finished inflicting his markedly depraved brand of evil upon young Quentin, and the man had rolled onto his back to go to sleep, Burnett had taken a red satin pillow and laid it over the man's face. While Christiansen suffocated, Burnett had taken an ice pick and plunged it through the pillow over and over again, until there was nothing left of the railroad magnate's face but red mash and feathers.

Christiansen's long, snake-like tongue had dangled out his wide-open mouth, blood dripping off its sloping tip to pool on his chest.

Young Quentin had dressed, then filled sacks with paper money and coins and silver and gold bric-a-brac, including a jewel-encrusted, solid gold pipe the magnate had kept in its own glass display cabinet in his library. Burnett had sneaked out of the house while the man's wife and children — yes, he'd been married with children — had slept, and quickly exchanged his collection of curios for cash that amounted to nearly ten thousand dollars.

With his newfound wealth he'd hightailed it west and, using the money to fuel the comet of his new life, he'd made a name for himself.

Yes, he'd come a long way.

He wasn't as rich as Christiansen, but he owned damned near the entire town of New Canaan and most of the land and even the mountains around it. His ranch up in those mountains was envied by some of the wealthiest men he knew.

Some of those wealthy and influential men were coming to New Canaan to hunt with Burnett, including the U.S. marshal, Blackwell. Blackwell was not rich, of course. No government man got rich as long as he worked for the government. But he did have power. Burnett always invited Blackwell up here to show him off to his rich friends. Blackwell was useful in demonstrating to others how powerful Burnett had become.

"You have to hand it to ole Quentin Burnett. Why, he has a chief U.S. marshal in his back pocket!"

Admiring laughter all around . . .

Consideration of the hunt brought Burnett back to the moment at hand. He needed to dress and to get his hunting party together, to organize his guides . . .

The girl in his bed.

Burnett turned to her. He enjoyed a morning ablution of sorts. It always took the edge off the dreams of suffocation.

All he could see of the girl was her dark head turned away from him on the red velvet pillow. A brunette. He lifted the sheet. She was naked. Her brown ass jutted toward him, her knees drawn up toward her belly. The soles of her feet, which rested one atop the other, were much paler than the rest of her except for the crack between her plump butt cheeks.

Mandy or Candy was her name, though he doubted it was her real name. A *mestiza* from Mexico. She'd been shipped up by a regular Mexican supplier from Tucson. A nice lay, though that's about all she'd done — just laid there! She wouldn't last long. If the girls didn't know how to attract repeat business, Burnett cut them loose, sometimes merely giving them a small canvas sack of the clothes they'd come with, and a sandwich, and shoving them out the Inn's back door.

Most often, they simply disappeared. Burnett didn't worry about what became of them.

Of course, he left the trivial work of dealing with the help to Dixie.

What would he do without Dixie? She literally ran things around here, though she did her share of bedroom business, as well. There were some men who didn't mind diddling an older woman as long as she came cheap. Besides, Dixie had her talents that this girl — this Mandy or Candy or whatever in hell her name was — could only dream about.

Burnett missed that part about her. In

fact, Dixie was still a fine looking woman. But he'd tired of her. That's why, despite their being married, he'd turned her out of his living quarters and onto the second floor.

At least, he hadn't kicked her out of the Inn entirely. She still earned a rather decent living for herself, Dixie did. Burnett paid her extra for performing all the tedious tasks that were part and parcel of running such a complicated business, and doing all the hiring and firing of the secondary help — the bartenders and bouncers and the men who swamped out the place and ran the gambling layouts.

Even the stable boys.

Dixie was seeing to Burnett's soon-to-be wife now.

Burnett felt a quickening of his blood as, giving himself a quick sponge bath and dressing for the hunting trail, he considered the Broyles girl. Nothing kept a man young like the prospect of fresh blood in his bed. He'd admired the girl since he'd first seen her ride to town with her father to buy supplies from the mercantile.

Jennie Broyles had turned more than Burnett's head, the businessman had noticed. When she came to town, nearly every man on the street got a crook in his neck, and Burnett had noticed a small crowd of men of all ages gathered around the mercantile while Jennie Broyles and her father had loaded their wagon.

The girl had an earthy charm about her. Tan and outdoorsy, with brown hair that flashed red when the sun hit it a certain way, she carried herself well. Not with a queenly insouciance, but in a way that said she had a spirit as big and bold as any man's.

She'd be a fine trophy, that one. Not unlike the trophy head of a regal elk or grizzly bear. Only this trophy would be clinging to Burnett's arm when he invited his moneyed friends to these mountains to dine and dance and then to head up into the higher reaches to hunt game trophies.

Burnett was adjusting his foulard tie when a knock sounded on his door. He grimaced at the intrusion. His hired help knew that he liked to take his time dressing in the mornings, especially after he'd sat up late drinking and smoking with friends. Cursing under his breath, he dabbed more water through his thin hair, which, he noticed with chagrin, was losing more and more of its brown to a grizzled gray.

Oh, well. He needn't worry so much about his looks. His charm and magnetism were in his raw power and dominating spirit. Women were attracted to him in much the way the females of the animal world were attracted to the males of their own species — a primitive draw toward the stud best equipped mentally and physically to provide best for them and to inoculate them with the seed of stalwart children every bit as indomitable as their sires.

After all, you didn't have to scratch very deep for proof that we were all savages.

Burnett closed the door of his sleeping quarters, crossed his parlor outfitted with several game trophies and an oil painting of the New Canaan Inn mounted above the fieldstone hearth, and opened the main door of his quarters. Dixie stood in the dark hall, looking her own somber self. She didn't appear to have had much sleep. Her cheeks were drawn, her eyes puffy.

"I told you to stay with the new Mrs. Burnett," Burnett grumbled.

"She's dead asleep. I slipped her a sedative in some tea I coaxed her to drink . . . finally . . . at four a.m."

"If she hangs herself, I'm holding you personally responsible."

"You do that, Quentin. Let me come in. I need a drink. A splash of the good stuff."

"Oh, Christ!"

Burnett drew the door wider and turned away. For some reason he had a difficult time refusing Dixie. She took too good care of him and his business for him to balk at her surliness and unreasonable demands. Besides, she never ordered him around in front of the other help.

Smart, Dixie was. She knew that would get her a black eye and a fat lip . . . for starters.

"You know where it is," Burnett said, pulling on a velvet rope hanging down behind the deep leather chair angled before the fireplace.

A bell would ring downstairs, and the help in the kitchen would scramble to bring his coffee.

"Well, since you're here," Burnett said, turning to Dixie and throwing his arms out, displaying his fawn-colored, buckskin hunting suit. "How do I look? Anything out of place?"

Dixie glanced over her shoulder at him while she removed the stopper from a glass decanter. She looked him critically up and down. "You're gaining weight, Quentin," she said, drolly, then splashed whiskey into a cut glass blue goblet.

She strode to him, her lacy wrap and sheer nightgown spreading like wings to each side of her still-lithe frame. She set the goblet on a lamp table, then straightened his tie and, her right eye glinting with mockery, said, "If you keep eating that venison stew I keep having the cook make for you — with fresh cream, as you always demand — you're going to need this vest taken out."

She gave his bulging gut a poke, and winked.

Burnett chuckled, his ears warming. He still couldn't help feeling the occasional pang of lust for his former wife. He was vaguely, unconsciously aware of a very strong pull toward Dixie, though he wouldn't have admitted it to anyone, least of all himself, despite the fact that she was the only woman — only person of either sex, actually — whom he'd ever been able to converse openly with.

There was a click. Burnett turned to see last night's *mestiza* poke her head out of his bedroom. The girl's eyes widened when they met Burnett's and then shifted to Dixie.

As she pulled her head back into the room with a start, and began to close the door, Dixie barked, "Mecina, downstairs! Now! Get yourself cleaned up and ready for business. It's payday out at the Circle 6, and you know how those boys always demand the Mexican girls! They'll be riding into town in a few hours to stomp with their tails up."

"Sí, sí, Senora!" the girl cried, hurrying out of the room, chocolate brown eyes as wide as silver dollars.

As she crossed the room, she said something in Spanish to Dixie. Burnett had never learned Spanish but Dixie had picked it up over the years from the Mexican doxies, and used it to communicate with those who had no English. Dixie barked commandingly back in what sounded to Burnett's unschooled ears as fluent Spanish.

The girl cowered, lowering her head, and made for the door.

As she did, Burnett found himself admiring her slender, brown body with small pert breasts, large nipples, and gently rounded hips. Her hair, coarse as straw, hung straight down to just above her splendid ass. She'd not been much of a lover. What a waste of such fine features! Last night, when he'd been bucking against the girl from behind, Burnett had made a mental note to have Dixie give the girl a few pointers.

As the young *puta* slipped out the door and into the hallway, Burnett glanced at Dixie to find her regarding him peculiarly.

What was that look? he vaguely wondered. Reprimand? Jealousy?

He was about to ask when harried heels clomped in the hall, growing louder.

"There's my coffee," Burnett said.

He pinched his pants up higher on his stout legs and sagged into his leather chair as Dixie went to the door. One of the kitchen girls — a stocky, round-faced, German blonde whose name Burnett could never remember — stood in the hall with her little, pale fist raised, about to knock. She swallowed in fear of Dixie — all the help feared Dixie even more than Burnett — and offered the steaming china coffee cup and saucer with a little curtsy and evasion of her eyes.

"Thanks, Madeleine," Dixie drawled, taking the saucer in one hand. It rattled a little, as Dixie had acquired a slight palsy, most likely due to overdrinking and overworking. "Now, get back down to the kitchen. Tell the cook he'd better have the bacon frying. Mister Burnett's guests will be rising soon and needing to eat an early breakfast before they head into the mountains."

Madeleine nodded nervously, wheeled, the hem of her pleated white kitchen dress billowing out around her barrel-like hips, and hurried away.

"That reminds me," Burnett said as he accepted the coffee cup and saucer from

Dixie, "I'd best get down to the dining room soon myself. I have to make sure the guides are awake. They were up far too late, drinking with the rest of us."

"I'll make sure they're up in a minute," Dixie said, sipping her bourbon and dropping lithely into the chair across a cherry coffee table from Burnett. As was her habit, she was barefoot, and as she dropped into the overstuffed leather chair, she drew up one of her nearly bare legs and tucked it beneath her, crossing the other one over the knee.

She closed the wrap around her the way a moth closes its wings.

"I wanted to talk to you about your new wife, Quentin."

"Oh?"

"Yeah," Dixie said, taking another sip from her glass. "I know you like the simple country girls. But you might want to reconsider this one. Send her back to where she came from. I'll find you another one. One you can actually tame."

Burnett grinned in delight over the rim of his smoking cup. "She's that wild, eh?"

"Wild?" Dixie laughed ironically. "This one's liable to cut your balls off and feed them to you, Quentin."

CHAPTER 10

Burnett threw his head back and laughed.

Odd, how he'd hated Dixie's salty mouth when he was married to her but no longer minded it so much, now that she was no longer adorning his arm but taking on the brunt of the tedious chores around here. Now she was an amusing business partner.

"I'm serious, Quentin," Dixie said, leveling a frank gaze at him. "She hates you. How could she not? You burned her cabin and killed her father! You might have tried a more subtle proposal. You might have gotten gussied up, ridden up there in your chaise, and taken the girl some flowers."

Burnett had been sipping his coffee. Now he jerked his head up, spewed coffee from between his lips, and threw his head back, roaring. Dixie laughed, then, too, and they laughed together, hysterically, for a long time.

They'd never laughed together this way

when they'd been married. Now they kept each other laughing for nearly three straight minutes.

Burnett laughed until he feared his ribs were going to break and tear through his sides.

Finally, he and his ex-wife sagged back in their chairs, panting, exhausted.

"All right, all right," Dixie said, finishing her bourbon and pushing herself up out of her chair. "I've had my say, and, obviously" — she chuckled again — "it's fallen on deaf ears."

"Let me go have a look at the girl," Burnett said.

He thrust his hand toward Dixie, who took it and pulled him to his feet. Burnett looked down at her. He found himself staring down into her low-cut sleeping gown, at the twin orbs pushing out from behind the fine silk cloth.

Lust tugged at him. Odd to find himself still attracted to the woman he'd kicked out of his bedroom nearly seven years ago, now. But there you had it.

She was even older now than when he'd dissolved their marriage because he'd needed a newer, younger conquest . . .

Dixie followed his gaze, then stepped back, flushing slightly, and drawing her wrap more tightly about her shoulders. She shook her hair back from her cheeks. "Are you sure you want to do that? You might not get out of the room alive, Quentin."

"Oh?" Burnett laughed, gesturing at the door. "We'll see about that!"

Burnett followed Dixie down the hall and up the short flight of stairs to the third story. They stood outside the closed door of the little attic room reserved for the disciplining of wayward whores. Isolation was a handy tool when physical punishment proved counterproductive. The girls had to look their best for the clientele, after all.

"We'll see about that," Burnett repeated as, thrusting his shoulders back, he turned the doorknob and stepped into the room.

Dixie followed him inside.

The Broyles girl lay on the bed, facing away from him.

"Hello?" Burnett said, raising his voice commandingly. "Turn around here and let me get a look at you."

The girl didn't move. Burnett frowned. Was she asleep?

He was about to speak again, louder, when she rolled lazily toward him. She lay on her back, covered with the bedcovers, regarding him with cold, brown eyes that owned a thin sheen of tears. Her cheeks were swollen from crying.

When she spoke, however, her voice betrayed no emotion whatever.

"You want to do more than look, don't you?" the Broyles girl said. "You didn't burn my cabin, murder my father, and haul me off here to this smelly attic just to look, did you?"

She blinked. She stared frankly up at Burnett as though awaiting an answer to her question.

Burnett hesitated. He started to chuckle nervously but stifled it and glanced at Dixie standing behind him. Dixie arched a brow at him as though to say, "See — what did I tell you?"

Burnett turned back to the Broyles girl and again put a commanding edge in his voice. "You're to be my wife. You might as well get used to the idea. When you do, you'll . . ."

He let his voice trail off. The Broyles girl threw the bedcovers back, revealing her long, splendid, naked body.

"This is what you want, isn't it?" she said, flaring her nostrils but otherwise continuing to betray little emotion. "You want to fuck me. So . . . get out of those funny-looking clothes, and climb in here. Show me what kind of husband you'll make. I have certain standards, you know. If I'm going to marry the old, fat tinhorn who killed my father, he'd better at least be a stallion under the sheets!"

She angled her body on the bed so that her bare feet were near Burnett's thighs. She spread her legs, giving him a bold, unrestricted look at her muff and the pink petals of flesh inside it.

She raised her hands to her breasts, pushed them up toward her neck, and then lay the backs of her hands against her pillow, to either side of her head with its comely mess of tangled auburn hair.

"For . . . for . . . for Christ's sake!" Burnett said, thoroughly taken aback. He found himself taking one stumbling step backward and glancing at Dixie, who continued to look at him without saying anything. She didn't need to. Her eyes said it all.

"Come on!" demanded the Broyles girl, spreading her legs still wider. "Get out of those silly clothes, old man, and show me how you'll satisfy my wildcat desires. That's what you wanted, wasn't it? A mountain wildcat? Well, now you have one. A virgin one, at that. A hungry virgin! You must take the horns with the hide, Mr. Burnett. If it's a wildcat you wanted, it's a wildcat you have. And I have very strong desires that need satisfaction, Mr. Burnett. Come on. Climb in here and show me what kind of a man you really are!"

She'd pushed up onto her elbows, her cheeks flushed with fury, brown eyes afire. A single tear rolled free of the right one and dribbled down the side of her nose. She brushed it violently away.

"What's the matter, Mr. Burnett?" she raged. *"Aren't you man enough?"*

She fairly screamed that last sentence.

Burnett's heart raced. His cheeks and his ears were hot with humiliation. He felt in his loins a weird tug of animal desire for this naked, wild, alluring creature. At the same time, he sort of felt the same fear he'd encountered when, still half-asleep, he'd watched that pillow thrust toward his face, threatening to suffocate him.

As the girl rose still higher on the bed, Burnett lurched around, grabbed Dixie's arm, and said, "Let's . . . let's go. Let's get out of here!"

He shoved Dixie out the door, glancing once more at the crazed girl now crawling toward him on the bed, breasts swaying beneath her, her hair hanging wildly down both sides of her face.

Her eyes were like those of an enraged

feral creature. Burnett stumbled backward once more and slammed the door. Inside the room, the girl let out a shrill, enraged scream that sounded like the scream of a mountain lion he'd once heard as it had pounced on its prey.

He turned the key in the lock and swung toward Dixie. Even she seemed surprise by the venom in the display she and Burnett had just witnessed.

"I hate to say I told you so, Quentin," she said, breathless, laughing incredulously. "But I told you so!"

"Christalmighty!" Burnett said. *"Christalmighty!"*

Hawk pulled his wooden-handled Colt from the holster hanging from a peg over his cot.

Still curled naked against him, Saradee Jones stared up at him, smiling with annoying serenity as he clicked the Colt's hammer back and shoved the pistol between her plump, pink lips.

She didn't flinch or pull back or otherwise resist the intrusion of the gun into her mouth. She didn't even blink.

In fact, she closed her lips around the barrel, as though she welcomed it there.

Her cornflower-blue eyes stared up the cocked gun at Hawk, her eyes wide and expectant, almost as though she were awaiting the bullet she did not fear. Or knew would not come.

"You," Hawk said around the hard knot of grief in his throat. "It was you. Last night . . ."

He glanced around as though he might spy his beloved wife, Linda, hiding in a corner. But of course she wasn't here. She was dead. Jubal was not in his bed across the hall. There was no hall. There was no Jubal. The boy was dead, lying belly up in a pine box six feet underground back in Nebraska, beside his mother.

Hawk was in the narrow lean-to addition of old Van Hootin's stable in the Idaho mountains. It was the female regulator and general no-account outlaw, as deadly as she was beautiful, he'd made love to last night, believing in his grief-ravaged, storm-wracked mind that Linda had come back to him.

"You," Hawk whispered, his eyes wide and glassy with shock.

The barrel of the Colt in her mouth, Saradee nodded slowly, staring up at him, the lamplight reflected in her pretty blue eyes — the crazy, taunting, eminently alluring eyes of an outlaw sorceress.

Hawk said, "I told you the next time I saw

you I'd kill you."

Staring up at him, eyes winking in the lamplight, Saradee nodded again. She tried to speak around the barrel of the pistol in her mouth. Her words was badly garbled, but Hawk made out what she said:

"Go ahead."

She blinked slowly.

Her mouth stretched a little around the barrel in her mouth, smiling. She was taunting him as she always did. Taunting him with her beauty that masked a devil's heart. The coal-black heart of a demon birthed in hell's burning soup and freed in this world in the form of a buxom, golden-haired succubus to drive men mad.

Hawk pulled his finger back against the eyelash trigger. It would go only so far, however. It was as though the trigger was jammed. It would not go back as far as it needed to release the mechanism that would drop the hammer upon the firing pin to detonate the powder and blast the bullet out of the chamber and through the barrel and into the head of the vixen gazing brashly back at Hawk, daring him to do it.

Knowing that he wouldn't.

That he couldn't.

Because as much as he hated her and wanted to kill her, he was under her spell.

He looked down at her breasts lightly pressed against his belly. Her nipples felt like rosebuds against his skin. He looked at her left hand splayed against his right side, over his ribs and near the silver cross that hung from her neck. Her other hand was pressed heel-down on the cot to his left. Her hair spilled down around her doll-like face to caress him like silk.

He felt such deep betrayal for what she'd done to him last night, masquerading as his dead wife, that he urged himself to go ahead and shoot her and to scour this buxom siren from his back trail once and for all.

But he couldn't do it.

Hawk pulled the Colt's barrel out of Saradee's mouth. Some of her spittle clung to the site at the end of the barrel. He held the hammer with his thumb while, keeping the revolver aimed at her face, he pulled the trigger, then gentled the hammer down against the firing pin.

"She was so real," Hawk said, looking around the room again, vaguely hoping that this was the dream and that if he looked around hard enough . . . if he hoped strongly enough, with all his heart . . . he would awaken and be in his room again in his house in Crossroads, and Linda would be the woman curled beside him.

And Jubal would be in his bed across the hall.

Somehow, he knew that wasn't going to happen. Somehow, the storm inside his mind had abated, and he was back in the real, present moment.

And this was his life now — this shabby room, this moth-eaten cot, this outlaw demon curled naked against him, his loins warming against his will as he remembered the vigor of their coupling.

Saradee looked at his midsection. She smiled devilishly up at him and then placed her hand on his stiffening shaft. She leaned over him, the tendrils of her hair sliding across his chest and belly. She licked her lips as she smiled at him again and then lowered her head and closed her mouth around him.

Hawk lay back in surrender, staring up at the low ceiling beams gauzy with spiderwebs to which the black specks of half-devoured flies hung.

Chapter 11

"I'm ready for breakfast, lover," Saradee said as she dressed.

Hawk shoved his shirttails inside his pants and pulled the suspenders of his whipcord trousers up over his shoulders. "You know I don't want you calling me that."

"But we are lovers, Gid," Saradee said, turning to him, bare-breasted. Biting her lower lip, she shook out her thin chemise and then dropped it over her head, covering the upturned bosoms. "Whether you want us to be or not."

She strode over to where he stood by the door, his back to the window. She looked up at him, again her eyes glinting mesmerizingly in the growing morning light. "We were meant to be together, Gideon. We're too much alike, you an' me, not to be together . . . always."

"How'd you find me here?"

Her smile broadened. "I have my ways."

"I want you to leave."

"Before breakfast?" Saradee exclaimed. "That's not bein' a very good host, Marshal Hawk."

Hawk sat down on the cot to pull his right boot on. "Shut up and leave me. Why do you keep following me? Tormenting me?"

"Because you want me to. Deep down, you know it's true."

"You're an outlaw."

"So are you."

"I have a cause. I kill bad people. People who deserve to die."

"So do I!" Saradee said, as though she were talking to a simpleton. "You know as much as I do, Marshal Hawk, that there's few folks on the frontier over the age of thirteen or so who don't deserve a bullet."

Hawk pulled on his other boot. "Don't you have a gang around somewhere you could drift back to? Maybe some banks to rob in Mexico?"

"My last gang disbanded as soon as we got back north of the border. Dangerous to hang together. You should know that, you bein' a lawman an' all." Saradee touched the deputy U.S. marshal's badge he'd pinned upside down on his vest last night, and pecked him on the mouth. "Even if you are an *upside-down* lawman."

Hawk leaned forward, elbows on his knees. He scrubbed his hands through his thick, dark-brown hair and then lowered his head and laced his hands across the back of the neck. "What's gotten into me?" he groaned. "Last night was so real!"

Saradee stood buttoning her blouse. "It was real, lover. As real as it's always been. Just you an' me."

"I saw my wife last night. In here." Hawk was talking to the floor, mostly trying to work it out in his own mind. "I saw my son . . . I saw Jubal . . . in his room across the hall."

"Oh, that's why you went outside. I was wondering. You came back in smiling like I never saw you smile before. It warmed my heart!"

"Oh, Christalmighty — why can't you shut your consarned mouth, woman!"

Saradee frowned, pouting. She walked over to Hawk and knelt before him. "That's no way to talk to the woman who made love to you last night, Marshal Hawk."

"I thought you were my wife."

"Oh, come on, Gideon," Saradee laughed. "No wife ever made love like that!"

Hawk jerked his head up, anger boiling in him. "Can't you understand — I think I'm losing my mind! Last night . . . I wasn't here. I was back in Crossroads. You were Linda. She was so real I could taste her and smell her and feel her the way I did before. And when I walked outside, I thought I was walking into . . ."

Hawk let his voice trail off. What was the point in going over it? Especially with one who was as crazy as Saradee. She was likely even crazier than Hawk was.

Hawk reached back for his Russian .44. He held it in both hands before him, looking at it. He turned the wheel with his thumb. "Maybe it's time I finished it."

"Don't be silly, Gid." Saradee closed her hand over the top-break revolver. "You got more killin' to do. Why, you just got started."

"If I'm goin' crazy . . ."

"You're not goin' any more crazy than the rest of us."

Hawk gave an ironic snort at that.

"The frontier's full of bad men, Marshal Hawk, Mr. Upside-Down Lawman, sir. And you're the man to turn their lights out!" Saradee pulled the Russian out of his hands and holstered it. "Now, then, maybe we'd best go see to the two young folks inside the cabin."

"Huh?"

Saradee ran her hand through his hair. "The girl and the boy in the cabin, Gid. I bet they're up and hungry. The girl didn't eat a bite last night, though who could blame her, with her father so recently dead an' all?"

Hawk jerked another incredulous look at her. "How did you . . . ?" He shook his head. There was no point in finishing the question. She wouldn't give him a straight answer.

He never knew when she was trailing him. When she *was* trailing him, she was like a ghost, or the shadow of a ghost. Always staying back just beyond the periphery of his perceptions, waiting until just the right moment to make her presence known.

A sorceress. A succubus. Sometimes, a guardian angel, albeit one with black wings.

She always maneuvered her way back into his life when he was at his weakest, or when he needed her most.

A thought occurred to him. He studied her now as she knelt before him, smiling at him, her hands on his knees.

Was she real? Or was she no more real than Linda had been last night?

No more real than Jubal had been in that imaginary room across the imaginary hall . . . ?

Hawk touched his fingers to her face. She felt so real that she had to be real, but, then, if he'd gone mad, how would he ever know for sure?

Saradee closed her hand over his wrist, drew his fingers to her lips, and kissed them. "I don't know about you, Gid, but I'm so hungry my belly's under the notion my throat's been cut." She rose. "Come on, now. No more brooding and mooning around. Let's go in and stir us up a batch of pancakes. I got the fixin's if you don't!"

She grabbed her twin Colt pistols off the chair back and strapped them around her sensually rounded hips. Hawk grabbed his own shell belt and holsters, and donned them, then set his hat on his head.

The sun was on the rise now, and the increased light pushing through the shed's single window revealed the shabbiness of his quarters in sharp contrast to his and Linda's bedroom in Crossroads.

He looked back at the shabby room as Saradee went out and strode toward the cabin. Then he followed her, his feet feeling heavy, his shoulders aching from renewed grief.

Linda and Jubal had been so real, he felt as though he'd lost them once again.

Hawk followed Saradee into the cabin. She stopped near the eating table and turned to the blind boy and the girl both sitting on the edge of the bed on the cabin's far side. Jacob tilted his head this way and that, listening, his nostrils working as he sniffed the air like a dog.

"The blond-haired woman!" Mercy said, glancing from Hawk to Saradee and back again.

Saradee arched a brow at Hawk.

"Yeah, right," Hawk said. "The blond-haired woman." He grabbed a handful of feather sticks from the wood box and opened the stove door. "Saradee here's gonna whip you up some pancakes. I'll get a fire started and then I'm gonna take a stroll, have me a dip in the stream."

By the time Hawk had the cookstove stoked, Saradee had the coffee pot ready to boil and was working on the pancake batter, chatting with Mercy and Jacob with the buoyant ease of an old friend.

Hawk grabbed a towel, a cake of lye soap, and his rifle and headed out to the stream. He crossed the creek via the wooden bridge and then walked up stream a ways, weaving around trees and shrubs.

When he came to the deep, dark pool that he'd been using to bathe, he dropped the towel and the soap, and leaned his rifle against a blow-down pine. He kicked off his boots and skinned out of his clothes, piling everything relatively neatly atop a boulder, topped by his black hat.

He picked up the soap and stepped off the bank without hesitation.

The cold mountain water closed around him, pinching his lungs and taking his breath away. It was a good, mind-deadening feeling, and that was what he needed even more than a bath. He needed to have all mind-corrupting thoughts washed away by the tooth-splintering cold water.

Feeling better at the palm of the water's frigid hand, he swam around for a while, the jumble of convoluted thoughts fading from his haunted mind, his senses returning. Now he could smell the creek and the air and the pines, and he could hear the morning birds and see the chickadees and nuthatches and mountain bluebirds flitting amongst the forest boughs.

He saw the sunlight filtering through the trees, causing the dew on the grass and on the leaves of the wild berry shrubs to glow like beads of honey.

Hawk moved into the shallows on the creek's far side and lay in the two feet of water for a time, aware of only the creek murmuring around him.

Finally he stood, soaped his chest and belly, and scrubbed his armpits and then his legs and his feet. He felt as though he were ridding himself of sweat and trail grit in the same way he'd rid himself of the tangled, dark web of thoughts that had turned his mind to a lightning storm.

When soap bubbles glistened over every inch of his large, dark frame slabbed with ridges of hard muscle, his shoulders as broad and hard as a yoke, he lay down in the creek to let the water wash the soap away, leaving his skin scoured and tingling.

He tossed the soap over to where his clothes were piled, and then he lay back against the creek bank, lolling in a foot or two of water sliding and eddying around him and making sucking sounds as it lapped against the bank. He draped his arms across a tangle of roots angling out of the bank, stretched his legs straight out before him, and crossed his ankles.

He lay back, tipping his face to a dollop of warm sunlight pressing down through the trees. He closed his eyes and let only the sounds of the mountain forest fill his head.

A man's voice came to him, swathed in the sounds of the creek and the birds and the whisper of the breeze nudging the branches.

Hawk opened his eyes and dropped his

chin, frowning, staring, listening.

After a time, the man's voice came again. It was followed by a horse's low whicker.

Someone was coming.

CHAPTER 12

Vance Dodge sat his copper dun and stared down at the two still, bloody forms of the Miller boys.

C.P. lay on his back, staring through half-open lids at the sky. He had an almost-dreamy look on his face, as though in his last moments, before that hole had been punched into his forehead, he'd watched a pretty bird swoop down out of the sky to carry his soul to heaven. Del was a mess. He's been shot through his left eye. He'd been shot elsewhere, but the eyeshot had sealed his fate.

Both were bloody messes. Someone had killed them hard, obviously without any trouble and without hesitation.

Dodge snorted at the thought of C.P. being swept off to heaven, and spat a wad of chew onto the grass off the right side of his horse.

There was no way either of the Miller boys

were in heaven.

That half-smile on C.P.'s face was downright bizarre. Not only because no pretty bird had carried his soul away to heaven, but because it was in such sharp, grisly contrast to the entrails that had been pulled out of C.P.'s belly by some wild creature of the forest. The liver-colored viscera trailed off for several yards through the weeds.

"Somethin' dug out his liver, most like," offered Frank Sunday as he calmly sat his saddle, building a quirley. "Dug it out and dragged it off to eat it. Not long ago, neither. Probably woulda stayed around here to dine at its leisure, but it heard or smelled us comin'. Lone wolf, most like. Maybe an older one abandoned by the rest of the pack. Whoever killed these two polecats gave him a good meal. One he likely won't see again soon. I wonder if he thanked the man."

Sunday chuckled.

Dodge scowled at the bespectacled gunman from Oklahoma. "Well, thank you for that, Frank. That's right helpful — to know that some creature burrowed into C.P.'s belly and ran off with his liver. You know, that's the most I've heard out of you in one shot since we started ridin' together three years ago."

"He's all excited," said George Reynolds. "He always gets that way when he sees blood!"

"I'm just sayin', that's what it looks like to me," Sunday said, licking his quirley closed.

"Again, thank you," said Dodge, his voice edged with sarcasm.

Reynolds chuckled ironically and turned his own incredulous gaze on Sunday. "Since you have such an inquiring mind, Frank, do you have any thoughts about who might have shot C.P. in the first place, making it possible for your wolf to come in and dig his liver out of his belly? That's who we're after. The killer. Not the wolf."

"Who gives a shit about the Miller brothers?" Sunday said, scratching a match to life on his saddle horn. Cupping the flame to his cigarette, he said, "Those two lowdown dirty dogs had bullets comin'. I'm just a little sorry it wasn't me who shot 'em."

Chick Holt and Hacksaw Campbell had ridden a broad circle around the two dead men. Now Holt and Campbell sat their horses near each other, Holt facing Dodge while the lean, wiry Hacksaw continued to scour the ground with his busy, colorless eyes, the breeze blowing at his long, brown hair.

"I didn't care for the Millers, neither,"

Holt said. "But they rode with us. Burnett hired 'em for their gun savvy. They were good with them guns, too. I recommended 'em both to Burnett after I seen their cold-steel work in that fuss along the Apache River. That little fuss remained *just* a fuss because the Millers killed the seven squatters who were threatening to burn out Squire Hedges. The Millers shot 'em when they was meetin' at a roadhouse near the river one night.

"Them squatters were ex-Rebs with mighty big chips on their shoulders. Hated Yankee landowners. The Miller boys alone took 'em all down in that barn that night, and burned the barn afterwards. I won't tell you what they did to them graybacks' women, but you prob'ly know."

"What Chick is sayin'," Dodge said to Frank Sunday, "is that whoever shot the Millers must be better than the Millers. And when he shot them, he attacked us. Us and Burnett. He can't get away with it. To *us, now,* he's a rogue griz with the taste for human blood. *Our* blood. We need to track him down and send him off to where he sent the Millers."

"Who in the hell up here could have shot the Millers?" asked Sunday, smoking and looking around speculatively. "The squatters up here is ranchers. Cowmen. They're not gundogs."

Dodge looked distastefully down at the eviscerated C. P. Miller again. "Well, one is. Unless the bastard who done this was just ridin' through."

Hacksaw Miller stood off a ways from the group, his horse's reins in one hand, both hands on his hips. His gray *sombrero* shaded his face. "Whoever he was, he rode down from the western ridge. We seen him sitting that mouse-brown dun of his right here. Looks to me, judgin' by his tracks, he just sat here as though he was just calmly waitin' for the Millers to ride up on him."

Hacksaw moved a little forward and toed the ground between spidery, dusty green wolf willows. The ground between the willows was gravelly, but with tufts of nutritious needle grass growing up through the thin soil. "They stopped right here. There's their prints. The Millers faced the sumbitch, and he shot 'em out of their saddles."

Hacksaw glanced at the two brothers and then gave Dodge a sharp, fateful look. "He had to have been faster than the Millers. And that's sayin' somethin'."

Dodge glanced around at the men sitting closest to him. Anger burned in him. There was also the slight prickling of fear, though he wouldn't have admitted it even if he'd been conscious of it.

To Hacksaw, he said, "Which way did he ride when he left the Millers?"

"That way."

"Toward the Broyles cabin," said Dodge, angrily.

"He came back this way. The same horse — I can tell by the prints — came back through here but a little wide of the dead men. He was leadin' it by now. Someone was leadin' it, anyway. Must've been him."

Chick Holt said, "I bet them Broyles kids was on the horse. Why else would he be leading it?"

"A neighbor, then," Dodge said. "A neighbor who seen the smoke and came to help the Broyles. He stopped here and watched us ride toward town with the Broyles girl. He killed the Millers, rode on to the Broyles place, and probably rode back to his own place with them kids."

"There's a cabin just over the next ridge to the north," said Hacksaw Campbell, pointing. "An old prospector named Van Hootin built it. Had him a few diggin's in these parts. I ran into him a time or two when I was shootin' meat for the Inn. Last I heard he was dead. Maybe someone's taken over his claim."

Hacksaw Campbell had been in Burnett's employ the longest of any of the other riders. He was a good tracker, but he was known to be a little soft in his thinker box. He was more of a follower than a leader. That's why Dodge ran Burnett's wolf pack.

"Well, it looks like we're gonna go see who's home at Van Hootin's cabin." Dodge leaned forward and slid his Winchester carbine from its saddle scabbard. He racked a cartridge into the action, eased the hammer down, and slid the rifle back home. He loosened his three pistols — a Schofield and two Colt Army 44.s — and booted his coyote dun around the dead men and the blood-splashed willows.

"Hey, Frank," he said as he rode, staring straight ahead at the western ridge, "let's go feed that old wolf of your'n some more liver." He gave a mocking grin over his left shoulder. "What do you say to that?"

"You know what I say to that," Sunday said, smoking leisurely in his saddle as he gigged his horse after Dodge. "Just use your imagination."

Dodge chuckled.

He led his men up the ridge, following the switchback trail. He himself was not a good tracker — he preferred keeping his head up and looking forward, and that's how he always defended his lack of tracking skills — but even he could see the relatively fresh horse and boot prints in the pine needle-peppered trail below.

When he'd crested the ridge, he continued to follow the trail through a little open meadow, with more forest abutting both sides. The trail angled out of the meadow and along the shoulder of a mountain. To his right was a deep, brush-choked gorge. To his left jutted the forest-clad mountain slope.

Hacksaw Campbell rode two riders behind Dodge. He lifted his voice to call, "Down in the canyon straight ahead of you is Van Hootin's cabin."

Dodge jerked a hard look back at Campbell, gritting his teeth, silently berating the man to shut the hell up. Did he want to warn their quarry of their approach?

Campbell flushed and looked sheepish.

When Dodge turned his head forward, his heart hiccupped. A black-clad man stepped out from the trees on the left side of the trail.

"Whoa!" Dodge said in surprise.

But he didn't even get his horse stopped before the black-clad man snapped a Henry repeating rifle to his shoulder and aimed grimly down the barrel at Dodge, whose blood turned instantly to ice as he became chillingly aware of the fact that he was going to die right here, right now.

Hawk quickly but calmly drew a bead on the lead rider's forehead, just beneath the brim of the man's gray Stetson, and fired.

The Henry punched Hawk's shoulder as flames lapped from the barrel and the bullet drew a round circle about an inch above the lead rider's nose. The lead rider's horse continued walking toward Hawk as the rider himself jerked violently in his saddle.

He sort of straightened but then his gloved hands released his reins and, eyes blinking wildly, he leaned back and to one side and then rolled down his horse's left hip.

He hadn't hit the ground before Hawk went to work again with the Henry, levering, aiming, and firing; levering, aiming, and firing. Two more riders went flying backward off their screaming and pitching mounts.

"Holy shit!" shouted a lean rider in a gray *sombrero.*

He whipped up his Bisley revolver from the soft leather holster thonged on his right thigh, but his horse pitched so violently that he dropped the weapon and grabbed his saddle horn to keep from being thrown. Hawk drew a bead on the man's head, but just as the rogue lawman squeezed the trigger, the horse whipped violently to its right, and Hawk's bullet sailed wide.

The other two riders fought to keep their horses under control while triggering pistols at Hawk. The horses were pitching too wildly to get off accurate shots. Hawk calmly racked another round into his Henry and blew one of the last two out of his saddle.

Or *sort of* out of his saddle.

The man fell down the horse's left side and smacked his head against the ground. His hat flew off and his pistol went flying, as well. He got his boot hung up in the left stirrup. When the frightened zebra dun wheeled violently, the rider was whipped through the air toward Hawk. The man's boot jerked loose of the stirrup and the man himself flew past Hawk, screaming.

He hit the ground and rolled.

When he stopped rolling and tried to gain his feet, Hawk blew a .44-round through his chest, hammering him back down. A revolver cracked behind Hawk, and, cocking the Henry once more, he spun back toward the dancing horses. There was one more seated rider, but this man was just now swinging down from his frightened mount, trying to keep his prancing horse between himself and Hawk.

He snapped off two quick shots over his saddle but then the horse buck-kicked violently, wheeled, and ran back in the direction in which another rider was galloping — toward town. The fleeing horse had exposed the man who'd last fired at Hawk. Now the man looked dumbfounded by his lack of cover. He gazed around, crouching, making herky-jerky movements, blinking against the dust rising around him.

He turned toward Hawk, who was just now drawing a bead on him.

The man jerked back and raised his hands, the right one holding a smoking Smith & Wesson. "Wait!" he screamed, hatless and dusty, bearded face slack with shock and fear. "Hold on, now, dammit!"

Hawk squeezed the Henry's trigger.

The bullet tore into the last standing gang member's belly. Stumbling backward, the man jackknifed forward and triggered his Smithy into the ground near his right boot. The bullet ricocheted off a rock near the boot and the man jerked his head up as the ricochet turned his left ear to jelly.

"Ohh-*ahhh*!" the man cried, sitting down hard on his ass. Clutching his belly with his hands, he tipped his head back, blood dribbling down from what was left of his left ear. "Ohhh . . . *goddamnit*!"

Hawk looked around. Three riders, not including the gutshot gent missing the bulk of his left ear, were down and not moving. Their horses had run back down the trail. One was standing in the meadow about a hundred yards away, reins drooping as it milled, nervously lowering its head to pull at grass clumps.

Hawk racked another round into the sixteen-shot Henry, then held the rifle barrel down along his right leg. The gutshot rider was a big, bearded, square-jawed man with thick, curly, dark-brown hair. He wore a duster over a wool vest and pale-blue linsey pullover.

The man removed one hand from his belly and raised it to his ear, stretching his lips back from his teeth. He was breathing hard, eyes bright with agony. He looked at Hawk.

"Who the hell are you, man?"

Hawk walked slowly up to him, his face a stony mask beneath the broad brim of his hat. He peered down at the gutshot man.

"Gideon Hawk."

The man's eyes found the deputy U.S. marshal's badge pinned upside down to Hawk's buckskin vest. "Christ, you're a *lawman*?"

"So to speak," Hawk said. "Who're you?"

The man threw his head back, snarling like a leg-trapped mountain lion. "Chick Holt."

"You work for Burnett?"

"I . . . I reckon . . . I *did* work for Burnett. You killed me, you son of a bitch!"

"I stand corrected." Hawk glanced around at the dead men and then turned again to the dying Holt. "Where will I find Burnett?"

"Don't you worry, you bastard," Holt said between groans. "He'll find you."

Hawk grinned. "I 'spect."

He raised his Henry to Holt's head. Holt closed his eyes and drew his head back and to one side a little, awaiting the bullet. "Oh, shit!"

Hawk finished him with a .44 caliber slug through his left temple.

Footsteps sounded behind Hawk. Pumping another cartridge into the Henry's breech, he wheeled.

"Easy, Marshal."

Saradee came toward him clad in her hickory blouse and light-blue denims, which fit her like a tailored glove. Her hat's braided horsehair chin thong danced across her chest and over the silver crucifix glinting where it nestled inside her cleavage. "I'd just thought I'd see if you needed a hand."

She stopped near Hawk and looked

around. "I guess I could have saved myself a trip."

"How're the younkers?"

"They both ate their fill of pancakes."

"I wasn't sure how you'd be with kids," Hawk said, pulling the loading tube out from beneath the Henry's barrel. "I was a little nervous you might boil 'em up and eat 'em."

"Nah, these mountain kids are too stringy." Saradee kicked one of the dead men. "Who're these fellas?"

"Quentin Burnett's men."

"Is Quentin Burnett gonna miss 'em?"

"Probably." Hawk was pinching .44 cartridges from his shell belt and thumbing them into the loading tube. "That's why I'm gonna take 'em all back to him. He might want a last word."

"You're gonna need a hand."

Hawk shook his head. "You stay here with the younkers. Just don't boil 'em up and eat 'em."

Saradee moved up to stand in front of him, fists on her hips, gazing frankly and a little worriedly into his eyes. "Last I heard, Quentin Burnett was top dog of the kennel out here. You're not gonna ride into town thinkin' it might be a nice send-off for yourself, are you, Gid? Kill Burnett and go out in a blaze of your own glory?"

"I don't see no glory in dyin'," Hawk said. "And like you said, I got a whole lot more men . . . and some women . . . to kill."

Saradee smirked as though she'd just been complimented. "All right, then. I'll stay here with the younkers. I promise I won't boil 'em. You say hey to Burnett for me, will you?"

"I'm sure he'll be right flattered that an outlaw of your caliber says hey."

Hawk started to walk back in the direction of Van Hootin's cabin. Saradee fell into step beside him. "Marshal Hawk?"

"Mm-hmm?"

"You like younkers, do you?"

Hawk shrugged.

"Maybe we should settle down somewhere and make a few of our own."

Hawk stopped and turned to her. He stared at her hard. He didn't say anything. He didn't have to.

Saradee sighed and pulled her mouth corners down with chagrin. "It was just a suggestion. Maybe you don't mind, but I don't like the idea of growin' old alone!"

Hawk gave a grunt and continued walking toward the cabin. After a time, he threw his head back and laughed. "What makes you think you're gonna grow old, Saradee?"

Hawk laughed again.

"Very funny," Saradee said, indignant. "You're a real funny guy, Marshal."

CHAPTER 13

Hacksaw Campbell drew back on his horse's reins, slowing the mount, and glanced behind him.

He was across the meadow from where the gang had been ambushed, and he'd just entered the trees. He curveted his paint gelding and scoured his back trail, panic a living, breathing, screaming beast inside of him.

The man who had appeared seemingly out of nowhere and commenced killing the gang was not behind Hacksaw. Hacksaw couldn't see the rest of the gang, only a couple of their horses that were now grazing on the meadow's north side, at the edge of the pines. He couldn't see the shooter, either, who was most likely the last man standing.

The other four — Dodge, Holt, Sunday, and Reynolds — were dead. Dead or as good as dead.

Campbell's heart was slowing its frenetic

pace but he was still breathing hard, shoulders jerking. His lungs felt like sandpaper. His knees felt like warm mud.

Now that he had time to reflect instead of merely react, embarrassment began to slightly edge away the terror he'd felt and that had compelled him to hightail it as fast as possible from the scene of the shooting.

Christ, he'd never seen a man so calmly and casually dispatch others. The big, mustached man in the black hat had stepped out of the trees, turned toward Campbell's gang, lifted his rifle, and didn't give Dodge any chance at all before he blew him out of his saddle. The man had appeared out of the forest like an apparition.

A black-clad apparition with a Henry rifle.

He'd had green eyes. Campbell had noticed that. They were incredibly bright and vivid, looking out from the shade cast over the top half of his face by his hat brim.

He'd stared calmly but purposefully down the long barrel of the Henry repeater, and dispatched Dodge first and then Sunday. Hacksaw would be dead, too, if his horse hadn't pitched and turned as the green-eyed devil in the black hat fired at him. When the horse had wheeled, screaming, and started galloping back the way in which the gang had come, Campbell had given the horse its head.

What had he been expected to do? Turn around and take a bullet for no good reason?

The green-eyed bastard had still been working away with his Henry until Hacksaw gained the meadow.

A green-eyed demon loosed from the bowels of hell was what he'd been. What he *was.* At least, he sure as hell had seemed so.

Hacksaw drew a deep breath, swallowed, and scrubbed the sleeve of his wool tunic across his horse's head, mopping up some of the cold fear-sweat. His heart still drummed against his breastbone. If his horse hadn't spooked and run away, Hacksaw would be lying dead with the others.

Just as dead as the Millers.

Still, guilt began working at him now, casting its slithering tendrils across his back. Maybe he shouldn't have run. Maybe he should have at least tried to stop his horse, turn back, and return the green-eyed demon's fire. Christ, this looked bad. His running looked bad. Maybe he'd be better off lying dead instead of having to negotiate the humiliation of having turned tail and run.

But it was his horse that had run. Hacksaw

had just been along for the ride . . .

That's not how Burnett would see it, however.

Burnett.

What was he going to tell Burnett?

Carefully studying his back trail, staring out across the meadow shimmering in the high-altitude sunshine, Hacksaw swung down from his horse's back and squatted, pulling absently at tufts of fescue. He considered his options.

Maybe he should hoof it back to the scene of the shooting. Maybe he should try to sneak up on that green-eyed demon with the Henry repeater, and drill him. If the man had returned to Van Hootin's cabin, Campbell could follow him and lie in wait in the timber around the cabin or in the brush by the creek, and pink the bastard when he showed himself.

Maybe even shoot him through a window.

Hacksaw had never before considered himself a coward. He'd killed a few men. Not a lot, but a few. He was as good with his long gun as he was with his pistols, by god. He'd ridden shotgun for a few stage lines in Indian country, and he'd even ridden stock detective back in southern Dakota for a time. He'd shot seven men in fair fights. He wouldn't go so far as to say he'd never batted an eye at engaging in a lead-swap, but he'd never before turned tail like he'd just done.

Hell, no. Never. He'd met shooters straight on.

But it wasn't he who'd run just now, Hacksaw reminded himself. It was *his horse.*

Doubt bit him with the fierce pinch of an autumn blackfly.

He was a good enough horseman that he could have stopped the paint if he'd wanted to. He could have turned back and drawn his pistol and engaged that green-eyed fiend and maybe even have killed the son of a bitch.

Then he'd have been Burnett's hero.

Instead, his horse had run and Campbell had let it run because, for the first time in his life — since he was five or six years old, anyway — he'd been driven blindly and at lightning speed by the cold, raw, burning chill of sheer panic.

He could think about going back and shooting the green-eyed devil. But even as he did, the fear lingering in his bones and muscles told him he wouldn't.

As if to cement that notion in his brain, he jerked with a start as something moved on the far side of the meadow. Something dark. Hacksaw drew a sharp breath, his heart hiccupping.

Then the warmth of chagrin rose in his cheeks once more when he saw a stout, black branch tumble from high in a tree to drop into the brush beside the trail.

The branch broke into several pieces and bounced.

The wind had picked up and broken off a dead branch.

That was all.

"Shit," Hacksaw said, running his arm across his forehead again. "I gotta get a hold of myself."

That might take a while, he decided.

He took a few more minutes to consider his options. He could avoid Burnett altogether and just ride on out of these mountains. Hell, he could leave the territory. Head for Colorado or Utah or even Arizona, for that matter.

But no. His pride pinched at the notion of more running.

He'd ride back to New Canaan and tell Burnett exactly what had happened. His horse had bolted and Hacksaw had let it run, because he'd seen nothing good in his dying. After all, that was the truth. That was reasonable. The green-eyed demon had gotten the drop on the gang. He'd gunned them all down like ducks on a millpond.

Hacksaw had saved himself, and now he could inform Burnett of the killings and where the gang had been ambushed by the green-eyed devil.

Hacksaw could ride back out here with a couple more men and kill the monster once and for all. This way — by informing Burnett of what had happened and by killing the killer — he'd redeem himself.

Convinced he was not a coward, after all, Hacksaw drew another deep breath. He chuckled confidently, spat into the dust, swung up into the leather, and booted the paint in the direction of New Canaan.

Quentin Burnett felt good. No, not good. He felt extraordinary.

He felt mildly intoxicated. He hadn't had a drink yet today. In fact, he was sitting in the dining room of the New Canaan Inn enjoying a cup of coffee and taking his time with a plate of bacon. No eggs, no bread. Just coffee and bacon.

That was Burnett's traditional breakfast.

Usually, he'd wolf down the bacon in about three minutes and then sit back and read the morning paper while sipping his coffee while the hired help scurried around him, serving other customers. But this morning, he'd eaten only one strip of the bacon and had nibbled the end off a second one.

He felt too good to be hungry.

He felt good despite the fact he'd wanted to be in the mountains by now, hunting game trophies, but his guests were all still sleeping off hangovers with the doves they'd retired with last night.

Why wouldn't Burnett feel good?

He finally had what he'd been looking for without fully realizing it. He finally had a woman who excited him no end. A wild woman — a beautiful, young, wild woman of the mountains — who he was as much afraid of as he lusted after.

What an intoxicating combination!

He felt like a kid with a new toy. Only this toy could rip his head off. Or, as Dixie had so aptly remarked, this toy could, if given the chance, cut his balls off and feed them to him!

Burnett chuckled as he sipped his coffee, blowing some of the coffee over the rim of his cup and onto his bacon.

"Good lord, what're you laughing about?"

Burnett jerked his head up. Dixie stood by his corner table over which presided the head of a massive bull elk Burnett himself had killed. Dixie had finally dressed and combed her hair so that it almost glistened.

The dress was a purple affair of metallic-like material and velvet trim. It was Dixie's customary attire for the daylight hours, when she was running around the place, managing the help. At night she wore something more revealing, to attract and satisfy the small but loyal stable of her own personal clients who still found her desirable despite her relatively advanced age.

"She excites you, doesn't she? All the more so because she wants to kill you more than all the others combined." Dixie smiled. "Including me."

She sat in the chair across from Burnett and leaned forward, entwining her hands on the table and continuing to smile at him ominously. "Quentin, that girl up there is downright dangerous. If you think she's going to marry you, you're mad."

Burnett chewed a strip of bacon, showing his teeth. "I once had an Indian friend. His name was Iron Tail. A Sioux from up north. He only had one arm. He had for a pet a rare, black cougar with eyes as yellow as that ornament you're wearing around your neck.

"The cougar accompanied Iron Tail everywhere. They came into the Inn together, in fact — the cougar on Iron Tail's moccasin-clad heels. I didn't object. They seemed to be joined at the hip, and the beast was a great curiosity. It was the most loyal creature you could ever imagine. More loyal than the most loyal cow dog. It would snarl at anyone who made a sudden move around Iron Tail, or raised their voice around him.

"One time I worked up enough courage to ask ole Iron Tail what had become of his arm. He told me that before the cougar had come to be his pet, it had attacked him while he slept one night in the camp he'd shared with several other Sioux hunters, chewing his arm off.

"When Iron Tail recovered, he tracked the cougar and, after many failed attempts, he finally trapped it. He did not kill it. He sensed in the cougar a special bond. Because it had eaten his arm, it shared his spirit. They were brothers, in a sense. For nearly a year, Iron Tail kept the cougar on a short log chain. At first, he beat it and otherwise abused it mercilessly. Then he started feeding it, but only a little at a time. Sometimes he would withhold food and water, then give the beast just a little food or just a little water now and then.

"Gradually, the cougar quit hissing and snarling at Iron Tail. It started to regard him with fear and respect. Its world, in fact, seemed to consist of Iron Tail and only Iron

Tail. After another six months on the chain, Iron Tail released the cat. You'd think it would have run away, wouldn't you? But it didn't. It came over to Iron Tail, who held a spear over it, in case it attacked. But it didn't attack. It gave a purr and lay down at his feet."

Burnett grinned as he chewed another strip of bacon.

"You see, the cougar recognized the feral bond between them, and chose to stay and serve old Iron Tail, whom it considered its lord and master despite, or maybe *because of,* the abuse he'd heaped upon it."

Burnett swallowed the bacon and sipped his coffee. Dixie stared at him, her lower jaw hanging in shock. When she finally found the words with which to speak, Burnett held his hand up, cutting her off.

He'd just spied something out the window to his right.

"What in god's name?" he said, pushing himself up out of his chair and turning to face the window.

Hacksaw Campbell was riding up to the New Canaan Inn, and all around him were saddled horses bearing the bodies of what appeared to be dead men.

Chapter 14

Burnett pushed out through the Inn's batwings and stood atop the veranda, staring out into the street.

Hacksaw Campbell sat his paint gelding in front of the New Canaan Inn, looking dubiously at the four horses milling around him and over which bloody corpses had been slung. Campbell scratched his three-day growth of beard stubble and then turned to Burnett. He opened his mouth to speak but no words came out.

"What in the hell is this?" Burnett said as Dixie came out of the saloon behind him, pulling a dark wrap around her shoulders against the morning's mountain chill.

She scowled distastefully at the grisly scene before her.

"Uh . . . well, Mr. Burnett," Hacksaw said, haltingly. "I, uh . . . I, uh . . ."

Burnett walked down the porch steps and into the street. Burnett stood beside the horse that he recognized as Vance Dodge's dun, and stared at the back of the head of the man slung belly down across the saddle. Burnett grabbed a fistful of the corpse's hair, trying to avoid the blood, though there was so much of it that the maneuver was impossible, and pulled.

The face, slack with death, appeared.

It was Vance Dodge, all right, eyes not quite closed. There was a quarter-sized hole in the man's forehead, just above his nose. The bullet had exited the back of Dodge's head, blowing out a good bit of brains, it appeared, too.

Burnett released Dodge's head. Dodge's face slapped the stirrup fender. Burnett looked at the other horses over which the rest of Dodge's gang lay belly down. All except Hacksaw Campbell.

Burnett turned his exasperated gaze to the gang's sole survivor, and said, "What in Christ's name happened here, Hacksaw?"

Hacksaw glanced around at the death-bearing horses again, and again gave his beard stubble a pensive scratch. "Well . . . I was ridin' out of the mountains . . . and . . . and I heard the thunder of hooves behind me . . . and then all of a su-sudden I looked back and . . . and these four hosses were runnin' to beat the band, like they was tryin' to catch up to me."

Hacksaw paused to study each horse in turn, as though he were trying to puzzle them out. "The bastard who . . . who ambushed us must've thrown Dodge and the others over their saddles, and . . . and slapped 'em home, and . . . and they caught up to me, sure enough."

The sole survivor looked stricken.

Burnett wanted to know what he was the sole survivor *of,* exactly. Or *who.*

He walked over to glare incredulously up at Hacksaw, and, fists on his broad hips, he said, "You're not telling me anything I can't see with my own eyes, Hacksaw. What I want to know is who killed these men. Who shot 'em, goddamnit!"

Hacksaw poked his hat back off his forehead and looked down at Burnett. "You know how Dodge told you about the man he sent the Millers after?"

"Yes, I know, Hacksaw. It was only yesterday. Are you tellin' me the man who killed the Millers killed all of these men, as well? If so, why are you still breathing? Did you stand with the others?"

That seemed to knock Hacksaw back in the saddle a bit. Both literally and figuratively.

"Well, hell, there were just so many of 'em,

boss," he said, wheedling. "And . . . and they sprung up out of nowhere!"

"How many were there?"

"Oh . . ." Hacksaw raked his hand down his face, scowling as though it were hard to remember. "Three . . . maybe four," he said. "I can't remember. They sprung up out of nowhere, ya see, boss."

"Just three or four men took down six of the best gunmen north of the Red River?"

"There . . . uh . . . there might've been more than that. They was hidden away in the trees when they opened up on us."

"They didn't give you a chance — that it?"

"That's right, boss. We was ambushed!"

"How did you make it out with . . ." Burnett tilted his head this way and that, scrutinizing Hacksaw's face and body. ". . . with nary a scratch on you?"

Hacksaw flinched a little at the question. He looked flushed and nervous. His Adam's apple bobbed as he swallowed. "I . . . uh . . . I reckon I just got lucky. My horse threw me an' I took cover."

"And returned their fire, I would assume."

"Oh, of course. I fired till I was out of bullets and then, with all the others dead, I took off after my horse. Without ammo, I was no good, and I knew you'd want to know what happened. So I headed for town. When I was halfway here, these horses came gallopin' up after me."

"I see, I see," Burnett said, nodding slowly, skeptically.

He glanced around to see that several shopkeepers and other townsfolk had gathered on the boardwalks and alley mouths surrounding him and Hacksaw, drawn by the grisly cargoes of the six horses as well as the testy conversation between Hacksaw Campbell and his employer, the richest and most powerful man in this neck of Idaho.

"You ran out of bullets, you say?" Burnett said. "Well, look there." He looked at the well-filled cartridge belt encircling Hacksaw's lean waist. "Why, you have plenty of cartridges in your belt loops, Hacksaw."

Campbell looked down. The flush in his long, horsey face deepened. "I refilled those from the box in my saddlebags . . . after I ran my horse down," Hacksaw said.

"Let me smell your pistol."

"What's that?"

Burnett held out his hand. "Let me smell your pistol, Hacksaw."

"Why, boss?"

"Turn over the fucking pistol, Hacksaw, or I'll have you tarred and feathered and drawn and quartered!"

Hacksaw jerked and clawed at the lone Bisley jutting from the holster belted to his waist. His second holster was empty. He fumbled the revolver out of its sheath, flipped it around so that he held it butt forward, and, with a sour expression, slowly lowered the weapon to Burnett.

The businessman took the Bisley and sniffed the barrel.

By now, the town marshal, Bob Nye, and Nye's three deputies had walked up to stand a few feet behind Burnett. One of the deputies was holding the bit of the horse carrying Chick Holt's bloody carcass. Burnett handed the Bisley back to Nye.

"Take a sniff of that, Bob. Does it smell like it's been fired to you?"

Nye touched the tip of the Bisley's barrel to his thick, salt-and-pepper mustache, and sniffed. He gave the pistol back to Burnett, saying, "That ain't been fired since it was cleaned about a day or so ago."

Burnett held the pistol down at his side and stared stonily up at Hacksaw Campbell, whose shoulders sagged with chagrin.

"My horse bolted when the bastard opened up on us," Hacksaw said.

"Did you say *the* bastard? Meaning there was only one shooter?"

"Yes, that's right. My horse bolted and

ran. It all happened so fast and I was so startled, as we all were" — Hacksaw glanced at the dead men surrounding him — "that when my paint finally stopped, I was a coupla hundred yards away. The shooting had ended."

"One man?"

"That's right," Hacksaw said with a sigh. "But he came out of nowhere. And there was no hesitation in him. He just stepped out of the trees and raised that Henry, and . . . *shit!* . . . we didn't have a chance."

"One man," Burnett said. It wasn't a question this time. He looked around, speculatively, then gave his befuddled gaze back to Hacksaw. "What'd he look like?"

"Big, tall bastard. Looked like he might have some Indian blood. Had a thick, black mustache and green eyes. A black hat, a black vest lined with wool. On his vest he wore a deputy U.S. marshal's badge. Only, he wore it *upside down.* I remember that."

"He wore what upside down?"

"The deputy marshal's badge."

"Shit," said Bob Nye, standing behind Burnett. "That's Gideon Hawk."

"Rogue lawman from Nebraska," added one of his deputies, Burl Loman, who held a Winchester repeater on his right shoulder. "Crazy son of a bitch. There's a four-thousand-dollar federal bounty on his head."

"What the hell is he doing here?" Burnett said, half to Nye, half to himself.

"Holin' up in the mountains, looks like," said Nye. "He sees himself as an avenging angel. When your men burned Broyles out, they put themselves in Hawk's gunsights. If he knows you sent them, Mr. Burnett, then you're likely in his sights, as well."

Burnett nodded as he stared off toward the snow-capped peaks to the west, which were glowing brightly now in the late-morning sun. Burnett turned to Nye. "Best form a posse and ride after him, Bob. We got us a kill-crazy wildcat in the mountains, sounds like. Let's hunt him down and bring him to town. I wanna see this rogue lawman. I heard about him in the newspapers. Been on the loose for a while now."

"A good three years," Nye said. "Ever since some judge and prosecutor freed the man who hanged Hawk's son. He's been gettin' even for that ever since. Like I said, he's one crazy bastard. Rogue lawman — bullshit. He's more like a rogue grizzly on the blood trail."

Nye stood gazing nervously, wide-eyed, into the mountains.

"Well, what're you standing here for,

Bob?" Burnett said, testy. "Form a posse and let's get after him. Saddle me a fast horse. Seems as though you want a job done right, you gotta do it yourself. Besides, I'm ready to go huntin'!"

"You got it, Mr. Burnett." Nye glanced at his deputies as he turned and walked away from Burnett. "You heard the man. Fetch every rider you know who's good with a Winchester. Griggs, saddle some hosses, includin' the best for Mr. Burnett!"

As the lawmen headed off, Burnett turned back to Hacksaw Campbell. Hacksaw peered down at the Bisley in Burnett's hand. He didn't say anything. He looked like he might have had a constriction in his throat.

Burnett raised the pistol. He aimed the barrel at Hacksaw. He raked his thumb across the hammer, making clicking sounds as he raised and lowered the hammer against the firing pin.

Hacksaw looked down in dread at the Bisley in his boss's thick hands.

Burnett looked up at Hacksaw. "I suppose you want this back."

Hacksaw didn't say anything. He just stared apprehensively at Burnett.

Burnett suddenly flipped the gun in his hand. Hacksaw jerked with a start. But then he saw that Burnett had only turned the gun so that the worn walnut grips faced him.

Burnett grinned as he handed the gun to Campbell, who accepted it tentatively, as though it were a venomous snake. His muscles relaxed as he dropped the pistol into its holster and secured the keeper thong over the hammer.

"Bury these men," Burnett told him. "Give them each a grave with a marker — you understand?"

"I understand, Mr. Burnett. I'll give 'em a proper send-off."

"See that you do."

Burnett would kill the coward later, after his work was done. Why pay an undertaker?

When Hacksaw had gathered up the reins of the dead men's horses, and led the cavalcade of corpses off toward the cemetery, Burnett turned to Dixie, who stood on the porch, staring skeptically toward the western mountains.

Burnett turned to them again, too, and did not like the chill that rippled the skin across the back of his neck.

Chapter 15

Hawk dropped to one knee on the roof of a bakery three buildings north of the New Canaan Inn, and stared to the south along New Canaan's broad main street. He was partly concealed from the street by the front corner of the tall building on his right.

As he looked toward the front of the New Canaan Inn, he smiled. Burnett was just then handing up the pistol of the man who'd turned tail and run when Hawk had opened up on the gang. The rest of the gang lay slumped across the backs of their horses milling nervously around Burnett and the man who'd fled.

The mounts didn't cotton to the smell of the death on their backs.

From both sides of the street, a good twenty or thirty townsfolk stood observing the grisly scene in hushed silence. The four town lawmen who'd been standing near Burnett were now walking off in the opposite direction.

Hawk was too far away to hear everything that had been said down there, but he'd heard clearly enough Burnett ordering the lawmen to form a posse and to head for the mountains, on the trail of Hawk himself.

"Crazy son of a bitch," one of the deputies had said. "There's a four-thousand-dollar federal bounty on his head."

Again, Hawk grinned.

Burnett and the others were rattled as well as distracted.

Hawk rose and poked a half-smoked cigar between his teeth. As he walked to the edge of the roof, he took a couple of puffs off the cheroot, to get it drawing soundly again, then dropped into the saddle of his grullo waiting near the bakery's rear wall.

Taking the reins in his hands and puffing the cheroot, he glanced around.

The only people near him were several Chinese of various ages boiling water on outdoor fireplaces, to the rear of the steam laundry and bathhouse that sat beside Burnett's Inn. Two of the Chinese were wizened old men in coulee hats.

As Hawk rode past them, he tipped his hat to the Chinese gents, who bobbed their heads at him. They had too much work to do — likely boiling the bedding from Burnett's saloon and whorehouse — to pay the big stranger on the grullo more than a passing glance.

Hawk stopped the gelding near the rear of the sprawling Inn. He took several more pensive puffs from the cigar as he studied the layout of the place. Finally, he took one more deep drag off the cheroot, dismounted, dropped the cheroot, and mashed it out with a boot heel.

He patted the grullo's neck, letting the reins hang to the ground. "Stay."

He glanced around once more, then climbed the stairs.

At the second story was an unlocked door. Hawk went in, drew the door closed behind him, and found himself somewhere in the middle of a dim hall with red carpet and a similar design of paper on the walls. The bracket lamps had not been lit.

There were few sounds in the musty hall around Hawk, but he heard a man muttering and groaning from behind a door just down the hall on his right. Hawk moved in that direction, wondering where he was going to find the Broyles girl. He paused outside the door on the hall's left side. The door was open just far enough to show him a gray-haired, mustached man sitting on the edge of a bed, naked save his socks.

He was vomiting into the white enamel slop pale he was hugging on his naked lap. A brown-skinned whore lay naked on the bed behind him.

Hawk was about to move on, but then he saw a wool vest hanging from a chair back. On the vest was the moon-and-star badge of a U.S. marshal.

Hawk gave a caustic snort, brushed a thumb across his own, upside-down moon-and-star, and continued walking along the hall, hoping to find a girl alone — one who might tell him where he'd find Jennie Broyles. But all the other doors were closed. The girls were probably sleeping off the drink and sex of the previous night.

Ahead was a broad stairs up which pale light washed.

Hawk paused at the break in the hall, and looked around the corner, over a scrolled, varnished rail and down the carpeted stairs. Below, lay the Inn's main drinking hall. Hawk could see part of the ornate bar and a few tables. Footsteps sounded, echoing in the heavy silence. A woman moved into Hawk's field of vision. She had long, wavy blond hair and wore a dark-blue dress of a shiny metallic fabric. She held a dark wrap tightly around her shoulders, as though she were deeply chilled.

As she reached the bottom of the staircase, she removed a hand from the wrap to pull her gown above her ankles, and started up the stairs. When she lifted her head to look up the staircase, Hawk drew his head back into the hall. He could hear the woman coming up the stairs. Her footsteps were slow, thoughtful.

Hawk slid his Russian .44 from the holster angled over his belly.

He pressed his back hard against the wall, head turned toward the top of the stairs. The woman entered his field of vision. She turned toward him and stopped with a startled gasp.

Hawk cocked the Russian, grabbed the woman, jerked her toward him, and threw her against the wall. He closed his left hand over her mouth and pressed the Russian against her temple.

"If you scream, I'll drill a bullet through your brain," Hawk said, keeping his voice low.

The woman looked at him over his large, brown hand, her blue eyes wide. She appeared more startled than terrified. Her eyes seemed to own a cast of recognition.

"You know why I'm here," Hawk said. "Don't you?"

She nodded once.

"Where is she?"

Hawk slid his hand from her mouth, ready to close it over her lips again if she started to scream.

"I'll show you," she said quietly, staring frankly into Hawk's own eyes.

"You won't scream?"

"I'm not a screamer, Mr. Hawk."

Hawk removed his hand and took one step back. Instantly, he liked and trusted her.

Holding the hem of her dress above her ankles, she moved tentatively to the top of the stairs and glanced down. She beckoned to Hawk with a toss of her head, and he followed her up the second flight of carpeted steps, this staircase narrower than the main one. The third story hall was as quiet as the second story had been.

Dixie strode down the hall until she came to a door. She opened the door and started up another flight of steps. These steps were mere unfinished planks. Hawk followed her to the third story and to a plain door with a key sticking out of its lock.

It was early-morning or early-evening dark up here. The only light came from two small windows at each end of the hall. This attic area was only partly finished. It appeared to be used mostly for storage — there were scattered, dilapidated pieces of furniture, stacks of steamer trunks, several rolls of carpet, and dusty drapes hanging from ceiling beams.

Dixie turned the key in the lock and opened the door.

Hawk pushed her inside, and closed the door behind him.

"Did you finally work up your nerve?" said a girl's voice, pitched with dry mockery.

Hawk turned to the bed on his right. The Broyles girl sat with her back against the headboard, staring straight across the room. She lowered the bedcovers to her knees, exposing her naked body. She turned her defiant gaze to Hawk — and frowned.

As her eyes scrutinized him, recognition flashed in the brown orbs, and she pulled the covers back up to her neck.

"Mr. . . . Hollis . . . ?"

"It's Hawk, not Hollis. I've come to get you out of here."

Jennie threw the covers back and bounded out of the bed, ripping a sheet from the bed and holding it over the front of her well-curved body. She stopped and looked at Dixie. "What about her?"

Dixie turned to Hawk. "Take me with you."

Hawk frowned. "Why?"

"He's crazy. I didn't realize just how mad

until today. I also didn't realize that I've been as much a captive as she's been since she got here." She tossed her head toward Jennie.

Hawk thought it over.

"All right." He turned to Jennie. "Get dressed."

Too anxious to worry about modesty, Jennie dropped the sheet and grabbed a pair of drawers off a chair abutting the far wall. While she dressed with Dixie's help, Hawk cracked the door to stare out into the hall toward the stairs. The Inn seemed eerily quiet. There was no movement on the stairs.

He continued to watch the dingy hall until Dixie said behind him, "All right."

Hawk turned to the women. Jennie was clad in a low-cut, cream-colored dress with lacy straps curled over her delicate shoulders. The frock was a cross between an evening dress and a Mother Hubbard. Hawk gave a silent, sarcastic snort. Obviously, the attire had been Burnett's idea. The dress was a cross between something a whore would wear and something a housewife would wear.

"If I can get to my room," Dixie said, "I could gather us both something more fitted for riding."

"No time." Hawk widened the door and

stepped through it. "Come on. Hurry. Stay close."

As quietly as he could, he walked down the narrow stairs. When he gained the second story, he stopped at the bottom of the third-story stairs, and cast his gaze down the hall toward the door to the outside staircase.

The hall was empty, silent. Hawk beckoned to the women breathing anxiously behind him.

When he and the two women were halfway down the hall, a door opened just ahead of Hawk, on his right. A lean, gray-headed man stepped out of the room in which he'd seen the U.S. marshal puking his guts into the thunder mug. Hawk stopped suddenly. Both women behind him gave a quiet gasp.

The man donned his gray hat, and, puffing a pipe, turned to speak through the open door behind him. "I'll be back, honey. You be waitin', now, you hear. I enjoyed them French lessons."

He grinned and drew the door closed. The badge on his wool vest glinted.

He turned toward Hawk and started to take one step forward, but froze. His eyes were nearly the same color as the badge. They also glinted in the dull light sifting through the shadowy hall.

Those eyes flicked toward the badge pinned upside down to Hawk's black leather vest. They flicked back up to Hawk's face. The man's thin-lipped mouth opened beneath his thin, carefully trimmed gray mustache.

"God . . . damnit," the U.S. marshal said, with quiet dread.

Hawk said, "You gonna go back into that room, quiet-like? Or is this gonna be your last dance?"

The U.S. marshal swallowed nervously, but he kept his unflickering gaze level with Hawk's. "Gideon Henry Hawk," he said. "Rogue-fucking-lawman."

"I have to admit that has a ring to it."

"You won't make it."

"We'll see."

Slowly, the U.S. marshal slid his coat back behind the walnut grips of the Colt Army jutting across his belly from its cross-draw position over his left hip.

Hawk unsnapped the keeper thong from over the hammer of the Peacemaker holstered on his right thigh.

"Oh, Jesus," said Dixie.

"Stay behind me," Hawk ordered her and Jennie.

Hawk stared at the U.S. marshal. The federal man stared back at him, thin lips quirking a thin smile that faded slowly.

The federal man jerked his hand to the walnut grips and then gave a bellowing cry as Hawk's Colt thundered twice, sounding like shotgun blasts in the tight confines and hurling the federal lawman backward, where he piled up at the base of the hall's right wall.

Behind the door he'd just come from, a girl screamed.

"Go!" Hawk said, stepping aside and gesturing for the women to run on ahead of him. "Take the outside stairs!" Hawk glanced down at the federal man writhing at the base of the wall, staring up at him. Hawk's Colt smoked.

The federal man looked at the Colt, then at Hawk. "No," he begged.

Hawk angled the Colt toward the marshal's head and finished him with a bullet through his brain plate.

Again, the girl in the room screamed.

Replacing the Colt's spent cartridges with fresh from his shell belt, Hawk ran to the open door over the outside stairs. He holstered the Colt and ran through the door and down the stairs. Dixie and Jennie had just gained the yard behind the hotel.

They froze, looking about wildly. The

thunder of approaching riders rose around them.

CHAPTER 16

Hawk's heart thudded as the rumble of the approaching riders grew louder.

"Take my horse!" Hawk grabbed Jennie around the waist and threw her up onto the grullo's back. "Give him his head and he'll take you to my cabin!" He threw Dixie up behind Jennie, jerked his Henry rifle out of its scabbard, and slapped its rear stock against the grullo's rump.

"What about you?" Dixie shouted, casting an anxious look behind her as the grullo lunged off its rear feet.

"I'll be along!"

Hawk watched the grullo and the two women gallop straight off through a fringe of pines behind the hotel. He whipped around as riders barreled out of the gap between the hotel and the Chinese laundry. Hawk rammed a cartridge into the Henry's action, aimed at the first rider exploding from the gap, and shot the man out of his saddle.

He'd been hoping the man would be Burnett himself, but as he'd fired, he'd spied a badge on the man's shirt. He was one of the town marshal's deputies. Hawk dispatched two more riders in less than two seconds after he'd drilled a bullet through the heart of the first one, emptying two more saddles.

That set the rest of the gang's horses pitching and the men shouting, panicking.

One of the riderless horses wheeled to run, but Hawk grabbed its reins and swung up onto the frightened beast's back.

As he did, more thunder rose behind him. He glanced back to see another contingent of posse riders, apparently attracted by Hawk's shooting inside the hotel, explode out of the gap between the hotel and another building.

"There he is!" a burly, bespectacled man in a bear coat and black opera hat shouted from the back of a cream mare, aiming a pistol at Hawk.

Burnett's bullet sailed wide as Hawk neck-reined his horse, ground heels into the appropriated mount's flanks, and rode straight toward Burnett and about six other men on horseback. Hawk raised the Henry in both hands and fired into the yelling, cursing, scattering crowd.

Burnett's eyes grew wide as Hawk bore down on him. "Ach!" the fat man cried, raising his arms as though to shield his face from a bullet.

One of Hawk's bullets blew his hat off his head. Burnett's horse jerked violently. Its rider lost his hold on the apple and tumbled out of the saddle to hit the ground with a loud thud and another scream.

Hawk killed two of the men trying to control their horses near Burnett and then galloped along the rear of the main street business buildings, dodging around privies and woodpiles.

"After that bastard!" Burnett bellowed. "I want him *dead*!"

Hawk grinned at the confused, horrified shouting behind him.

As a pistol barked and a bullet cut the air to his right, thudding into the corner of a frame building just ahead, Hawk swung his horse to the right and picked up a trail that cut through the pines and angled across an open beaver meadow. His galloping horse splashed through a network of narrow streams, and then Hawk was on the far side of the meadow and following the trail up through pines that stippled the first slopes of the mountains surrounding New Canaan.

When he'd ridden what he judged was probably a thousand feet above the town, he reined his mount, a blue roan, to a stop and looked back along the curving trail he'd taken into this rocky, pine-clad country.

These first slopes of the higher reaches, under a cobalt sky tufted with white puffs of snow-white clouds, would have looked like an alpine heaven if Hawk hadn't spied the pack of angry devils galloping up the slope behind him, closing on him fast.

Horses and riders flashed between the trees.

They were still yelling and cursing, infuriated by Hawk's brash attack on them, killing several of their number, and likely further drawn by the four-thousand-dollar bounty on his head.

"Come and get it, you hoopleheads!" Hawk shouted.

Then he grinned, always game for a chase.

He pointed his horse up trail and rammed his heels into its flanks.

He rode hard, climbing ever higher.

But not far behind, the posse kept coming, triggering shots. The bullets plunked into the ground well behind Hawk, screeching off rocks.

He was crossing a stretch of steep, open

ground about three thousand feet above New Canaan when another rifle belched below and behind him. His horse screamed. Its right leg gave. It hit the ground on its right wither. Hawk threw himself wide so the horse wouldn't roll on him.

Dazed, on his hands and knees, Hawk looked up the slope. The horse was breathing hard, frothy blood boiling out of its nose.

"Bastards!" Hawk gritted out, and finished the horse with his Russian.

He pulled his Henry out of the saddle sheath, racked a round, and looked down the slope at the posse riders galloping toward him, two and three abreast. Burnett was about fifth back in the line of twelve or so men.

Using his dead horse for cover, Hawk cut down on them, triggering five quick rounds and grinning in satisfaction as two posse riders went flying off their horses. The others bellowed curses, swung down from their saddles, and dashed for cover.

Hawk triggered three more shots, then looked around for a better place to shoot from.

Up the slope behind him was a nest of rocks with a craggy rock wall rising over it, offering rear cover. The rock wall was about fifty yards away.

Hawk glanced at the posse men hunkering behind shrubs and trees and low hummocks, chomping at the bit to get at him. Deciding he'd best make his move now, before they all got comfortable and started their barrage, he triggered two more shots toward the cowering posse and then started running up the slope.

He traced a zigzag course around trees and shrubs and small boulders. Behind and below, the posse commenced firing on him.

Slugs spanged off rocks and thudded into tree boles. One nudged the heel of his right boot and another kissed the nap on his left shirtsleeve.

The rock nest was a little more than ten feet away from him now . . .

He scissored his arms and legs, running hard.

Another slug burned a furrow across his left side, along the top of his rib cage. Hawk heaved himself up off his heels and dove over the rocks that formed the nest's perimeter. He hit the ground and, cursing against the pain in his side, rolled.

Rolling off his right shoulder, he found himself in the small, gravel-bedded, oval-shaped area inside the rocks surrounding it. The posse's rifles were kicking up a near-deafening cacophony. Bullets sizzled around

Hawk's head and screamed off the nest's rear wall.

A quick reconnaissance told him there were good-sized rocks to both sides of the open area, as well, which meant Hawk had some high ground he could hold . . . as long as his ammo didn't run out.

A cold stone dropped inside him.

All the ammo he had was in his .44s, the Henry, and on his shell belt. He'd left two boxes of ammo, one for his pistols and one for the rifle, in his saddlebags draped over his grullo's butt. Since the sixteen-shot Henry was likely almost empty, he probably had between thirty and fifty rounds.

Rifles thundered. Bullets thumped and spanged off the rocks surrounding Hawk's nest.

Hawk crawled up to a slight, V-shaped gap between two of the largest boulders forming the wall of the nest overlooking the slope, and snaked his rifle barrel through it. He set his sights on a man in a red shirt and black neckerchief just now aiming a Winchester from around the side of a stout fir tree.

The Henry leaped and roared.

The man in the red shirt jerked back, dropping his rifle. He disappeared behind the fir for a second, and then Hawk caught brief glimpses of him rolling down the slope behind the fir.

A bullet crashed into the face of the large rock on Hawk's left, and he pulled his head back behind the boulder on his right as he racked another round into his Henry's action.

He snaked the Henry through the V-shaped gap once more and returned the posse's fire, cursing when he saw no more men go down. They'd obviously seen what had happened to the son of a bitch in the red shirt, and they were revealing nothing but the briefest glimpses of themselves as they fired up the slope.

Hawk returned fire, pulled his rifle out of the V-notch, and cursed again.

Three more wasted shots.

Quickly he reloaded the Henry from his shell belt and turned back to the notch. As he rammed another shell into the breech, he spied movement out of the corner of his left eye. He wheeled in that direction, tightening the tension in his trigger finger.

"Hold your fire, lover!" Saradee leaped over a shoulder of the upthrust of craggy limestone, and squatted on her haunches, keeping her head low as the bullets sliced through the air just above her and Hawk.

"What the hell are you doing here?" Hawk

barked. "I told you to stay with the younkers!"

"When have I ever done anything you told me to do . . . except after dark?" Saradee added with a lusty smile.

Hawk canted his head to one side and narrowed a mock-suspicious eye at the beautiful, busty blonde. "You didn't boil 'em up and eat 'em, did you?"

"Mmmm!" Saradee licked her lips and rubbed her belly. She cast a quick glance over the rocks and down the slope. "What you got goin' here, lover?"

"Just a little misunderstandin'."

"Sounds like a big disagreement to me."

"How many shells you got?"

"What I have on my belt, in my pistols, and the nine in the Winchester." She patted the barrel of the carbine in her gloved hands.

"Christ!"

"That ain't enough?" Saradee lay belly down on the ground and crabbed up to peer through a notch between rocks, to Hawk's left. "How many are doggin' you, anyway?"

"Just shy of a dozen."

"Shit!" Saradee cried, slamming her fist against the ground. "I have a fresh box of cartridges in my saddlebags. I didn't think I'd need it."

"You thought wrong!"

"Don't get your drawers in a twist, lover," Saradee said. "My horse is just down the other side of this slope. I'll fetch the cartridges and be back in — !"

Saradee gave a squeal as she lifted her head above the sheltering rocks. A bullet fired from below blew her hat off her head to hang by its thong down her back. Saradee dropped back to her knees.

Hawk chuckled without mirth. "Saradee, you're purtier'n a speckled pup. But you're soft in your thinker box. You managed to slip in here without getting your pretty ass shot, because I was keeping those boys distracted. But now that they know you're here, you're not gonna *leave* here with your head on your shoulders. Burnett's men are gonna see to that!"

Hawk laughed again and triggered three shots downslope, evoking one yelp before he pulled back as bullets peppered the rocks to either side of his rifle.

"That's all the thanks I get?" Saradee gritted her teeth as she aimed her Winchester down the slope.

"Thanks for what?" Hawk said, firing the Henry.

"For not letting you die alone, I reckon!" Saradee said, triggering her Winchester until the hammer pinged benignly onto the firing pin.

She pulled the carbine out of the notch and started to slide fresh cartridges from her cartridge belt. As she did, she cast Hawk a bizarre smile. "Kind of romantic, ain't it, lover?"

"What is?"

"Dyin' together."

"Dyin' *together*? There ain't no such thing." Hawk aimed through the notch, trying to find another target, wanting to whittle the posse's number down low enough that the rest might give up on him and hightail it back to New Canaan. "We might die shootin' side by side, but we'll still die alone. We come into this world alone, and that's how we leave it."

He fired, then cursed when his target pulled his head back behind a tree bole just in time to avoid the bullet, which merely chipped bark from the trunk.

"We'll get a pine box if we're lucky," Hawk said, pumping another round into the Henry's chamber. "But probably not. Nah, we'll be snugglin' with the snakes, most like. These boys will leave us right here. Food for the mountain lions."

When Hawk had triggered the Henry once more and pulled it back out of the notch, he was surprised to see Saradee snuggling up close against him. She wrapped an arm around his neck and kissed him on the mouth. He discovered that his situation wasn't so dire that he couldn't appreciate the soft, moist feel of the girl's lips against his.

"Hawk, I love you so much that sometimes I fear my heart is going to burst wide open!" she exclaimed, gazing at him dreamily through her big, blue eyes, around which her blond hair was blowing in the wind. "And you know what?"

"What?"

"I think we're gonna float straight up to heaven hand in hand, and those pearly gates are gonna fling wide for us, and angels are gonna be there to greet us, blowin' their golden trumpets."

Hawk studied her, as usual appalled and enthralled by the girl at the same time. He looked at her cleavage exposed by the open first few buttons of her hickory shirt. While bullets continued to screech through the air and hammer the rocks around them, Hawk lowered his head and planted a wet kiss between her splendid breasts.

"You know what, Saradee?"

"What's that, Marshal Hawk?"

"I'm gonna miss you. Not as much as I

miss my wife or my boy, but, may the gods forgive me, I am gonna miss you."

"There you are — see?" Saradee said with delight, kissing him once more as the posse's lead sung around them. "You're under my devil's spell!"

"I reckon." Hawk laughed. He could laugh about it now, because he had so little time to live. Maybe ten more bullets were all he had left in his guns.

Then the torture of this life — all the bitter memories and strange hauntings and his hammering lust for this beautiful devil lying here beside him in this virtual stone coffin — would end.

Chapter 17

Saradee gave a yowl and looked at her arm.

Hawk looked at it, too. Apparently, a bullet had ricocheted off the stone wall flanking the nest and carved a burn across the outside of her upper right arm. Blood oozed through the tear in her sleeve.

Hawk moved to her, startled by his own concern. "You all right?"

"It's just a graze." Saradee blinked slowly and smiled, pleased by the attention he showed her. "I'm fine."

Staying low, Hawk removed his bandanna and quickly knotted it around her arm. He didn't reflect on the absurdity of his concern for a woman he'd wanted dead for years. Nothing had made sense in Hawk's world for a long time.

When Hawk had finished tending her arm, Saradee gave his hat brim a playful tug, and then they went back to work with their rifles. The posse was closing on them, working its way up the slope and yelling back and forth to each other. They were staying hunkered low behind whatever cover they could find.

When Hawk had run out of bullets for his Henry, he used his pistols.

A half hour after Saradee had taken the bullet burn, Hawk sat back against the rocks, and drew a deep, fateful breath. He hadn't been able to reduce their numbers by nearly as much as he'd wanted. Soon the posse would overtake the nest.

"How many bullets you got left?" Hawk asked Saradee, who was just now triggering one of her pretty Colts down the slope.

She sat back against a rock, legs stretched wide before her, facing Hawk.

"Not enough."

"Save one for yourself."

Saradee curled her upper lip at him. "You save one for me. I'll save one for you."

Hawk gave a caustic snort.

She narrowed a suspicious eye at him. "What's the matter? You've been wanting to trim my wick for years."

"You got that right." Hawk smiled, though he really wasn't sure he wanted to see her dead anymore. And that part frightened him. If they had to die, though, they might as well die together. Hawk himself had no fear of death. In fact, he welcomed it.

Saradee grinned, then swung back to the notch between her two covering rocks. Hawk fired several more rounds through his own notch, wounding one posse man in the leg as he was trying to run up the slope.

Hawk pulled back from the notch once more and checked the loads in his Russian. "I'm down to my last round."

"Yeah," Saradee said, leaning back against her own rock, breathless. She ran her sleeve across her dusty cheek. "Me, too."

She holstered the near-empty Colt and crawled over to Hawk. She wrapped her arms around his neck and kissed him. Hawk holstered the Russian. He wrapped his arms around the blond succubus lying across his lap. He tipped her back in his arms, lowered his head to hers, and returned her tender kiss.

He savored the warmth of her lips, the playful press of her tongue against his. She groaned as she pulled him down tighter against her. Her breasts swelled against his chest. He could feel the warmth of her crotch against his own, igniting his desire.

Saradee jerked in Hawk's arms, grabbing one of her pistols from its holster and firing at something behind Hawk. He whipped his head around to see one of the posse men stumbling backward, dropping his rifle and clamping his hands over the blood geysering from the hole in the center of his chest.

The man looked down at the hole, bug-eyed, and sobbed. Then he dropped out of sight.

"Hey, that was supposed to be my bullet," Hawk said.

"Sorry, lover — it was automatic."

"Hold it, Hawk . . . and whoever you are!"

Hawk looked up to see Quentin Burnett aiming a rifle at him and Saradee. Two other men stood to each side of Burnett, also aiming rifles.

Hawk looked at Saradee. He looked at the Russian in his hand. The revolver had one last bullet in it. Saradee closed her hand over the Russian and pulled it out of Hawk's hand.

"If we can't die together. . . ." She tossed the revolver away.

Burnett glanced at the two men beside him. One was New Canaan's town marshal, the dark-eyed, belligerent Bob Nye. The other was a beefy, young, curly-headed deputy. "Nye, Deputy Loman — get in there, cuff 'em, and make sure they don't have any more weapons!" He glanced over his shoulder and yelled, "Someone, fetch rope. Plenty of it!"

"What — you're gonna hang us?" Saradee asked, leaping to her feet.

"Holy Christ — look at that," said the beefy Deputy Loman as he stepped over the rocks at the nest's perimeter, letting his gaze sweep the blonde up and down. "Where did you come from, honey?"

Saradee spat in his face.

Loman jerked his head back, grimacing. "Goddamn bitch!" He started to whip up the butt of his rifle to smack her with it, but Hawk, who had also gained his feet, smashed his fist against Loman's right ear, laying him out cold.

"Don't shoot him! Don't shoot him!" Burnett ordered Nye, who'd aimed his rifle at Hawk's head and was starting to draw back the trigger. Nye winced, then loosened his grip on the rifle.

Burnett turned toward the five other surviving posse members, who were climbing the slope behind him, their rifles raised, and repeated, "I want this man taken alive!"

"Why, Mr. Burnett?" asked Nye. "The four-thousand-dollar bounty is good if he's alive *or* dead. I say we kill him and hedge our bets. He's a tricky son of a bitch!"

"That he is, that he is," Burnett said, looking Hawk up and down with keen, almost admiring interest. "But he's a rare and exotic creature. Look at him. Look at the size of him. Note the savagery in his eyes. He's a spectacle. He's been hunted a long time — a particularly dangerous and wily predator. Mad, to be sure. No, no. You don't so quickly kill such a brute as this. Hell, no — you trap him, parade him around town, call in eastern newspaper reporters, call in the territorial governors who put a death warrant on his head, throw one hell of a party!"

"I think he'd rather you hanged him," said Saradee.

"Oh, we'll hang him, young lady. That will be the capstone of the party." Burnett looked at her through his glinting glasses, his eyes narrowing lustily as he raked her curvy form with his gaze. "Who are you? What are you doing here . . . with him?"

"I'm proud to call myself his woman."

"His woman, eh?" Burnett glanced at Hawk, who said nothing.

Hawk's mind was focused only on how to get out of the current bind he was in. He could not be incarcerated. Every fiber of his being chafed at the notion. He should have killed himself. For some reason, he'd found himself reluctant to leave Saradee here alone to fend for herself.

Why such chivalry?

In the past there'd been only one thing he'd wanted to do to her more than he wanted to kill her, but now, suddenly, his priorities were being realigned.

Probably more a sign of the madness that was infecting him, growing inside him.

"Two vital specimens," Burnett said, shifting his shrewd gaze between Hawk and Saradee. "It figures he'd choose you."

"I'll take that as a compliment," Saradee said, cocking one boot forward and thrusting her shoulders back, breasts out.

While Nye held his rifle on the prisoners, the deputy placed handcuffs on Hawk first and then on Saradee, securing their hands behind their backs.

"Christ, you are something." Burnett swallowed as he studied Saradee, flushing.

He glanced behind to shout, "Hurry up with that rope. I want these two tied securely!"

The man bringing the rope broke into a run up the slope. All the others were surrounding Hawk, Saradee, and Burnett, rifles aimed. Burnett held his own rifle low across his waist. He was squeezing it as though he were trying to kill a snake with his bare hands.

"You can get that look out of your eye, old man," Saradee said. "Like I said, I'm his woman. No one else's. When he hangs, I'll hang with him."

"Just his woman, eh?" Burnett glanced at the other men around him. A couple appeared wounded, though not seriously. "How would you like to get a peek at these two together, fellas? That would be something to see, wouldn't it? Two savages toiling as though in the gutters of Bedlam!"

The others chuckled lustily. All except Nye, that was.

"I don't think we oughta fool with Hawk, Mr. Burnett," the marshal said. "He's like a wounded griz. There's a reason it's taken years for anyone to run him down despite that four-thousand-dollar bounty on his head."

"Yes, but it's *we* who had the *cojones* to catch him," Burnett said, staring at Hawk again admiringly from behind his glinting spectacles. "And, since we lost a lot of men in the process, we're owed some fun."

"I say we have some fun with the girl right now," said Loman, his lumpy chest rising and falling heavily as he eyed Saradee. He adjusted his crotch. "I'd like a piece of that right now. How 'bout you boys?"

"Hell, yeah," said two of the others at nearly the same time.

Another man said, "Look at them tits!"

"I told you," Saradee said, flaring her nostrils at the goatish men surrounding her, lusting after her. "Only Hawk beds me."

"We'll see about that!" Loman lurched toward her.

He got Saradee's right boot in his groin for his efforts. It was a sound, devastating blow. She'd hammered the boot's pointed toe deep into his loins.

Loman jackknifed forward, red-faced and howling, cradling his smashed oysters in his gloved hands.

The others laughed.

Burnett said, "She'll do. She'll do right well. No, we'll save her . . . for later. I got something special in mind for her and Hawk."

To the man who'd come up with two ropes coiled over his arms, he said, "Tie them both and bring the horses. Tie them good. We're headed back to New Canaan to celebrate our capture." He grinned lewdly at Saradee, his eyes lingering on the upturned points of her breasts. "And to have some good, old-fashioned fun."

Hawk dropped his head and put some slack into his shoulders as the man with the rope approached him, a reluctant cast to his eyes. The man looked as though he were approaching a leg-trapped bear with the intention of throwing a saddle on his back.

"Someone hold him," said the man with the rope. He wore a bowler hat, a shopkeeper's vest, and sleeve garters. His left ear had been creased by a bullet, and there was blood on his broadcloth pants leg. "Hold him good. He's playin' possum, but he's a devil! He's waitin' to bust my nose — I can read his mind!"

Burnett said, "Nye, you and Loman hold Hawk's arms. Gibson, Simms — keep your rifles on the girl. If Hawk so much as twitches a finger, shoot the girl right between her big tits!"

The others chuckled nervously, ogling Saradee.

"Boys," Saradee said snidely. "I'm surrounded by boys."

She turned to Hawk and watched as Nye and Loman drove him belly down to the ground and hogtied him. They weren't taking any chances.

When they were through with Hawk, they did the same to Saradee, taking their time with her, letting their hands get a good feel of her curves. Saradee accepted the assault stone-faced. She'd been through it all before.

Hawk lay on his stomach, staring up at Burnett and the others, who were now waiting for the horses to be led from the bottom of the slope.

Fury was a hot fire building in Hawk. But he had to keep it under control, lest it burn too hotly too soon and consume all its fuel. He had to conserve that fuel for later, for when he saw his chance to kill as many of these men as he could and to affect his and Saradee's escape.

Even if he died in the process.

Saradee . . .

Why in hell was he referring to her in his own mind as his partner?

Ever since he'd first met her, he'd wanted to kill her, to scour her evil but intoxicating presence from his back trail. Now, however, he wanted to save her even more than he wanted to save himself.

My god, had he fallen in love with her?

And, if so, what did that say about the man he'd become?

When the horses were brought up, one was led aside for Hawk, the other for Saradee. Three men lifted Hawk up over the saddle of one of the horses. They bound his hands and feet under the horse's belly.

They did the same to Saradee.

When most of the other surviving posse members had mounted their horses, Burnett pinched his pants up at his thighs and squatted down beside Hawk, grinning at him mockingly. "We're gonna take you to town and have fun with you, Hawk." He glanced at Saradee. "A whole lot of fun."

Hawk said blandly, "Go to hell, you limp-dicked old tinhorn."

Saradee laughed.

"No, no." Burnett straightened. "You go to hell, my friend!" He smashed the butt of his Winchester against Hawk's head.

Everything went black and painful and loud. The loudness dwindled gradually, but the pain faded only a little as Hawk drifted into deep unconsciousness.

Chapter 18

The pain in Hawk's head grew keener as he felt himself floating slowly toward consciousness, toward the loud noise he'd heard before. He groaned against the pain of what felt like rail spikes driven straight down through the top of his head.

The noise grew louder.

He realized it wasn't the same loud noise he'd heard before.

What he'd heard before was the tolling of many cracked bells in his head. What he was hearing now was the din of yelling and loudly conversing men. His other senses began coming alive. The smell of cigarette and cigar smoke touched his nose. He could feel himself being rocked to and fro, as though he lay in a rowboat on troubled waters.

Then he smelled something terrible.

The smell was so invasive — the stench of some horrible rotten thing pickled in hog urine — that it was like one of those rail spikes being hammered up through his nose and into his brain. He was catapulted out of unconsciousness, choking against the disgusting fetor, and opened his eyes to find himself in a large, nicely decorated bedroom filled with well-dressed, middle-aged men.

Smoke hovered over and around Hawk who looked down to see his naked body lying spread-eagle on a bed. A small, hairy hand waved something under his nose. There it was again — the horrible hammering stench setting his brain on fire.

"Get that away from me!" he croaked, and the little, well-dressed man with the hairy hand pulled the smelling salts away from him, recoiling from Hawk as though from a suddenly conscious mountain lion.

"He's awake," the little man — a sawbones, most likely — told Burnett, who stood near Hawk's side of the bed, hands in the air, his fists full of money.

Burnett turned to Hawk, grinned, and then turned back to the crowd of sitting or standing men — fifteen or twenty or so — several waving money in the air with one hand while holding drinks and cigars or quirleys in the other hand.

Several sat with half-dressed whores on their knees or straddling their laps. A couple more whores stood near the door to whatever bedroom Hawk was in, fashioning alluring postures while holding trays filled with drinks.

Hawk was slow to get the layout of what was happening . . . until he turned to his left and saw that what was rocking the bed, making it feel like a rowboat on troubled waters, was Saradee.

She was also naked.

Not wearing a stitch.

She knelt on the far side of the bed, lunging at three men who were mocking her and laughing, lurching forward to make faces at her or to poke her or grab her breasts, then bounding back when Saradee threw herself toward them, snarling and cursing at the tops of her lungs.

Though they were all in their late middle age and holding drinks, their eyes rheumy from whiskey, they were like young boys teasing a chained lynx.

Deputy Loman was laughing and holding a double-barreled shotgun on Saradee.

Hawk looked around, blinking, certain he must be dreaming.

Having a nightmare.

Burnett barked, "He's awake, everyone. The co-star of this evening's performance. Are all bets in?"

A man with shoulder-length silver hair parted on one side leaned forward on his silver-handled walking stick and shouted, "I got a thousand says he'll finish within two minutes when he gets goin' on her, Quentin!" He was grinning at Hawk, his pale-blue eyes ogling the naked captive almost rapturously.

Hawk rose onto his elbows, scowling at the man. He started to rise when a shotgun was thrust into his field of vision from his right. Town Marshal Bob Nye grinned down the length of his own double-barreled shotgun at Hawk, bald threat in the man's flat gaze.

"Go ahead, Hawk," Nye snarled. "Go ahead — try somethin'. I want ya to!"

"Easy, Marshal — easy!" reprimanded Burnett. "Only shoot him if he steps off the bed. We got us a festive night ahead!" Burnett turned to the man with thick, silver hair. "A thousand for under two minutes it is!"

Burnett took the man's money, then turned to Hawk. Burnett pointed at the silver-haired gent, and said, "Know who that is, Mr. Hawk? That there is the territorial governor of Idaho. Showed up late today to join my hunting party, and decided to join tonight's private, by-invitation-only festivities!"

Hawk looked at the obviously moneyed crowd around him. He blinked against the wafting smoke. The room was thick and hot and it smelled of sweat and drink and the whores' mingling and conflicting perfumes.

The men in the room must be part of Burnett's hunting party.

They were postponing the hunt to privately gamble on something so repulsive that Hawk couldn't wrap his mind around exactly what it was.

Hawk turned to Saradee, who glanced over her shoulder at him and then sank down onto her butt, putting her back to the headboard. She raised her knees to her breasts, and hugged them, covering herself from the glassy-eyed oglers as much as possible.

She wore nothing. There were no bedcovers. The only bedding at all were two silk-covered pillows and the red silk sheet beneath her and Hawk.

"Welcome to the party, lover," she said with a brittle grin. "I thought you were gonna sleep through the whole thing, damn ya!"

Hawk looked around again, fury a wild animal growing inside of him. He looked at Nye, still aiming the shotgun at him. He wondered if he could grab the gut-shredder before Nye shredded him.

The thought must have shown itself in his eyes.

"Look out — he's gonna make a leap for it!" yelled one of the moneyed crowd, pointing apprehensively at Hawk.

"Not to worry," Burnett assured the man, holding up a placating hand. "If he steps foot off the bed, Nye will blast him to Kingdom Come. Same for the girl. Keep your eyes on her at all times, Deputy Loman. I'm sure that won't be hard!" Burnett added, laughing, evoking more laughter from the crowd.

"Relax, Hawk," Saradee said. "We're not goin' anywhere. I sure would like to get my hands on one of those shotguns, though." She turned her smoldering gaze to Burnett. "You know just where I'd like to stick it and pull both triggers!"

Hawk looked at Burnett. Fury exploded in him once more, but he reined it back. He didn't want to die here, like this — naked on a bed, a spectacle in a room full of wealthy demons. He had to live so he could kill Burnett.

"What the hell is this about?" Hawk asked, half to himself. "What do they want?"

"Take a guess, lover. Look at you. Look at

me. Take a guess.”

Hawk stared out at the crowd forming a semicircle around the bed. Most of the rich men were getting their drinks replenished by the scantily clad whores. They were savoring the moment, enjoying the anticipation of the spectacle ahead.

Hawk would be damned if he’d give it to them.

He wasn’t some wild animal to be humiliated in some rich man’s depraved circus.

“Forget it,” Hawk said. “I won’t give ’em the satisfaction.”

“I don’t think we have much choice, lover.”

“You heard me — forget it.”

“You don’t wanna die this way any more than I do, Gid. We gotta get our hands on some guns. We gotta fix that bastard’s wagon.” Saradee turned toward Hawk. “Pretend they’re not here. Pretend we’re alone.”

She caressed his cheek with the back of her left hand and gave him a sympathetic look. “It’ll be okay. I promise. We’ll have our revenge, lover.”

“Look, look — I think she’s enticing him!” someone yelled.

Instantly, the din in the room subsided as the gamblers cast their eager gazes toward

the bed.

Hawk looked around the room onc
“Go to hell!” he bellowed so loudly
lamps around the room rattled. He c
onto his hands and knees, ignoring
who thrust his shotgun toward H
head, and stared red-faced at the c
“You can all go to hell! I won’t be hu
ated, you sonso’bitches!”

“Oh, I sincerely think you will,
Hawk,” yelled Burnett, grinning the s
assured grin again that Hawk wanted
much to scrub from the man’s face w
one of the shotguns.

wondered if he could grab the gut-shredder before Nye shredded him.

The thought must have shown itself in his eyes.

"Look out — he's gonna make a leap for it!" yelled one of the moneyed crowd, pointing apprehensively at Hawk.

"Not to worry," Burnett assured the man, holding up a placating hand. "If he steps foot off the bed, Nye will blast him to Kingdom Come. Same for the girl. Keep your eyes on her at all times, Deputy Loman. I'm sure that won't be hard!" Burnett added, laughing, evoking more laughter from the crowd.

"Relax, Hawk," Saradee said. "We're not goin' anywhere. I sure would like to get my hands on one of those shotguns, though." She turned her smoldering gaze to Burnett. "You know just where I'd like to stick it and pull both triggers!"

Hawk looked at Burnett. Fury exploded in him once more, but he reined it back. He didn't want to die here, like this — naked on a bed, a spectacle in a room full of wealthy demons. He had to live so he could kill Burnett.

"What the hell is this about?" Hawk asked, half to himself. "What do they want?"

"Take a guess, lover. Look at you. Look at

me. Take a guess."

Hawk stared out at the crowd forming a semicircle around the bed. Most of the rich men were getting their drinks replenished by the scantily clad whores. They were savoring the moment, enjoying the anticipation of the spectacle ahead.

Hawk would be damned if he'd give it to them.

He wasn't some wild animal to be humiliated in some rich man's depraved circus.

"Forget it," Hawk said. "I won't give 'em the satisfaction."

"I don't think we have much choice, lover."

"You heard me — forget it."

"You don't wanna die this way any more than I do, Gid. We gotta get our hands on some guns. We gotta fix that bastard's wagon." Saradee turned toward Hawk. "Pretend they're not here. Pretend we're alone."

She caressed his cheek with the back of her left hand and gave him a sympathetic look. "It'll be okay. I promise. We'll have our revenge, lover."

"Look, look — I think she's enticing him!" someone yelled.

Instantly, the din in the room subsided as the gamblers cast their eager gazes toward the bed.

Hawk looked around the room once more. "Go to hell!" he bellowed so loudly that the lamps around the room rattled. He climbed onto his hands and knees, ignoring Nye, who thrust his shotgun toward Hawk's head, and stared red-faced at the crowd. "You can all go to hell! I won't be humiliated, you sonso'bitches!"

"Oh, I sincerely think you will, Mr. Hawk," yelled Burnett, grinning the self-assured grin again that Hawk wanted so much to scrub from the man's face with one of the shotguns.

The crowd fell nearly silent as Burnett turned toward the bed and pulled a small-caliber, silver-chased, pearl-gripped pocket pistol from the waistband of his trousers. He clicked the hammer back and aimed it at Saradee.

"Do your duty, Marshal Hawk. Perform the act we require of you . . . or I'm gonna kill her. Slow. One bullet, one limb, at a time." He slid his devilish gaze to Hawk. "You wouldn't want that, now, would you?"

Saradee slid her gaze from the barrel of Burnett's Merwin & Hulbert revolver to Hawk. Her eyes asked the same question Burnett had asked.

Hawk had no idea why, but for the love of

him, he didn't want her hurt.

"Take the gun away, you son of a bitch."

Burnett smiled and pulled the gun back. He depressed the hammer and stepped aside.

He turned to the room and said, "Gentlemen, I think we have two willing participants now. The bets are in!" He gestured to Hawk and Saradee. "Let the game begin!"

The crowd erupted with roars of encouragement and applause.

"Three minutes," someone yelled. "You gotta last three minutes, Hawk!"

"No, no — take your time, big fella. You gotta last *five* minutes — you understand? Five minutes or I'll have to sell my house . . . and divorce my wife!"

"And leave the country!" added another man.

The crowd roared at the joke.

Hawk turned to Saradee and tried to close out the cacophony in the room around him.

"Christ," he said, placing his right hand on her left cheek, curling his upper lip with fury and humiliation as he stared down at her. "If there was a way, I'd kill every bastard in this room!"

"Don't listen to 'em, lover," Saradee said, snuggling down against the bed and rubbing her breasts against his chest, curling one leg over his. “It’s just us. We’re the only ones here. It’ll be like all the other times.”

He could feel the tuft of fur between her thighs prick softly against his belly. He was surprised to feel a wave of erotic pleasure wash from his belly to his toes, even with the crowd staring at him.

Hawk looked at the slender wooden bedposts holding up the canopy over the bed.

“All right,” he said. “It’s just you and me.”

Saradee was massaging him with both her supple hands, smiling up into his face. It was as though she’d shut out the spectators completely. It was as if there really was no one else here but her and Hawk.

Two lovers making love.

“It’s all right if you want to pretend I’m Linda,” Saradee said in a little girl’s voice, brushing the backs of her fingers up across his cheeks to his temples.

Hawk shook his head, grinding his molars. “Be quiet.”

“We don’t need her here, do we?”

“Goddamnit, I told you to be quiet.”

“It’ll be all right,” she said, reaching down for him again. Her hands were warm and tender, so hypnotically artful in the way they manipulated him, toying with him gently, teasingly. “There, now. How’s that? Oh, yeah . . . you like that. Just like you’ve always enjoyed it, lover. All the years, and you didn't realize how much you enjoyed it, did you? Making love to a killer?"

"I did know," Hawk grunted. "That was the trouble."

"Because you knew we were cut from the same cloth."

"No."

"Yes."

"If you don't shut up, goddamnit — ! If we have to do this, let's just . . ." He let the thought trail away, shaking his head. "We were not cut from the same cloth."

Hawk was not aware of the crowd's sudden silence punctuated by only a hushed, awful exclamation now and then. Or an appreciative chuckle. He'd almost entirely shut the gamblers out of his mind.

Saradee laughed as her hands continued to tease him to arousal. "I don't think you ever needed Linda. I've always been enough."

"Oh, Jesus," Hawk croaked, glancing around briefly to see the spectators gathering closer for a better view. "Shut the hell up!" he told Saradee, pushing the gamblers from his mind again.

"You don't need Linda anymore. She's dead. I'm here. I'm alive, Hawk!"

"Shut up!" As much as he hated her, or

hated loving her, he was continuing to come alive in her hands.

"I'll always be here for you, Gideon." Saradee laughed her sweet, mocking, knowing laugh. "That's all you need to know. That's all you *need*!"

"Oh, Christ," Hawk said as the bittersweet pangs of his rising desire rolled through his loins. "Lord help me."

He looked down between them. He was fully erect. Her hands pumped him slowly but eagerly. The blond succubus beneath him smiled up at him, lips slightly parted to reveal her perfect, even teeth. It was a teasing, gently mocking smile.

A sweetly smiling succubus beneath him, urging his soul on to hell with her. And he was entirely willing to go.

"Lord have mercy on my wretched soul!" Hawk intoned, thinking of his son and wife, though their images were growing harder and harder to conjure. It was as though they were spiraling away from him, disappearing into the mists of forgotten time.

He sobbed as a dam of pent-up emotion burst inside him. He sobbed beneath the cacophony swirling around him.

"Lord have mercy!" he cried.

Saradee laughed. "Good luck with that, lover!"

Saradee slipped him inside her and pressed her hands down hard against his buttocks, sliding him in . . . in . . . in!

The room erupted with loud applause, ribald laughter, thunderous encouragement.

Hawk shut it out as best he could as, sandwiching Saradee's face in his hands, sobbing, he began hammering his hips against hers. His rhythm increased as his passion grew.

He glanced at the canopy shaking above him. The posters supporting it shook and swayed.

Nye and Loman stood to each side of the bed, about six feet away, their shotguns sagging slightly in their hands as they watched the mesmerizing spectacle before them.

Hawk thrust his hips against Saradee harder, harder, harder . . .

The four canopy posts started making soft cracking sounds.

Saradee wrapped her arms around Hawk's neck, entwining her legs over his back.

"Jesus Christ, they're really goin' at it!" one of the spectators shouted, laughing.

"Shhhh!" admonished another of the crowd.

"If they ain't careful, they're gonna break the bed!" another man warned, and snickered.

"Oh, my gosh!" cried one of the whores, aghast. "They're like two . . . *animals*!"

"You takin' notes, Betsy?" one of the male spectators asked the shocked dove.

A roar of laughter.

Occasionally, Hawk could hear men clapping and yelling instructions and encouragement, as though he and Saradee were boxers in a ring. Mostly, he saw and heard nothing at all. He only felt the heat of his passion rising while an entire universe of grief and anger and self-recrimination hammered away at his soul, pummeling him into submission.

Saradee tried to pull his head down to her, to kiss him, but he resisted. Propped on his outstretched arms, he ground the heels of his hands into the mattress on either side of her beautiful blond head.

She smiled up at him dreamily, eyes glinting in the lamplight.

Then he saw that she was frowning. A strange, incredulous light had entered her eyes. She lowered her hands to her neck.

Hawk saw that one of his hands was around her throat.

Chapter 19

"Hawk," Saradee rasped, trying to pull his hand away.

Hawk hammered against her faster, harder.

Faster, harder.

Faster . . .

Harder . . .

"Hawk," she said, but he could only read her lips. No sound escaped her mouth. His fingers were digging into her throat, pinching off her wind. She clawed at it desperately but she couldn't budge it. Her strength was no match for his.

The crowd roared around Hawk, but his brain registered the cacophony as though it originated from a half a mile away through a dense forest. He could see movement around him as the crowd drew closer to get a better view of the depravity in their midst, but Hawk registered only shifting shadows in the very periphery of his vision.

As he continued to hammer against Saradee, strangling her, she struggled violently against him, clawing at his hands, kicking her long legs at him, desperately trying to unseat him.

But Hawk was immovable. Her desperate struggles only exacerbated his desire.

He kept his hand fast against her neck, digging his fingers deeper and deeper into her throat.

Saradee let her hands flop down onto the bed. She stared up at him. Gradually, the fear left her eyes. It was replaced with a vague amusement even as her face turned from pale to light blue, and her eyes turned to isinglass.

"Christ, what's he doin'?" asked one of the men in the crowd, inching closer and closer to the pitching and swaying bed.

"He's strangling her!" The speaker guffawed nervously. "Good god — you ever see such a thing! Why, he's diddlin' her to death!"

Hawk glanced up at the canopy. It pitched and swayed in time with the bed.

He hammered against Saradee, the heat of his passion rising in his loins. Saradee lay still beneath him, glassily staring, unmoving . . .

"Lord have mercy on my soul!" Hawk bellowed, tipping his head back and gritting his teeth as the canopy posts splintered.

Hawk held his hips fast against Saradee, his loins spasming. The right front canopy post broke in two. Then the left one broke in two. At the same time, the rear posts were breaking.

The canopy fell down around Hawk's head and shoulders.

"Christalmighty!" Burnett shouted. "*Shoot* the son of a bitch!"

"Don't let him get away!" bellowed another man.

Hawk leaped off of Saradee. He shouldered the side of the canopy off of him. The crowd was right next to the bed. He glimpsed a shotgun held by Loman, who'd lunged forward to shove the gut-shredder beneath the canopy.

Hawk thrust his hands forward, ripped the shotgun out of the deputy's hands, pulled the hammers back, whipped the barrels forward, and tripped a trigger.

Thunder racked the room.

Loman screamed as he was blown off his feet and backward.

Again, Hawk shouldered the canopy up and away from him. Nye lunged toward the bed, aiming a shotgun. Hawk aimed his own shotgun at the marshal's belly and sent him flying violently and bellowing shrilly back against the wall.

Hawk tossed the empty shotgun aside and jerked his head toward the door.

Apparently there had been a pileup that was just now clearing as the men who'd fallen on each other in their frenzy to leave the room gained their feet and ran off down the hall.

Two doves who'd been hammered under the fleeing gamblers' feet were quietly sobbing on the floor. They didn't look so much injured as scared. They both cast bright-eyed, fearful gazes toward Hawk.

Burnett had been the last one to the door. He stood in front of it now, his pistol in his hand, staring in shock and horror at the naked, blood-splattered Hawk. The rogue lawman stepped off the battered bed, shouldering away a corner of the fallen canopy.

Hawk curled his upper lip at Burnett.

As though he just now realized he was holding the pistol, Burnett snapped his pistol up. As he tightened his finger on the trigger, he jerked forward and fired the Merwin & Hulbert into the floor halfway between himself and Hawk.

Burnett screamed, staggered forward, and dropped to his knees.

A wooden-handled Bowie knife protruded

from his back.

Jennie Broyles walked in behind him, clad in blue denims and a red and white checked wool shirt, her hair pulled back into a horse tail. Dixie, dressed similarly, walked into the room behind Jennie.

The women stood to either side of the raging saloon owner, who tipped his head back and gave a bellowing cry as he reached over his shoulder and pulled the knife out of his back. He tossed the knife on the floor and looked in pain and horror first at Jennie Broyles and then at Dixie.

"You . . . you . . . bitch!" Burnett bellowed.

Dixie smiled down at him, but there was no humor in her eyes. "Good riddance to you once and for all, Quentin. I hope the devil straps you with his oldest whore for all eternity."

Burnett jerked his gaze to Hawk. He looked around again, as though hoping to find someone remaining in the room who might offer assistance.

But there were only the two dead lawmen lying in thick, growing pools of their own blood and the two sobbing whores. The din of moments before had drifted downstairs, where the moneyed gamblers were apparently fleeing the building.

Hawk picked up an unfired shotgun and strode toward Burnett, mindless that he was naked. He looked like a savage — naked and blood-splattered. Saradee lay unmoving beneath the collapsed red canopy.

"Please don't shoot me," Burnett said, breathless, eyes pinched with pain.

"All right." Hawk tossed away the shotgun. Gritting his teeth, he reached down, grabbed Burnett by his coat collar, and jerked the man to his feet.

Burnett bellowed miserably as Hawk dragged him savagely across the room and then hurled him through a window. The big saloon owner screamed as glass shattered around him.

There were several crunching thuds and yelps as Burnett rolled down a sloping roof.

Silence.

Another thud as Burnett hit the street out in front of the saloon.

Hawk walked over to the window. Jennie Broyles and Dixie moved to another window, to Hawk's left, and looked down into the street. Hawk could see Burnett lying in a pool of light cast by the Inn's first-story windows.

He was the only one on the street, the gamblers and other clientele apparently having fled the bloody violence. The only sounds were distant dogs barking and Burnett moaning as he lay on his back in the street. A slender, dark, hatted figure in a shapeless coat walked up to Burnett.

"Jacob," Jennie said, placing her hands against the window.

Then she swung around and ran out of the room. Dixie followed her.

Hawk looked back down into the shadowy, lamplit street. Jacob looked straight ahead, pricking his ears to get his bearings.

"Please," Burnett said between moans, raising a hand toward the slender, blind boy standing over him. "Help me!"

Jacob reached behind him and pulled what appeared to be a knife from the back of his belt. The boy crouched over Burnett. Hawk grinned as he saw the boy making a sweeping motion across the top of Burnett's forehead with the knife.

Burnett squealed like a gutshot javelina.

Jacob's knife worked deftly for a brief time. Then he straightened and held up something small and dark and ragged-edged and dripping. Burnett's scalp.

Burnett squealed again, louder, clutching his head in his hands.

"Look, sis," Jacob said, turning toward the Inn's veranda. "I got the first hide for the wall of our new cabin!"

Hawk had to chuckle at that.

"What's so damn funny?"

He whipped around and jerked his startled gazed toward the canopy-draped bed. Saradee sat on the edge of the bed, massaging her throat with both hands and looking over her shoulder at Hawk.

"You 'bout killed me." She worked her jaws, clearing her throat. "Like to have snapped my neck!"

"No," Hawk said, dully.

Saradee rose slowly and walked toward Hawk in all her naked splendor, hips rolling, jutting breasts jostling.

"No," Hawk said, shaking his head in disbelief. "No. I killed you. Once and for all, I killed you."

"If you'd wanted to, lover," Saradee said, reaching up and wrapping her arms around his neck. "If you'd really wanted to, you would have."

She kissed him tenderly, then gazed lovingly up into his face. "What do you say we round up our duds and head downstairs? I could use a drink. I got a sneaking feelin' we're gonna have the whole place to ourselves. That's a lot of busthead, lover!"

"No," Hawk said again, still shaking his head. "No." He blinked his eyes as though to clear them. "No. No. You're not here.

You're a dream."

"If I was," Saradee said, pressing her lips to his once more and lifting his hands to her breasts, "I'd be one hell of one — wouldn't I?"

ABOUT THE AUTHOR

Western novelist **Peter Brandvold** was born and raised in North Dakota. He has penned over 100 fast-action westerns under his own name and his pen name, **Frank Leslie**. He is the author of the ever-popular .45-Caliber books featuring Cuno Massey as well as the Lou Prophet and Yakima Henry novels. The Ben Stillman books are a long-running series with previous volumes available as ebooks. He also wrote twenty-nine books in the long-running *Longarm* series for Penguin Putnam. Head honcho at "Mean Pete Publishing," publisher of lightning-fast western ebooks, he has lived all over the American west but currently lives in a small town in western Minnesota with his dog. Visit his website at www.peterbrandvold.com. Follow his blog at: www.peterbrandvold.blogspot.com.

The employees of Thorndike Press hope you have enjoyed this Large Print book. All our Thorndike, Wheeler, and Kennebec Large Print titles are designed for easy reading, and all our books are made to last. Other Thorndike Press Large Print books are available at your library, through selected bookstores, or directly from us.

For information about titles, please call:
(800) 223-1244

or visit our Web site at:
http://gale.com/thorndike

To share your comments, please write:
Publisher
Thorndike Press
10 Water St., Suite 310
Waterville, ME 04901